I0713665

CAPTAIN RANDOM AND THE BATTLE OF RODAS

HAYDEN GRIBBLE

Dedicated to all who keep trying

Also by the author

The CAPTAIN RANDOM Adventures

Captain Random vs the Sandman
Captain Random and the Eater of Souls
Captain Random and the Rainbow Chasers
Captain Random and the Stratos Conundrum
Journeys in the Randomverse

Other titles by the author

The Man In The Corner
Tales From Another Me
Child Out Of Time: Growing Up With Doctor Who In
The Wilderness Years
The Lurking
Don't Panic! The Unauthorised Dad's Army
Handbook

In the light of the bright moon stood a figure bathed in darkness. An eerie calmness betrayed the malicious storm in his heart, as the fire of a thousand suns raged through his veins. He had stood upon the precipice of death for centuries and witnessed the destruction of all he once held dear.

His planet was a battleground. It had been for as long as he could remember. Since the old times, many had said to him when he was young, so long ago. As he had sat in the libraries of the citadel, taking in his studies whilst the carnage of war was happening all around him, he had watched as explosions far away had rocked the mighty timbers high above. The tremors and terrible sounds of destruction haunted his every waking moment. Even as he slept, the horror of battle poisoned his mind every second of his life, like a tinnitus that wouldn't go away.

Some days he'd cry. Only to himself, not to those who looked after him. An orphan like him had to be tough on a planet like his. Any sign of weakness, the slightest glimmer of deviation from normality, a slip of keeping his head down and getting on with life as best he could like everyone else, was dealt with harshly.

His people were sick enough to let a war rage
throughout time, both sides refusing to concede
defeat. Whole families were regularly torn apart.
Mothers and Fathers were captured, enslaved, or
slaughtered and their children equally so if they
were not careful. Just to be alive was supposed to
make little boys like him grateful. So how could
he openly admit how scared he was?

As time moved on, he noticed that it never
rained on his world. As the madness of war bore
its way into his soul, he soon began to realise
why.

If everyone like he had spent a lifetime holding
back the tears, why would a planet so broken
weep for itself?

Time marched on like the good little soldier he
became. Suddenly, any shred of emotion he had
felt; the sorrow he felt for missing his Mum, the
not knowing if she was alive or dead, in danger
or safe, the hope that one day the killing would
end for everyone in his world, drained out of
him.

It had all happened in the heat of battle. The
years of cowering from laser fire, of dusting
himself down when the building he was in had
split into pieces and the heat of the flames that
had licked at his flesh seared into significance
when he had to face the enemy.

All children, no matter how hard they had
studied, no matter their brilliance in whatever
they did ended up picking up a gun. It was
expected of them. After the horror of it all had
engulfed him once and for all he finally saw the
sense in all the madness.

He had to do it.

He had to kill.

If he didn't, he would be killed himself.

He'd just be another corpse rotting in the street,
forgotten.

If he wanted to find his mother again, he'd have
to fight.

He'd have to win.

On the day of the Battle of Endos, the continent
he had grown up on, the bloodiest war that had
stained his planet took place and in the face of it
all, in the heart of the storm as all around him
perished, he remained.

His life came at a price.

Captured by the enemy he had been brought up
to despise, he was tortured mercilessly. For years
that felt to him like decades falling away through
the hourglass of time, he felt the pain of being a
red face.

The pain of his whole life was stretched out before his very eyes. The things they did to him would make any other man die and yet he survived.

For all that the blue faces did to him, the horrors they imposed upon his person mentally and physically one thing kept him alive whilst his fellow prisoners succumbed. He had to see her face again. He had to know she was still alive.

He had to keep fighting.

Before long, his captors, the Sapphire Regime as they were known, began to fall back against the might of their enemies to which he belonged; the Crimson Empire. Every rumour that whispered around his tiny, dank cell, the one he was forced to share will fellow prisoners of war, was that they were winning. No act of recrimination would stop them, the Crimson Empire was a tidal wave of hope that told him to keep going. They would be rescued soon. As long as they kept fighting back, he'd be out soon and then he could find her.

But it wasn't to be. If the Battle of Endos had told him to carry on no matter what, then what happened on the day of its end would crush whatever spark of love and hope he had left in his heart.

One morning an explosion of sheer apocalyptic velocity shook the prisoners around their cage. As they struggled back to their feet, dazed and confused by what had happened, he peered through the bars toward home. He forced his eyes open as the shockwave continued to wash towards them and as he gazed at the awesome destructive horror before him, his eyes filled with tears for the last time.

Endos was gone.

The Sapphire Regime had wiped it out.

She was gone.

If she had even been alive still, any hope of that had burnt like the rest of Endos.

He cried out in horror, gripping the bars and pulling at them so hard that one of them began to creak, no match for the grief that was exploding from within him.

He was restrained but it had taken many guards to do it, far more than it should to contain a man who had spent years at the Sapphire Regime's merciless hands. He had even killed a few of them in the struggle, driven insane by the finality of what he had witnessed, he possessed a strength no one could understand.

Finally, the man was subdued enough to be put to execution for the murder of the guards and yet, the promise of death didn't stop him.

On the day of his trial, which lasted mere minutes before he was brought before the firing squad, he had laughed in the face of his accusers. He had been laughing to himself since he had awoken after he had witnessed the burning of Endos. A deep, low rumbling chuckle that sat in his throat.

As he stood manacled to the post, awaiting the inevitable, he told himself that this was not the end. When the volley of lasers pierced his flesh and sent his body back at such a velocity that the pole snapped in two, his burnt and twisted body hit the dust at such speed that a cloud engulfed him. The laughing had suddenly stopped. They felt no need to check for life signs. No one could have survived such an ordeal.

But this was no ordinary man.

This was a man whose spirit had been possessed by the devil.

A man whose heart had become black with evil.

The very core of his being had become rotten, corrupted by the lunacy of the world in which he lived.

As he blinked his eyes open, his beaten, bloodied body thrown onto a heap of the corpses of his fallen comrades, he felt the strength begin to flow through him again. As he rose off the pile he slipped quietly away before his captors had a chance to burn them and attempt to hide their shame.

He felt his flesh as he walked back to where Endos had once been, finding it odd how quiet the world had become outside of his cage in the prisoner-of-war camp. It was wet, torn to ribbons and sore with infection. He liked it. It made him feel alive.

How he was still alive was a mystery to him. He lived to keep going. This was no second chance. He was still on his first and he was determined to make it work for him.

As he heard footsteps approach him, he was disturbed from his thoughts of the past. The clicking of boots against the floor of his private chamber grew louder and yet he still faced the window, looking out upon the world he called home.

The home he was about to act upon his salvation.

Suddenly, the footsteps stopped and clicked together in a salute.

'Supreme ruler,' came the voice, a strong, feminine tone that echoed around the desolate chamber.

'Are we ready?' came the reply from the man at the window, his hood hiding his features.

'Yes, my Lord,' was the reply.

'Good,' the man's voice was harsh and yet possessed a velvety tone, polite and dripping with malicious intent. 'Prepare your troops, Admiral.'

The Admiral nodded in response and turned to leave.

'Oh, and Admiral?' said the hooded voice.

'My Lord?'

The hooded figure turned to face her, his blood-red eyes shattering the darkness that surrounded them.

'Failure is not an option.'

The Admiral gulped. A bead of sweat formed on her brow.

'Of course not, my Lord.'

He continued to glare at her as she left his presence before returning to the glorious view of battle outside.

His name is Kalor Maloso. His world of chaos is known and shunned by the universe that surrounds it. But the war that has shattered it is soon to come to an end. Its name was a stain on the cosmos.

Rodas.

Book One

DECIMATION

I

Worlds away from hell was a little ship that transgressed the stars like a butterfly fluttering through the sunrise. Its sleek, curved quicksilver exterior betrayed the chaos that ensued most days within the body of it all. In the years it had sailed the galaxy it had seen much, just like its inhabitants. To those who had seen it, they had instantly fallen in love with the look of such a beauty. For any who had stepped on board, which was few in number, the thought that immediately crossed their minds was that it needed a really good spring clean. Then again, it was to be expected when three teenagers, whose days were like cracks in the pavement, who spent most of the time righting wrongs and eating and sleeping, lived on board.

To them, it was home. To anyone else, it was the Venus II. The only ship in the history of the universe to have escaped the war-torn planet Rodas and on board were the only two life forms who had the pleasure of doing just the same.

But recent events had brought about an abrupt end to the adventures of the occupants of the Venus II. At the orders of the captain of the ship, the AI robot who acted as chief science officer, medical officer, counsellor and reluctant housekeeper to his teenage friends had set the coordinates to return to their home world.

As the Venus II made its way home, the four travellers inside were all contemplating the horror of what they were doing. And although two of them were going back to the place they had escaped; the other half were wondering just how awful their immediate future was about to become. But none of them, not even the robot who seemed to have an answer for everything when a question was asked, knew just how dangerous their return was to be than Random.

'Knock knock,' came a voice from outside the door.

Random's deep thought was ended abruptly by the interruption.

He licked his lips. His mouth was drier than a desert in raining season.

'I'm not here,' came his response.

'Oh, okay then, can you let Random know when he's back that Anji wants to see how he is?' was the jovial reply.

Random allowed himself a little smile. 'I'm not sure she wants to,' he said as he got up to unlock the door. As it hissed as it slid up into the ceiling the face of Random's friend Anji stared back at him.

Her chirpy question clearly betrayed the concerned expression that was etched on her face. Random had grown used to seeing her worried over the years they had travelled together. They had seen so much, but this was new territory.

'You've been in here for hours. Skateboard was beginning to wonder if you wanted some food so I said I'd come and ask you.'

Random sat on his bed. His quarters were a state. Anji looked around as she made to sit beside him, dodging the piles of dirty clothing and books. She spotted many trinkets and souvenirs he had picked up from their multitude of adventures. A laser gun from the time they helped liberate the planet Genocia from a creature from the beginning of time sat half slumped down the wall near the foot of his bed. A file of sand, encapsulating the gorgeous multi-coloured memories of Spectronia sat on the window sill that sat above the bed and looked out onto the twinkling majesty of the stars as they blazed past as the ship was currently in hyperspace. Anji took them all in a way she never had before.

'I'm surprised you keep this stuff,' she said as she made herself comfortable and crossed her legs on Random's bed.

'They are a reminder,' he said bluntly.

'Of past glories?' she asked.

'Not quite,' said Random glumly.

Anji placed a hand gently on Random's shoulder. He felt clammy; like his trademark yellow t-shirt was clinging to his skin for dear life. 'Talk to me. Please. What happened on that moon?'

Random sighed. 'I wish I had never insisted we check out that distress signal.'

Merely hours earlier, the travellers had intercepted an SOS signal that was emitting from a remote ice moon situated in a cold and forgotten corner of the universe. It had been a welcome distraction from their current predicament, thought Random, who had just rescued his other human friend and Venus II incumbent, Jake, from the fabled fountain of youth and who had de-aged back to the very beginning of his puberty.

Plus, it was instinct, for Random at least, to help when it was asked for, or needed.

Only on this occasion, he regretted caring so much.

On the ice moon, he had proceeded alone to explore the signal at his own insistence. He was fine with risking his own life but he was not as ready to throw his friends in the line of danger. Indeed, most of his free time was actually spent rescuing them after they had either ignored his

pleas or he'd inadvertently misread a situation and placed them in peril at his own hand. He was sick of the responsibility of it but too much of a coward to send them home. They were his friends after all, so why wouldn't he want them around to share in the good times? But on this occasion, he had a funny feeling that things would not be so smooth…and he was right.

What followed when he finally found the origins of the signal, would change the course of his life forever.

'I met the Oracle,' he said.

Anji furrowed her brow. 'Who?'

'The Oracle. There are corners of the universe where the oracle is a myth. A creature that can see all of the cosmos, all of what will happen. All that should be. All that might be if nothing is acted upon. Others deny her existence completely, as did I until I met her. How foolish I feel now.'

'What did she do to you?'

'Nothing. It's what she showed me that scares me.'

'Fine, what did she show you then?'

Random stopped staring in front of him and faced his friend. 'Home.'

Anji realised the implications. Random had told her a long time ago, back when they first met that he had run from his home world. She sympathised with him at the time and even more so now as she had fled hers just like him. But then she remembered the little boy she knew back then, his purple skin unique and alien, those red/blue eyes glowing as he explained to her that was supposed to stop a war that was raging back there.

'How bad is it there?' she enquired.

'Hell,' came the response. 'Rodas is falling. The planet is turning to ash and dust. The flames of battle that have been raging there since anyone can remember are about to burn their last.'

'And you've got to put an end to it falling? Is that what she said?'

'Anj, remember when I told you it was my destiny to put an end to it all?'

'Like it was yesterday,' she replied.

'Well, today is that day. I've got to stop it. No more excuses. No more time finding distractions. This all ends now.'

Anji shivered. The finality in Random's voice was haunting. She took his hand.

'We've fought wars before. We shall do it again. Together.'

Random snatched his hand away. 'Not this time.'

Anji frowned. 'What do you mean by that?'

'I can't allow you and Jake to get involved. This is my mess that I have to clear up, no matter the cost, but you two should never have to bear my brunt with me.'

Anji sighed and smiled a little. 'Random, we'd never leave you to fight alone. You've always done your best to protect Jake and me but we are older now. We're grown-ups. None of us are kids anymore. We can make our own decisions and nothing would make us change our minds. Nothing.'

Random frowned a little. 'Jake's a kid again.'

'Skateboard said he's sorting that out. Random, if this is what you were made to do surely, it's easier to do this with others?'

Random allowed a little smile. He wasn't so sure this time.

II

It was still early morning and yet Jake wanted nothing else but to go back to bed. Indeed, when he had awoken from a dreamless sleep he had wondered if he was stuck inside his own nightmare. Then, as he had hopped down from his bed and wandered over to the bathroom, with his room and the corridors of the Venus II looking more intimidating than usual, he spotted his reflection and realised he was in a nightmare.

So, it had happened after all. He was young again.

Why was it always him? At least, that's how it felt to Jake. He'd been sure that the fountain of youth was just a legend. He'd assured his friends they were wasting their time wanting to go on a silly quest to find it. Even as he had teetered on the precipice of a pond which Random had categorically said not to teeter off, he was still disbelieving that such a concept existed. Oh sure, he'd seen space whales, been to parallel dimensions and even watched as a whole planet had turned itself inside/out and managed to not blow up in the instance, but the fountain of youth? What a load of rubbish.

Whether that thought was still running through his mind as he was plunging head first into the very thing he did not believe in, he couldn't say.

But just as it's as likely to be driven in a car by a ghost, they'd found the fountain of youth alright. At least he could claim that he was the first being in the entire universe to have discovered it properly. If only it hadn't reset his adolescence by seven years, that's what he was thinking as he sat stirring his spoon absent-mindedly in his bowl of cornflakes.

Skateboard entered the mid-section of the ship via the cockpit and noticed straight away that Jake was away with the fairies, which was a rather common thing to find Jake away with but he made for the brooding teenager anyway.

'Do you mind if I sit down?' he asked inquisitively.

Jake turned his ache-riddled face towards him and moaned. 'I don't see anyone else sitting there.'

Skateboard was caught a little off balance. 'Pardon me, sir, but unless that's a turn of phrase it doesn't really answer my question.'

Jake put his head in his cornflakes and groaned. 'Look mate can't you just leave me alone I'm busy.'

'Doing what?' asked Skateboard.

Jake didn't have time for his friend right now. 'I don't know, something to come along and stop me from being bored.'

'May I help you with that?' asked Skateboard.

'I don't know. May you?'

Skateboard's wheels squeaked out a sigh. 'I'm sorry Jake if I am speaking out of terms but when you were eleven were you this obtuse?'

Jake picked his face out of his bowl and rubbed the cornflakes off his eyes. 'I'm sorry mate. I'm feeling as stroppy as a toddler in a toy shop and my dad's forgotten his wallet.'

'An…interesting analogy, sir. I have taken the liberty of carrying out a biometric scan with my sensors and I have noticed that your GnRH levels are through the roof.'

'In English?' asked Jake.

'It means that your hormonal fluctuations are erratic. This will explain the irritable behaviour that you are currently displaying. I suggest taking it easy whilst the effects of the fountain of youth wears off.'

'How long will that be?' Jake enquired.

'It's hard to say. It could be days or it could be weeks.'

'Uh, what!?' groaned Jake again.

Skateboard moved to reassure his young friend. 'It's all temporary, sir. In time you will look back and laugh at all of this.'

'Oh, like Anji and Random did?' Jake said sarcastically. He huffed. 'Look. I'm sorry Jake. I know this whole thing is sending me haywire and we should be worrying about Random but…just this once I'm more worried right now about myself.'

Skateboard propped himself up next to Jake.

'I don't know. I feel like if I was me, the normal me, I can help more. I don't feel like I'm going to be able to do anything the way that I currently am. And I can't help thinking the worst. You and Random have spoken in the past about what a dangerous place Rodas is.'

Skateboard nodded. He hadn't told him half of the story. 'There are many dangerous places in the universe. Many of which we have visited. When you and Miss Anji joined us, you were both the age that you have regressed back to. I don't recall either of you bemoaning the fact that your ages were going to stop you from saving the people that you did or defeating the evil that you have met. Whatever I have told you about Rodas in the past, it will not prepare you for what you will see when you get there because nothing ever prepared you when you went to Genocia, for example. But you've always taken these things head-on with all the bravado and carefree nature that you've always shown, so what is it about Rodas that makes you feel so negatively?'

'Random seems scared of going back. He's never been like that before,' said Jake.

'Unlike our other experiences, this is going to be a very personal one for Random.'

'And you,' nodded Jake.

Skateboard paused for a moment. Jake was right. He hadn't really allowed himself time to think about it much but yes, the prospect of returning to Rodas filled him with as much dread as it did Random. He knew why also, but dare not speak of the subject with either Anji or Jake.

'Indeed, so it's going to be hard. But if we all look out for each other and support where we can, then we can be greater than the sum of our parts.'

Jake scoffed a little. 'Like little toy cars linking up to make one big robot.'

Skateboard had no idea what Jake was talking about. 'If you say so, sir.'

'I get the feeling this won't be as easy as it has been in the past. And if it's the end...'

'Why would you think that?'

Jake paused. 'Anji...and I have a pact. It's something we've said to one another whenever we've faced certain death, you know, day-to-day usual situations like that. Back on Earth, we'd be finishing school around about now. It's a big deal. You do your exams, all go your separate ways, drink legally, start going out with...you know, the fun stuff in life starts to happen. Anyway, we had both agreed, years ago now, that around the time this would be happening back home, we'd have a big leavers party called a prom and Anji and I…had agreed to go with one another.'

Skateboard was still listening but had noticed on his biometric scanners that Jake's hormones were about to explode through the roof. Not wanting to panic him further, plus as it wasn't life-threatening, he thought it was better if he didn't mention it and let the boy continue.

'So, I've…' he continued, 'I know I've fancied other girls in the past but with Anji, it's always been different and that promise we made, well, let's just say that promise has got me through a lot.'

'I understand, sir. As much as a robot with artificial intelligence can. I once felt the same.'

Jake looked surprised. 'You did? Skateboard you dark horse!'

'Well, it wasn't a relationship of sorts but, there was someone I met a little while back who I connected with.'

'Woah-ho, you're not holding back on the details there are you chum!' giggled Jake. 'Go on, what else happened?'

Skateboard was startled by Jake's juvenile take on his story and then reminded himself that his friend was currently experiencing a compressed period of adolescence.

'Maybe I'll save it for another day.'

'Spoilsport,' said Jake, who was genuinely miffed that he hadn't managed to get any gossip out of his metal friend. 'So anyway, now that we are both eighteen, well, I will be again soon, finishing up school and life would be changing for us and we'd be going to prom soon. So, I kind of hoped that Anji would want to still go and…oh, I'm an idiot. This is all so silly.'

'Why?' asked Skateboard.

'There is no prom is there? And look at me. It would be like I'd taken the babysitter if we did go!'

'Jake, I'm confused. Are you telling me that you want to go to a party?'

'No. Well, yes. Let me put it this way. I want us all to survive whatever is coming so that we can go to the prom. But what's the use anyway, we've probably missed it. I mean, what month is it? It's hard to tell in space, isn't it?'

Skateboard tried gesturing to the calendar that was hung unevenly above the worktop in the kitchen but then quickly gave up on that idea too as Jake's self-pitying was starting to break his biometric scan capabilities and he was beginning to feel like he needed a lie-down.

'You two can go to the prom whenever you want. The universe, as they say, is your oyster,' the little AI robot said trying to be helpful.

'Maybe if we get through this,' replied Jake.

'You don't have to come. In a way it would be a relief if you both didn't, to put it bluntly,' said Skateboard.

Jake looked a little surprised. 'Skateboard, are you trying to get rid of us?'

'In a way yes but in many ways no. Random and I know how dangerous Rodas can be, far more than you can ever imagine. I want to protect you all from ever getting hurt and yet Random needs you…we need you.'

Jake put his arm around his friend. 'I guess what we are both saying is we had better not get killed, eh?'

Skateboard's diodes purred. He didn't know how many more chances he and his friends would have to be all together. Moments like this needed to count.

Suddenly, the alarm klaxon began to shriek all across the Venus II. Little red lights replaced the normal lighting and all four crewmembers jumped out of their skins.

'What the bloody hell is that?' cried Jake. Both he and Skateboard ran towards the cockpit and were soon joined by Random and Anji. Skateboard busied himself with the onboard computer whilst Random slid into his pilot's chair and took command instantly.

'Have we hit something coming out of hyperspace?' asked Random.

'Negative, sir, it appears that there is a warning up ahead,' replied Skateboard.

'What kind of a warning?' asked Anji who was gripping the back of Random's seat as the ship's ride had become less stable.

'Sensors are picking up a blockade up ahead, roughly seventy kilometres from the edge of Ursa-17,' said Skateboard.

'How far ahead?' asked Jake. 'Maybe we should slow down a little bit. If there's something blocking our way, we could hit it.'

'Good idea Tiny Tim,' said Random mockingly, which made Jake glare back. 'Dropping out of hyperspace...now.'

All of a sudden, the bright, psychedelic features of hyperspace melted away and the Venus II came to a stop.

The four travellers look out of the cockpit and were stunned.

'Those ships,' said Jake. 'They look familiar.'

'They are,' said Anji with a level of disdain in her tone.

'It looks like we've encountered a space block,' said Skateboard.

Random tutted. He was always surprised by his metal friend's capacity for stating the obvious.

In front of them lay three huge battle freighters lined up in a row and several dozen hornet fighters in attack formation.

'Just when I thought I'd seen the last of them…' said Anji ruefully.

The comms system on the dashboard of the Venus II began to blink into life.

'There's an incoming message coming from one of those freighters,' said Skateboard.

'Put it through,' said Random instantly.

Obeying his Captain's order, Skateboard accepted the message. A hologrammatic display enveloped the viewscreen showing the face of someone that all four travellers knew very well.

'Admiral Bagari,' said Random.

'Captain Random,' replied Bagari in her usual unimpressed manner. 'I had a feeling I'd meet you here.'

III

Nkite moved quickly as the heli-fighter's laser fire continued to explode all around her. Round after round of the deadly blasts threatened to strike her down as she weaved the cavernous ruins of a long-desolated part of her hometown. She breathed heavily, carrying under each arm the two children she had found cowering in a delipidated building. As she struggled against their kicking and screaming, terrified of the danger she was trying to save them from, she stole her sights off the winding, crumbling road and looked high up in the burnt sky at her tormentor. She knew that the heli-fighter's pilot was toying with her. The chopping blades of the craft whipped in the air high above her and seemed more than content to give her the run around than finish her off for good. The sound of the heli-fighter roared alongside that of its open fire from the laser cannons to such an extent that Nkite couldn't hear anything else. The roar of chaos was now deafening. Inside the heli-fighter, the pilot grinned manically as his thumb continued to squeeze the trigger on top of his steering wheel.

'Like fish in a barrel,' he smiled to his co-pilot, who was looking pensive next to him.

'Can't you just finish her off now, sir?' he said
through green-tinted cheeks. 'I feel sick.'

The soldier scoffed to himself. A seasoned man
like he had resented taking on another co-pilot
since he had lost his last colleague, who during a
heated battle in the skies above the ruins of
Rodas had sadly fallen from his heli-fighter.
Granted, his superiors had not known that it was
the pilot himself who had pushed him but they
were never to know, lots of things happen in
battle. What he didn't tell them saved them time
on paperwork after all. He had rebuked even
more when he discovered that his new partner
possessed no experience of aerial combat
whatsoever.

Then his horror had been well and truly
confirmed when those in charge of his sector
revealed to him that his new partner would
eventually become his replacement as he was
being moved out.

He loved killing. Nothing else in life came close
for him in his quest for fulfillment. A desk job in
a never-ending war just didn't whet his appetite
as much as blowing people up. So, while he was
up there in the sky, blowing people up and
having enormous fun at the same time was what
he was going to do, and no one was going to stop
him.

'You know what makes killing these stinking blue skins so satisfying?' he purred. 'No matter how hard they run they can never escape. It's a battle with only one victor – the hunted.'

The co-pilot's stomach lurched as the heli-fighter continued its pursuit of the stubborn girl it has been chasing ever since it had spotted her leaving the ruins. The powers that be had started to task members of the Crimson Empire army with destroying the ruins of the capitol through any means necessary and they didn't care if anyone was caught up in the demolition project. Like rats fleeing the fire, they would soon run and those who did, no matter what side of the war they sat on, was fair game for a murder chase. They had shunned the war effort, so why save them? Recruiting them would only result in people like the pilot's newest recruit being handed a gun and if they were the future of Rodas, to him, he'd rather the gun was turned on them.

'I can't take this anymore,' cried the co-pilot as he hurled his breakfast out of his person and onto the ground far below.

'Your generation, you just don't have the stomach,' quipped the pilot. 'Right, I'm getting bored of this.'

He squeezed the trigger again and through his sighter, set his gaze firmly on the fleeing girl. 'Game's up, blue skin.'

Nkite weaved and ducked some more and then suddenly she stopped.

The heli-fighter that persisted in terrorising her did exactly the same.

For a brief moment, there was an air of calm that came between them and for the first time, Nkite could hear the cries of the children she had under each arm.

She put them down without looking at them, glaring upwards at their pursuers. 'Girls, find somewhere to hide. Now.'

The children did exactly as they were told and made for the relative safety of a nearby collapsed wall.

'You want to play games?' Nkite said out loud. 'Let's play.'

Without any hesitation, Nkite pulled her stick out of her backpack and tore towards the heli-fighter, which although not as high as it had been before, was still hovering at roof level above her. The nose of the craft pointed downwards as the pilot trained his guns. Nkite gritted her teeth. Just what she wanted him to do. As her legs pumped faster and faster, she used a pile of rubble as a ramp and threw herself off the end of it. At that moment, the lasers began to fire again. The pilot smiled sickeningly as Nkite flew through the air. His sights locked on to her frame as it flipped in mid-air.

Suddenly the windscreen of the heli-fighter cracked. Something had penetrated the glass.

The co-pilot, still wiping the sick from his mouth looked over at his sadistic pilot and gasped.

The pilot's twisted smile was indelibly stained upon his lips and his bulging eyes stayed motionless. Everything else was just as it should be in the cockpit except for one thing. A spear was sticking out of his chest.

The guns had stopped and the heli-fighter was starting to fall from the sky. The co-pilot pulled himself together and reached for the steering wheel but it was too late.

Even if it hadn't been his first day, or if he had been given more than just one practice run in a craft such as this, he was too close to the ground to stop it crashing now.

As the pilot's lifeless body fell forward, so did the heli-fighter and death for the co-pilot became just as inevitable.

Nkite continued her pirouette in the air and landed less than gracefully in a pile of sand and dust, hurting her ribs in the process just in time to see the heli-fighter explode in a ball of flames. As the fire began to die down, she shakily got back up to her feet and wandered over to its burning remains.

'I win,' she muttered. Nkite made for the children's hiding place and winced as she walked. She noticed a deep throbbing in her right ankle and her ribs felt sharp all of a sudden. 'It's okay, kids, you can come out now.'

She waited for a response and yet there was none.

As the sound of the flames that scorched the crashed heli-fighter grew distant, she refocused her senses.

'Kids?'

Nkite started to panic. The crash had occurred far away enough for them not to be caught in the blast, and then she remembered where she was. The capitol was teeming with Crimson Empire soldiers. No matter if they were in the air or on foot, they teamed the capitol like lice sucking what was left of the life force dry. They could have been picked up by foot soldiers whose attention had been alerted by the hullabaloo she had caused.

Despite her injuries, which had begun to gnaw at her attention, she hurried her stride towards the wall that the children had hidden upon and through her wheezing lungs she finally drew a sigh of relief as she rounded the corner and saw the pair of them, huddled together, paralysed with fear.

'It's okay, my loves,' she cooed. 'You're safe now.'

'Please, don't touch us!' shouted the bigger of the two girls.

Nkite's outstretching hand recoiled instantly, as though she were about to have it bitten.

'I mean you no harm. I'm here to help.'

'You're one of them, keep away!'

Nkite gave the girl a puzzled look. 'One of them?'

A searchlight from a nearby heli-fighter illuminated them briefly and it dawned upon Nkite what the little girl had meant.

The two girls that she had rescued, the two who looked back at her with pained, judging eyes, were red. crimson red.

Nkite shook her head. 'Look, it doesn't matter what colour I am or what colour you are.'

'It does to us,' said the smaller girl. Nkite saw the terror in her young eyes, a terror that no girl her age should ever witness and yet it was the same horror that had scarred her at her age. The girl turned to the older of the two and began to cry. 'Where's Daddy?'

The older girl turned back to Nkite. 'Leave us alone. Please.'

Nkite looked at the floor. She had risked her life for the children and saved their lives from their own race. A race who didn't want them alive. She couldn't guarantee them safety but she could get them to a safer place than where they were.

High above them the sky became busy with the sounds of battle once again.

Nkite grabbed the girls. 'Listen to me, if you stay here you will die. These people, YOUR people, are killing everyone who can't fight. You must come with me.' Nkite's eyes began to cry as she pleaded with them to come with her. 'Please.'

The older girl held her sister tighter. 'No.'

A chill shot down Nkite's spine. 'I'll carry you if you don't.' She winced again. Clearly to the girls she was in no fit state to rescue them by force. To them, it wouldn't be a rescue. It would be a kidnapping and blasphemy upon their names if they were to allow themselves to be taken by a blue skin.

'We'll scream in you do,' said the oldest sister defiantly.

With that, a little bit of the hope that kept Nkite fighting went out. She had risked life and limb and now, as the battle continued to rage all around them, as it had done for century upon century on Rodas, she knew she had to go.

The tears began to stream down her face. As she wiped her nose with the back of her hand, she heard more laser fire from heli-fighters like the one she had destroyed descending upon them. The whole area was about to burn and she could do no more than to save her own sorry skin.

Finally, she croaked one single word to the girls, telling them to run, turned her back and limped away, too ashamed to look back. As she crouched in and out of the debris and ruins of a once great city, one that the Crimson Empire was too ashamed to keep alive, like the people who dwelled there, her heart ached inside her chest.

She had held onto the hope of salvation for so long and yet, as she slipped quietly away, hearing the terrifying noise of gunfire emit from where she had just been, that flame started to diminish.

As she slinked and hobbled her way back to the hideout by the river, the dwelling she had been adopted into when she had been no older than the little girl who had just turned her away, she tried not to let any of the hurt stop her. That girl and her sister, she could have saved them, they could have survived, maybe they still did. They had scorned her and why? Because she was different from them. A difference that they had been taught was dangerous and evil.

Nkite dragged herself through the desert towards the river, her body burning with pain, she saw the shacks which made up her neighbourhood and collapsed to the floor, sobbing like a little child.

She had waited for salvation. She dreamt of it all her life. But her heart couldn't take it anymore.

A few distant lights burst the darkness of the riverbank as Nkite's fellow dwellers heard her cries.

She punched the sand over and over, the injustice of it all was too much to bear.

Salvation wasn't coming. Rodas was beyond redemption.

IV

'Get out of the way, Admiral.'

Random's anger at the Space Seals sudden appearance on the cusp of Ursa-17 was enough to boil his blood. Anji looked at her friend and could see his fists were clenched by his side.

'I'm sorry, Captain but I can't do that,' came the response.

'I wouldn't advise you to try and stop me,' Random said.

The Admiral sighed one of her trademarks, long and unimpressed sighs. 'Captain, you are a truly remarkable man. You are outnumbered sixty to one. If we liked, we could transport your friends out of there and leave you to try our patience, at which point one single blast from any of our freighters will totally destroy you. Now I know you're healing powers are beyond comprehension but I doubt your metabolism is good enough to withstand the vacuum of space now do you?'

'I wouldn't go making threats,' replied Random.

'And I wouldn't stoop that low,' Bagari responded. 'I was just pointing out that it'd be stupid to disobey my order.'

'I'm not one of your soldiers,' spat Random. 'You can't tell me what to do.'

'I'm the Admiral of this sector among many others and I am in charge of this space. So yes, I can. Look, I understand that this isn't ideal. Come aboard, I'll bring you up to speed on everything. Then we can discuss what the next steps shall be. How does that sound?'

Anji, Jake and Skateboard looked at Random, who stared unblinking at Bagari's image on the monitor.

'Sounds a lot nicer than being blown up,' he replied.

Bagari gave a little sigh of relief. 'We shall send you our coordinates now. Docking Bay 48 is free. I shall meet you there.' Bagari nodded to someone out of the image and disappeared from the screen.

Anji and Jake breathed a sigh of relief. 'Blimey,' said Jake. 'I thought we were going to war with the Space Seals for a minute there.'

'You're not afraid of the Space Seals, are you?' asked Random.

'No…but Admiral Bagari gives me the jeebies!' admitted Jake.

Random allowed himself a smile. He registered a new message that had come through the onboard computer. 'Docking bay 48, Skateboard. Take us in slowly.'

The Venus II turned and made for one of the massive battle freighters.

The fleet of hornet fighters that had blocked their route started to part like the red sea in the bible story as the travellers made their procession.

'Just when I thought I had seen the last of Admiral Bagari,' said Anji ruefully. Just over a year ago, she had spent a weekend training to become a Space Seal herself in the Academy. It had shocked her just as much as it had shocked her friends. At the time the crew of the Venus II had found themselves being unofficial freelancers for the Space Seals after it was discovered that from an earlier adventure, that an evil tyrant from another universe called Stratos, had infiltrated their reality from another. This had created a knock-on effect where anomalies had opened up in all corners of the universe and all sorts of weird and dangerous creatures had started to seep into the wrong reality altogether. Since it had been Random and his friends who had caused the first one, in Bagari's eyes, she thought they should tidy up after themselves. They eventually stopped the anomalies but in a break from their battles against parallel universe monsters, Anji decided to take a sabatical and ended up, to her surprise, enrolling in the academy.

Much to Anji's relief, it didn't last long.

Her stubborn streak and issues with those in authority had put pay to that but Bagari had been rather kind just before she had left so although her respect for the Space Seals was non-existent, she had bucket loads of it for Bagari. Where countless teachers, social workers and people in uniform had failed oh so many times before, Anji had finally found a person in authority to look up to and all it took was for someone to show her respect and value. It didn't make going back there any easier though.

When the Venus II flew through the forcefield barrier between the outer hull of the freighter and the docking bay, Anji began to worry a little about bumping into any of her fellow cadets. As they looked out of the viewscreen at the rows of soldiers, standing to attention in banks of ten, she gulped hard.

Random, Anji, Jake and Skateboard descended down the gangway, leaving the relative safety of the Venus II and onto the cold, non-descript floor of the battle freighter, a loud click echoed all around. Someone in the crowd of soldiers bellowed an order and everybody, every man, woman, diaphone and subjakeat alien lifeform snapped into a smart salute.

The travellers didn't know what to do. Jake gave a rather feeble salute back that looked like a wet fish slapping a teenager on the forehead.

'At ease,' came a familiar voice. The soldiers' salutes instantly disappeared as their arms snapped back down to their sides and their heels clicked again as they relaxed.

The voice belonged to Admiral Bagari and she walked to greet her old friends.

'No salute from you I, see?' said Random quizzically.

'You know me, Random, I am hard to please. To get a salute from me you'll really have to earn it.' She said back with a hint of cheekiness in her voice.

Random didn't feel like joking around. 'Might I hazard a guess as to why you've stopped me?'

Bagari nodded. 'If you'll follow me to my ready room, I shall brief you all personally.' She turned on the spot and led the travellers out of the docking bay.

V

'It's worse than you think, Captain. Much worse.'

Bagari unbuttoned the top of her tunic and made for a drink cabinet in the corner of her ready room. Jake took in his surroundings. The room was furnished beautifully. The walls and floor seemed to shimmer a pinkie, purple colour and there were three push sofas arranged neatly in a U-shape around a big desk, which was impeccably tidy and to which itself sat a few feet in front of a big leather chair and a huge wall of monitors and diagrams.

'Blimey, pays well does it, being an Admiral?' said Jake.

Bagari ignored the comment and instead busied herself with pouring drinks.

'Please, do make yourselves at home. I've been meaning to ask. Jake…have you always been so?'

'Annoying?' asked Anji.

'Young?' finished Bagari. 'Or is this a new thing?'

'Second puberty,' said Jake. 'I enjoyed the first one so much I thought I'd like to go through it all over again.'

Bagari frowned and shook her head. 'Anyway, back to more pressing matters.'

She finished pouring a filthy, dark-looking liquid into five tumblers, put them on a tray and proceeded to take them to the travellers, who had arranged themselves untidily on the sofas.

'Forgive me, Admiral, but I cannot drink,' said Skateboard.

'It's Alturian vodka and it's consumable by any humanoid or android in the known universe,' Bagari reassured.

'Vodka!' replied Jake excitedly.

'You're too young to drink,' said Random.

'Believe me, when you've heard what I have to say I think you'll all be asking for the bottle,' said Bagari. 'First, I'd like to ask you Captain why you chose this moment to return home?'

Random took the tumbler offered to him from the tray. 'Is it important?'

Bagari shot him a look whilst offering the others their drinks. 'I wouldn't be asking you if it wasn't.'

Random nodded. 'The Oracle. She sent me a distress signal. I answered it. Never been one to ignore them. She showed me what was happening on Rodas. How the war had developed while I had been away. She convinced me to come back.'

Bagari took to her chair. 'The Oracle…until now I thought they were just a myth.'

'I wish she was,' replied Random who took a brave swig from his tumbler. Jake and Anji gave him a disgusted look as he let the disgusting-looking liquid cascade down his throat. 'It's just like honey, honest!' he said.

Hesitantly, they too took sips and looked pleasantly surprised at each other. Skateboard produced a tiny metal straw from inside his casing and proceeded to take little sips as he listened on.

'Then she must have foreseen what we have been dreading for quite a considerable time,' said Bagari.

'And what's that then?' asked Jake, who even after one sip of the vodka was starting to feel a little merry.

'We've had news from the security border that protects the galaxy from Rodas that the leader of one of the warring factions has started putting together plans to break out.'

'Kalor Maloso,' said Random coldly. He had encountered him once before on the day that he and Skateboard had stolen the Venus II and become the only people in the history of the cosmos to break the security barrier that contained the war on Rodas and fled the chaos. 'We've met. Kind of.'

'In the past few years, the Sapphire Regime has all but crumbled.

    With little resistance left the Crimson Empire
are now committing genocide against their own
people.'
    'That's horrible!' cried Anji.
    'That's not the half of it,' replied Bagari. 'Since
he learned of Random's birth and escape he had
been conducting experiments to raise an army of
unbelievable force.'
    'Has he succeeded?' asked Random.
    'We are not sure. Intelligence tells us that he has
been conducting similar experiments for decades
but now he has acquired the technology he is
going further than he ever had before. It'll end
Rodas. His plans are to ultimately destroy his
own world and then spread his infection of war
across the galaxy. It's the universe's biggest fear.'
    Random scoffed. 'The universe's biggest shame,
more like.'
    Bagari scowled. 'How do you mean?'
    Random slammed his drink down, his anger
raging through his body. 'Rodas has always been
scorned. I didn't spend long there but you didn't
have to be a genius to see what had happened.
The people there. The billions of refugees from
both sides of the planet; took me a split second to
see how the rest of the universe had turned its
back on them. Their faces have haunted my life. If
the universe was so concerned about Rodas then
why did it never intervene? Think about it.

The countless lives that have been lost and for what? And now I'm forced to go back there to finish off a job that no one else ever dared to do. I mean look at you, sitting all safe and sound in that cosy armchair when you have an armada out there, all just to stop me from doing what I'm so-called "destined" to do. You could put an end to this war. You and all the other Space Seals. But no. You're all just watching. Observing from afar. You're no better than the rest of them Bagari and you know it.'

'That's not true, Captain and you know it,' said Bagari calmly.

'No! No, I don't know it! There are zillions of armies in the cosmos. All it would have taken was a warning from them all. But they all sat back and let it happen,' he continued.

'Captain there are treaties and agreements too many in number that I could bore you with that prove otherwise,' Bagari said springing out of her chair and meeting Random's frustration head-on. 'I don't like having to sit back whilst millions of people die, believe you me. I'm in this job to save lives, just like you are, but there are times when all I can do is protect and serve. Take our current location for example. We are allowed no further, not one inch closer to Rodas than here, and why? Because there are forces on that planet that the people in charge of this big, bad universe fear even themselves.'

Anji and Jake sat pensively, the electricity in the air was cracking.

Random's clenched jaw relaxed a little. He saw the sincerity in Bagari's eyes. He heard it ringing in his ears. It didn't make him feel any better.

'Why? Why is the universe so afraid of Rodas?' asked Anji.

'Because of the war. Because the people were stupid enough to start a conflict over the making of a colour,' said Random, showing that he had acknowledged Bagari's counterargument.

'Making of a colour?' parroted Anji. 'Which one?'

'Does it matter?' asked Random. 'The point is that Maloso and the Crimson Empire have got to where they might just be strong enough to get out…and take Rodas down with them. It's not just the people in charge who are worried about war spreading across the stars. It's the guilt of never putting an end to it. They can't sleep at night and now their dirty little secret might just pollute those they are sworn to blind from the obvious.'

Bagari didn't argue back. It was hard to. 'Even so, we cannot advance further than this point.'

'So that's it? Rodas is contained here if the security barrier goes? Who says that it will? It's impregnable, isn't it?'

'No, sir,' Skateboard interjected, tearing himself away from his delicious drink. 'We got out,

remember? So, us doing it will have given
Maloso the drive and hope to do it himself.'

'And according to our people on the ground, he
will,' said Bagari.

'And yet you won't let us stop him,' said Anji.

'It's not that,' said Bagari.

'Well, it sounds like you won't even let us try,'
slurred Jake, who had finished his drink already.

'I never said I wouldn't let you try.'

Random tried to hide his surprise.

'You mean?' squealed Jake.

'I'm not happy about letting anybody go down
there but I'm not allowed to do a thing. My
superiors have spoken. No-one is to enter Ursa-
17. But having seen the reports about what is
going on down there, I cannot stay passive. If you
youngsters want to go to Rodas, you can and I
give you my word that I shall say nothing. I have
to ask. All four of you. Do you really want to go?
You haven't seen what is happening down there.'

'We have to,' said Random.

Anji and Jake gave the same confident look.
'We're staying with Random.'

'I'd prefer if you two were to remain here,'
replied Bagari.

'As would I, Admiral,' said Skateboard, whose
drink was keeping him unusually quiet. 'I've
seen Rodas. I'm worried that if you two follow us
down there you won't come back to the same
people. War changes people.'

'So?' said Jake. 'We are sticking with you. No matter what.'

Random sighed. 'A part of me prefers you to stay. At least then I would know that you were safe, but another part of me wants you by my side.'

'We'll listen to that side then,' quipped Anji. 'But how do we get in? If by what you say the security barrier is still up then how do we get through.'

'I have a contact,' said Bagari. 'They can get you in. I'll send you the coordinates Skateboard.'

'Thank you, Admiral,' Skateboard replied.

'Bagari,' said Random. 'This could be the last time that we see you. If that's the case…thank you, for everything.'

Bagari looked at him. 'A lot can happen if you go down there. You might put an end to it all yourselves or it might be the case that the Space Seals change their stance. Whatever happens, I'll be keeping an eye on developments. Just make sure you all get back safe.'

Random said nothing. 'Right, you lot, finish your drinks. There's no time like the present.'

'Wait,' said Bagari. 'Before you go, we need to speak about the condition of your craft.'

'The Venus II? It's in brilliant condition,' said Anji.

'That's the problem,' said Bagari. 'It's a stolen, very famous ship. The only one that has ever escaped Rodas? It'll be seen.'

'We have cloaking capabilities, Admiral, I'm sure we will be fine,' said Skateboard, who had a horrible feeling that he knew what was about to be suggested.

'And the entire fleet don't want me to send you down there.'

'So, what are you saying?' asked Random.

Bagari raised her eyebrow. 'Let's create a show. You all try to escape, we open fire, the Venus II crash lands and you turn off your sensors so it looks like there are no survivors. No questions asked by anyone else, you get where you want to be and I don't have to write any reports or be dragged towards a disciplinary committee.

'You mean you want to shoot us out of the sky?' cried Jake.

'In a way, yes. We'll only leave surface damage; I'll make sure of that. It's the only way that can get you past the fleet's sensors and to the security barrier. You can switch the cloaking device on before you get there.'

Random pondered on the idea. Skateboard and the others looked on anxiously.

'Alright, fine,' he said finally. 'But please, mind the paintwork.'

'You'd all better run out of here too. Make it look as though you've escaped,' Bagari said.

Skateboard diodes whimpered. He knew it was inevitable that their ship would get scuffed a bit during this mission but now he was starting to worry about how long it would take him to carry out repairs.'

'Okay, Admiral. As I said, go easy. Don't actually blow us up.'

Bagari nodded.

'I'll drive,' slurred Jake.

'No, you won't, you've been drinking,' replied Anji.

'Right, come on you lot, let's go,' said Random. He looked at Bagari again and pelted out of the room, closely followed by the others.

Bagari gave them a ten-second head start and then raised the alarm from her desk. She smiled to herself. For all the annoyance they had caused her over the years, she was looking forward to shooting at them. Then she remembered where they were about to go. If this didn't work, her career would go up in smoke. Were they worth it? She grabbed her beret and made for the ready room door.

'Godspeed, Captain Random.'

Meanwhile, as the travellers fought their case away from Rodas, Kalor Maloso put the finishing touches to his master plan. He stood alone, brooding over a strategy map that sizzled a neon red into the darkness that was his domain. The warlord allowed himself a smile, something he was rare to do unless he had taken a life or ordered the death of many. He glared over the map, which showed a three-dimensional live feed of what was happening on the battleground. He watched in delight as the areas that had once been blue were starting to flash a crimson red. The audio of his troops putting to action his orders surrounded him and he closed in eyes in glee as he heard the declarations of liberation and the screams of their enemies being extinguished like flames in the night.

He opened them and proceeded to monitor the bombardment of the ruins that scattered around the capitol. Dozens of little dots buzzed all over the place like ants.

He thought to himself how he was rather like a giant, pouring scalding hot water upon them to wipe them out altogether. He found that good.

Kalor Maloso has grown weary of the weak and infirm.

He had no use for those who couldn't fight or did not wish to fight. All they did was take up valuable food and shelter, resources which in his mind should be the bare minimum his soldiers should be given. After all, no one except he had a home anymore, but why should they all go hungry? Maloso purred as he watched the sheer magnificence of his genius and switched the map off with a wave of his hand, plunging the room into darkness once more.

Without hesitation, he proceeded to stalk slowly across the vast gloomy room and made for the far wall. With a click of his long, bony fingers, a panel spun out of the rock face. Pressing a few buttons, Maloso stepped back as a low-pitched hum began to emanate around him. The ground started to shake as a trapdoor appeared in the floor and out of it a glass chamber began to rise. Maloso grinned, his demonic eyes glowing blood red. Before long, the long tubular chamber, and a bank of complex instruments came to a halt. Maloso considered the chamber for a moment.

So far, his plan had worked. But there was so much more he had to do. There was little resistance on Rodas that could stop him now, but he knew that at any moment, the threat of the one who could destroy his conquest of Rodas could return. The prophecy had been told and he knew better than anybody that destiny was something that could not be stopped.

Only he didn't know that. He knew that he could hold back death, that his purpose in this cosmos was to rule. It was his right and no coward was going to stop him.

That's what the people of Rodas had started to call their savour. A coward who ran away instead of fighting for them. All hope of salvation had left the planet at the same time that his little ship had somehow broken through the security barrier which contained the madness within Rodas.

Maloso opened the chamber door and stepped inside, laying down inside the empty tube. He thought to himself as he fixed a breathing mask around what was left of his rotting nose and mouth. If he could break through the barrier once then it would happen again. Only there would not be a barrier to pierce this time. If his plan was to work, then the coward would probably return too late and find himself on a dead planet.

As Maloso made to close the chamber door, his communication system fizzed into life.

'I'm sorry to disturb you, sir, but we have some urgent news.'

Maloso stopped in his tracks and bolted upright. 'I told you,' he said in his malevolent calm voice,' that I was not to be disturbed.'

The voice paused for a second and then continued with a significant amount of fear in its tone.

'Supreme Ruler, I can only apologise but we have received intelligence that the chosen one is on the outer edge of Ursa-17.'

Maloso's eyes grew wider. 'I see,' he said, calculating his next move. 'Then we had best be sure that we are prepared in all things, isn't that right, Commander?'

'Yes, Supreme Ruler,' came the reply. 'Shall I proceed with the plans?'

'That would be most satisfactory,' purred Maloso. 'And Commander? Oversee the experiment personally. We don't want to add yet another abomination to the pile now, do we?'

'No, Supreme Ruler.'

'Good. I shall now retire for the evening. If what you say is true and the coward is indeed on his way then I shall need every ounce of strength I can muster. Until then, make sure that your troops keep driving the Sapphire Regime out and kill anyone who gets in your path.'

'As you desire, Supreme Ruler.'

'Oh, and Commander?'

'Yes, Supreme Ruler?'

'If you disturb me one more time, I shall pull apart every inch of bone in your skull inch-by-inch while you are awake, do you hear me?'

The Commander whimpered. 'As you wish, Supreme Ruler.'

'Good,' said Maloso. The comms went dead and he was left alone again.

So Random was coming back sooner than he had thought. No matter, he said to himself. He calculated how long he would need in the chamber to combat this news. Several hours, perhaps? As he laid back leather straps snaked out from under him and fastened his limbs in place. Then another shot out and wrapped itself around his hooded head. Sighing heavily, he grinned. He looked forward to their meeting.

As he closed his eyes the chamber door shut automatically and an orange gas seeped out of invisible holes in the chamber as tiny little operating needles and sharp implements plunged down from the door and proceeded to plunge deeply into Maloso's hideous flesh. It began harvesting what was left of him, taking what valuable DNA it could.

He did not wince, he did not cry out in pain. It was all for the good of the Crimson Empire.

After all, if he didn't spend several hours a day in the chamber, there wouldn't be a Crimson Empire for him to rule.

VII

Two knocks at the door awoke Nkite from her dreamless sleep. She groaned loudly and refused to open her eyes.

'Gron. I know it's you, please not now.'

'How did you know it was me?' asked the gruff, elderly voice from outside Nkite's little shack.

'It's your knock,' she moaned.

'I didn't know I had a knock,' came the rather puzzled response.

'Well, you do and it's woken me up,' groaned Nkite as she turned on her rough straw bed. She waited a minute to make sure that her unwanted visitor had gone and then allowed herself to start falling back to sleep.

'Are you still awake?' came the old voice again.

'No,' said Nkite, she tutted loudly and shuffled off her bed, wiping individual strands of straw off her person as she got up. She reached for the door. 'Alright Gron, you win.' She opened the door. The silhouette of a hunched figure appeared before her, the luminous moon of Rodas shining aggressively behind him.

'I heard,' he said as he took a well-worn leather hat from off his head, revealing thick yet dropped white hair that matched the colour and texture of his beard, 'that you were a bit of a mess when you returned here tonight.'

Nkite stood upright as though a superior officer had ordered her to attention. 'That doesn't sound like me.'

'You're right, it doesn't,' replied Gron. 'May I enter?'

'If you must. I warn you, the place is a bit of a mess,' she said as she walked over to a little table. On top sat a metal kettle which was perched above some glowing vegetation. 'I think that water might still be hot, did you want some tea?'

'No, thank you. I had some earlier.' Gron shuffled his way into the shack. Although he had use of a crude walking stick, he used his other hand, the one with the beaten-up hat in it, to steady himself inside. 'But I'll trouble you for a chair as always if you don't mind?'

Nkite smiled as she made the tea. 'I never would. Please make yourself comfortable.'

Gron's bones ached as he lowered himself into the wicker chair that sat near Nkite's bedside. He watched her finish pouring the contents of the kettle into a metal cup and perched next to him on her bed.

'What happened?' he asked.

'You wouldn't want to know,' she said, not making eye contact with him.

Gron smiled. 'Do you remember when we first met? You came to my shop, the little one on the other side of the river. I caught you trying to steal one of my fish.'

Nkite scoffed. 'You're not wanting me to pay for it now, are you?'

The pair of them laughed. Before long Nkite fell into a serious mood again. 'If I'd had money to pay you Gron, I would have done.'

'That's exactly what you said to me. And I gave it to you, for free, remember?'

'Yes,' said Nkite. She was taken back to that day several years ago. 'I broke down. It was the first time anybody had been kind to me in a long time.'

'You poured your little heart out to me. You told me that you had lost your parents and that you were all alone. I told you, so was I. My family were long gone, I had only my shop and my relative safety to my name. Then you told me about what you had seen in the night sky around that time. We talked about it, remember? How the sorrow in our hearts just melted away when we spoke about that brilliant wash of purple in the sky. You had a look in your eye as bright as the sun. It was hope. It sparkled inside you. And now, my dear, I can see in the moonlight how that sparkle is diminished.'

Nkite's eyes began to well up with tears. 'They wouldn't come with me, Gron.'

'Who?' Gron asked kindly.

'They were just kids and they didn't want to be saved,' Nkite's lip began to quiver.

'Every time I set out on a mission; I swear that I will help someone. It's an offer that has never been refused. But now, the children…even the children don't want to be saved,' she started to sob. Gron began to cry too. He placed a sympathetic palm on her head and lowered his head.

'Oh, my child I am so sorry,' he whispered.

Overcome with grief, Nkite threw herself into his arms and sobbed heavy, heartbroken tears into his shoulder.

'How bad has it got that even children would rather die than go on?' she wailed.

Gron's face fell. Through the tears, he looked out of Nkite's open window and saw past the tranquil sight of their river pockets of sparks igniting in the night sky. He knew that the bombing was getting closer. He knew that it would only be a matter of time before their little corner of Rodas would turn to rubble and dust.

'Some people, no matter their age, just don't want to be saved, my dear. It's a sad fact of life. You don't know what their lives had been like. Maybe they weren't lucky like yourself. You found shelter and strength upon the riverbank. They probably never had the chance to see the light like you did.'

'But to refuse me…because of the colour of my skin?' she sniffed. 'To favour death over being saved by someone like me?'

'This world has long been poisoned. The night of the purple sky invoked a hope that had not been seen on Rodas in my life until then, believe me. Those who believe such ridiculous notions that we are different are wrong. Take you and me for example. Both of Sapphire complexion and yet do we look alike? We are all of the same race. The Sapphire Regime, the Crimson Empire, we are all one and yet we have never been further apart.'

'Try telling the Empire that, I've seen them slaughter so many people.'

'And it's begun to eat away at you. I know. Every day that you venture out I pray to the stars that you'll return safe. We need more people like you Nkite. You carry the flame that will one day take us to peace. But please, do not lose that spark just yet. The war must end sometime and people like you will make it happen, I am sure of it. Someone like you, who'd scare off soldiers by firing purple paint at them, do you remember when you used to do that?'

Nkite allowed herself a smile. 'If only that tactic worked now.'

'That takes guts and belief. War can destroy such gifts. Don't let that happen to you.'

Nkite picked herself up and looked into Gron's sweet old eyes. He'd seen so much. He'd been a soldier a long time ago.

But the war had moved on and worse was on its way. She just couldn't make that promise.

'Otherwise, my hope dies a little too,' he said.

'Now, that's just putting pressure on me,' she retorted before giving Gron a smile of appreciation. 'Thank you for coming.'

Gron took her hands in his. She was like a Granddaughter to him. 'Thank you for letting me in. If you ever need me, or find yourself at a loose end and want to listen to my stories, I'm just a hop over the riverbank.'

'Always. Now then Gron, time for me to help you. Let's get you back home.' She got up and offered her hand, to which Gron took it and using the walking stick in his other hand, lifted himself off the chair. He stood and admired her.

'Not all heroes are up in the stars, Nkite. You'll always be mine,' he smiled.

Nkite scoffed. She was about to reply with one of her usual witty retorts when suddenly she could hear something in the distance.

'What's that?' she said, making her way over to the open window.

'Ha, I wouldn't ask me. My hearing went years ago. The Battle on Blon-Fuge it was,' replied Gron.

'Ssshhh.' Nkite put a finger to her lips. It sounded like an army of noisy crickets but it was getting ever louder. 'Oh zark,' she exclaimed.

She ran over to the door, on which her satchel was hanging on a crude hanger that stuck out of it like a nail in a bit of wood.

'What, what is it?' asked Gron, the panic palpable in his voice.

Nkite fetched her binoculars from inside the bag and ran to the window again. Training the sighter, her jaw dropped when her eyes focussed on where the noise was coming from.

'No, please, no,' she muttered. She threw the binoculars onto her straw bed and ripped through her door onto the riverbank outside. Confused, Gron made for the bed and picked them up. His old hands trembling, it didn't take long for him to realise why Nkite had run away.

'Mercy,' he whispered as he lowered the binoculars. Terror began to flood his mind. 'The monsters…'

Nkite ran as fast as her legs would carry, losing her balance in the soft sand under her feet every now and then as she tore towards a large bell that stood incongruously next to the river.

'Wake up everyone, we have to go!' she screamed as loud as her lungs would allow. Some of the people living their lives on the riverbank stopped and saw her and too began to feel panic. 'To the boats, quick! Everyone, get to the boats!'

She reached the bell and using the rope that dangled below it, yanked it with all her might.

The loud ringing was deafening but it alerted the river folk that they had company.

Nkite continued to shout her warning as she watched the dozens of river dwellers leave their little shacks. Men, women and children, some as young as babies in arms enveloped out onto the sand.

'They're here. They're here!' she screamed.

As the river dwellers prepared themselves for evacuation, the terrifying image of hundreds of heli-fighters, their engines roaring like fire grew ever closer.

And Nkite watched as every single one of them was about to destroy them all.

VIII

As Admiral Bagari's ship continued to pummel the Venus II with its heavy artillery, Random was so lost in his thoughts that he barely registered that they were under attack. He sat, unblinking as the ship lurched sickeningly from one side to the other, the outer hull screeching as the searing heat of laser fire scolded its surface.

Anji and Jake, like Random himself, were clasped into their chairs as Skateboard magnetically fastened his frame to the dashboard as more and more sparks and tiny explosions erupted all around them.

'I thought she said she would go easy on us!' shouted Jake as the Venus II rolled to avoid a particularly nasty volley of missiles.

'She is!' said Anji, who was starting to feel pretty sick.

'Just twenty more clicks and we shall shut the engines down and trip their scanners. I've readied the cloaking device too, sir,' said Skateboard to Random but he wasn't listening. Skateboard channelled his optical sensors towards his friend and Captain expecting a response but there was none.

Random just sat there, staring past the viewscreen and beyond the stars.

If Skateboard had an arm to wave, he'd have frantically whirled it in front of his face to bring him back with them but it was no use. Random might have been there physically but not mentally.

'Nearly there,' Skateboard reassured, just as the contents of Jake's stomach emptied into his lap.

'Clean up in aisle…er…everywhere!' quipped Anji, who thought that humour might from deflect from the fact that her dinner was about to vacate her soon too.

'Three…two…one, cutting engines!'

As Skateboard spoke, he shut down all power except life support and, just as was planned, Bagari's battle freighter ceased firing upon them. The Venus II, now chard, a scorched mess of a ship, was drifting aimlessly behind a nebula cloud, out of sight of its attacker.

'We should be out of the way of their sensors now. This nebula cloud will help us get to the security mainframe,' said Skateboard. 'Feel free to unfasten your safety belts. The gravity inside the ship should be stable now.'

He looked back and saw the mess that his two human friends had created.

Skateboard's diodes sighed. 'I'll get a mop.'

As he turned off his magnetic feature and left the cockpit, Random stayed motionless, still staring blankly out into the wideness of space.

He couldn't move, he couldn't think about anything other than his mission at hand. Not for his friends, who were now being mopped up by his obedient and ever-faithful robotic friend. Not for the fact that the ship that he had called home most of his life had small fires inside its cabin that sprinklers were currently putting out. As the Venus II lurched through the nebula, on the other side of the cloud a net began to hone into his sight.

'We're here,' he muttered, diverting his friend's attention away from their clean-up job.

The travellers continued to see to themselves as they joined Random at the front of the cockpit. They watched as they drifted closer and closer to what to them looked like a giant net in space. Before long they could see the electric pulse that shook through the net, a blue energy keeping the danger far below it at bay. As they left the relative safety of the nebula, the image of the security mainframe became clear to see and beyond it and the people who worked within the net could be seen moving in their little command post which clung to the net like dew on a web.

Past it, there it lay. The planet that had haunted Random's dreams.

'What is that?' asked Anji.

'It's the security mainframe,' replied Random.

'And that stops anyone from leaving Rodas?' asked Jake. 'Why didn't it stop you two?'

'We knew how to get out,' replied Skateboard.

'Now we need to get back in,' Random added. 'Okay, Skateboard, let's open a channel.'

'We cannot do that, sir. If we do, we will risk making the mainframe aware of our whereabouts.'

'How do we do that?' asked Anji.

'They will contact us, apparently. Leave the comms open, Skateboard, we'll wait for their signal,' Random got up and made his way down to the mid-section of the ship, avoiding the puddles of sick his friends had failed to clear up yet. He ignored the sparks that were spitting at him from broken electrical cables and the singed walls and floor. He even ignored the little puddles of water that now swamped the room. His feet were wet instantly through his shoes but he didn't mind. Ignoring the calls of his friends as he embarked down the corridor back to his room.

More remnants of the attack littered his path and still, he ignored it.

'Everywhere I go I cause destruction,' he cursed himself.

'But you also leave hope.'

Random stopped in his tracks. That voice. He had heard it before but not for years. She had left him alone for so long after plaguing his conscience with pleas to go home.

That had all changed after the time Random used the powerful element the Zedron Flux to wipe out a race of gods known as the Osirans to save the peaceful planet of Spectronia. After the incident, the voices stopped never to haunt him again. Or so he thought.

'I thought you were leaving me alone now,' he spat. Random wondered if their return had anything to do with him being so close to home. As if he didn't have enough to contend with…

'You need our guidance. The Oracle foresaw what is to come. She knew you would need us but we were always here with you. We would never abandon you,' came another voice, this time that of a male.

Random sighed. 'Why now? Why not any other time since I left? The Oracle never told me, she couldn't tell me.'

The two mysterious voices burnt fiercely inside his mind, so powerful that he believed that they had manifested themselves whole right in front of his eyes. He'd never seen their images so clearly before. The unbelievably tall and gangly blue man and the normal-sized and fierce looking, her crimson red eyes aflame with the same determination that Random possessed. They stood before him, side-by-side, their ghostly vision hazy in the gloomy dark of the Venus II corridor.

'The Oracle can only do and say as much as she is allowed,' said the woman.

'Allowed? I've met gods before and they never seemed to believe much in rules.'

'Look what happened to them,' said the man. 'You have the power to change Rodas for the better. It's what you were destined to do.'

Random sighed. 'I don't feel ready. I've allowed myself to come this far and now...' he hammered his fists down upon the wall, leaving two dented panels looking like they had seen better days.

'We understand, we really do.'

Random scoffed. 'That doesn't help me much.'

'Then let your friends help you more,' said the woman.

'I can't! I've already led them here. How do you think I feel about that? I'm too much of a coward to let them go and I'm too selfish to admit I can't do without them.'

'To have friends is not selfish,' replied the man. 'Random, you must open your heart. You're about to embark on the most dangerous mission you've ever encountered. You're meeting your destiny head-on. You need them now more than ever. Don't leave them in the dark. If there is light, there is hope.'

At that moment, the visions faded away and Anji, Jake and Skateboard appeared in the gloom.

'Who were you talking to?' asked Jake.

'If I told you, you wouldn't believe me,' sighed Random.

Skateboard knew instantly who Random was referring to. 'The voices, sir?'

'Got it in one,' came the response.

'Random, while we were waiting for the signal, we thought you might want to hang out?' Anji asked.

Random smiled at them all. 'No. Sorry.'

Anji and Jake's smiles faded.

Random watched their changed expressions. He could see how hard they were trying to lighten the mood and he was ruining it. He looked down at the ground and allowed himself a little laugh. 'After all, you both stink of sick. I know that my room is a mess but still, at least it smells nice right now.'

The pair of them looked at themselves and laughed. 'Yeah, good point. We'd better get changed,' said Anji.

'Then can we hang?' said Jake. He was eager, just as much as Anji as they knew it might be the last time to have a laugh.

'Depends on how badly you still smell,' said Random cheekily. 'Of course, I wouldn't want anything else.'

As they both made it down the corridor, Skateboard was left alone with Random.

'I know, Skateboard, I know. Is the auto repair on?'

'It's functioning, sir. The question is, are you?'
Random turned to Skateboard. He couldn't answer.

IX

They had barely made it onto the boats before the shelling started. Just as Nkite had helped get the last remaining stragglers on board they set off down the long and dark river, completely exposed to the descending madness of war. Gron, who was sitting on the same boat as his beloved Nkite, had known this was coming. They all had. For too long they had sheltered away from the atrocities unharmed. It was only a matter of time until their abstinence in the long, bitter war would be punished. But in all that time, the river dwellers had been able to set up a contingency; a place to go if their peace was ever disturbed. They had defence mechanisms to help them get there but no way to attack. As the heli-fighter's artillery torched their homes, they had to get away.

Nkite watched as the homes of her neighbours burnt to the ground. The distant crackling or embers drowned out the steady rowing of the people who had manned the oars. Not one river dweller was able to take their eyes off the destruction of the place they had once called home.

Many of them cried. Men, women, children. Gron himself sat solemnly, forcing himself to close his eyes like he was trying to escape a nightmare. Against his chest, he clutched a tattered leather-bound book with all his might.

Nkite sniffed and picked up an oar to help the rower on her boat. It was one of a dozen that were fleeing the flames and as she began stroking the water, she cursed their luck. The escape plan that they had all learned, like a myth handed down through time to each and every new dweller, allowing for more time to escape than that which reality had allowed. She began to feel suspicious. How come nobody had alerted them of oncoming heli-fighters earlier? Whose turn was it to keep watch tonight? Now they had to negotiate roughly two miles of river before they could slope out of harm's way and through a complex system of underground caves.

Someone had given them away, she felt sure about that.

As she saw her own shack succumbed to the flames Nkite couldn't keep her suspicions to herself any longer.

'Who was keeping watch?' she shouted.

'Nkite, this is no time for blaming anybody,' came an older, female voice. It was that of Bakal, an elder of the river dwellers close to Gron's age, but lacking his calm head and tact. 'We must get to safety first.'

Nkite bit her lip. Bakal may have been an old woman, but she wasn't the kind of person she wanted to get on the wrong side of.

In the old days, she had been a fighter and led a resistance battalion across the jaws of a battleground known as Ellipsis. Despite heavy gunfire from the Sapphire Regime, she survived and was tortured and finally tried as a war criminal. Only she had escaped and Nkite had never found out how, but whenever Bakal spoke about the night she made it across the sand dunes to the river, the old woman's eyes turned to stone. Having been taken in by the other side, she had grown to appreciate acceptance and as the years wore on, she grew to love her quiet retirement out of the claws of her enemies and even grown to admire her blue-skinned neighbours.

Bakal placed a reassuring hand on Nkite's broad shoulder. 'First, we survive, okay?'

Nkite nodded and turned back to the task at hand. She noticed a few of the boats in front of theirs were already falling under cover of darkness as the reeds and overhanging trees afforded some visible camouflage from the heli-fighters whose engines and fire poisoned the night sky. Then she looked back and noticed that maybe, after all these years of luck, it looked like it might finally run out.

'Bakal,' said Nkite. She nodded into the distance and Bakal turned around.

A heli-fighter had spotted them and was soaring through the air.

The dwellers on the boat, which had managed to hold roughly thirty refugees, began to panic.

'Stay calm!' barked Bakal. 'Everybody, stay calm!'

The screams of the river dwellers became just as loud as the heli-fighter's engines.

'Raise shields!' cried out Bakal. Her words were echoed across the boats and one by one, a bubble-like protection formed and shimmered a calm blue over those in the boats. As Nkite remembered helping to fit the boats with this defensive capability, stolen by herself from an experimental craft the Crimson Empire was developing, she allowed herself a moment to feel proud.

Up ahead, she breathed a sigh of relief as the mountain containing their hideaway started to feel closer and closer. But then, she watched in horror as the heli-fighters opened fire on the boats. She bit her lip. If their defences were compromised or failed to work, it would be her fault.

She found the shield mechanism and promised the camp that it would work.

They had only managed to test them out with handguns and what few grenades they could thieve from the soldiers that had up until now left them well alone.

She had been told that the shields would be a match for anything. The plans she too had stolen and reported back to Bakal with said so also. But there was always a chance they wouldn't. Recent events in her life had taught her not to misplace her hope.

Voices cried out into the night sky as the laser fire exploded all around and began pummelling the boats. Nkite's heart beat faster than it had ever beaten before as she witnessed explosions of light all around her and her fellow refugees. The water boiled and hissed as the lasers burrowed deep beneath. As the fire sent the water rushing into the air like an inverted waterfall, the squadron leader of the heli-fighters led a flyover, surveying the magnificent chaos they had created below.

As the waves settled, she was astonished to see that their malicious attack had failed. All of the boats were still going. 'Why have they stopped?' she said as she turned to Bakal. The old woman dared not take her eye off them.

'We've bought time; that's all that matters right now,' she noticed that the boat had stopped. The rest of the refugees continued their journey into the cave.

One in fact had already entered through the narrow entrance and was safe from the barrage.

'Don't stop!' cried Nkite to her fellow passengers, 'keep rowing!'

The rowers snapped out of their trance, frozen with fear and even slight relief that they were no longer being shot at. But the fleet was starting to converge.

Nkite knew what they were doing straight away. 'Come on, come on, go!' She took up an oar herself and began pounding the river with it, imploring, willing her little boat with all her might towards safety. The faster they went, the more the water seemed to lap up and over the side into the cabin. Water was sloshing around the feet of the river dwellers. Nkite's face went pale.

'The shield...' she looked at Bakal, who seemed to have a telepathic understanding as to what Nkite was going to say next. She said nothing but looked at the half dozen heli-fighters that had adopted an attack formation. Nkite looked forward, trying her best to ignore the fact that they were now vulnerable and of all the boats in the river dwellers' fleet, they had now lagged behind so drastically that the other boats were almost all inside the mountain and yet they still seemed so far away.

Without warning, the heli-fighters opened fire on the boat.

'Plan B, now!' screamed Bakal.

Immediately, those among the dwellers who were not holding onto infants or loved ones deliberately rushed the port side of the boat, causing it to capsize instantly.

As the dwellers plunged into the water, the fire raged and spat against the hull of the boat.

Nkite, along with a few others had gone under but was now floating back to the top of the water, gasping for air in the little bubble that the boat had created.

She looked back, choking as the hideous sound of artillery raged against the hull above her.

She looked for Bakal, but could not find her. 'Is everyone okay?' she cried.

There was no reply. So many of her fellow refugees were half drowned, recovering from the shock of the cold water and were trying to hold on as best as they could to what had been their seats but now acted like sturdy beams of salvation above them.

Nkite still looked for Bakal but could not see her. She could not work out whether there were tears or river water dripping down her face.

So many old and young were struggling to hold on, clambering for safety as their eardrums were ripped apart by the fury of the heli-fighters' guns.

'The hull is going to give; we need to swim now! Hold on and swim!' she implored. 'If you can, just do it!' As she barked her order, a shard of the metal hull buckled above her head. 'Now, now!' she hollered.

With all their might, they kicked and kicked until the boat began to move forward. As she gritted her teeth, Nkite realised the horrible possibility that there could now be friends of hers floating helplessly in the water behind. She tried to shake the thought from her head as she and her friends pulled themselves inch by inch, closer to safety.

Nkite took a moment to stop kicking and taking a gulp of air, ducked her head underwater to see their progress. She saw the opening of the cavemouth was closer than she originally thought. Luckily, they were on a straight piece of the river.

'Keep going!' she screamed, hoping that her friends could hear her over the noise of the heli-fighters. 'We're almost there!'

With all the strength left in them, the dwellers kicked and kicked, sometimes hitting each other in their effort to reach the cave but nobody was giving up. Not one of them was giving in.

As more fire ruptured the hull above them and one refugee was sent sprawling by something that had struck him, Nkite swept him up in one arm and grimaced as the current of the river pushed them along.

With one final effort, the boat passed through the cave opening but the heli-fighters continued their assault, sending waves of artillery fire into the cave mouth opening and causing the rock formation that had allowed the boat's safe passage to close in a massive explosion of dust and rubble. Once the sound died down, Nkite knew they had made it. She sighed loudly whilst others among her whooped and cheered and some just sobbed.

'They made it!' came a cry from outside the boat.

'Quick, let's get this thing off them,' came another. Nkite could hear the sound of people jumping into the water. She held on tight to the wounded man whilst she let go of the bench above her head.

'It's okay, we're safe,' she smiled at him as she tried to keep both of them afloat. Her smile then faded as she saw the vacant, unblinking eyes of a man she had not known well but did know had a family elsewhere on this boat.

She tried to shake him back into life gently at first but then rigorously but it was too late. As the boat was lifted off them, and many were picked up and taken to one of the banks on either side of the river, Nkite held onto him tight as she drifted to dry land. A couple of dwellers tried to pick her up when she got there and she asked them to be gentle with the dead man.

Soaking wet, she pulled herself up without the help offered and looked through the gloom in the cave. Although it was dark, there must have been light coming through as she could make out figures and people all around.

They had made it. The river dwellers were saved.

'Are we all here?' she said to nobody in particular, the cold water dripping off her making a wet puddle in the rocks below her.

'We are missing a few from the last boat,' came a familiar voice. Nkite looked up and saw the crooked figure of Gron. 'All the children were saved. You saved them.'

Nkite ignored Gron's final three words. 'And Bakal?'

Gron shook his head.

Nkite's face fell. 'It's my fault. The shielding unit...it's all my fault.'

Gron used what little strength he had left to sit down beside her. He put a reassuring hand on her shoulder.

'Nothing is your fault, don't ever think that for one second Nkite.'

'What do we do now?' asked a woman who was clutching a crying baby to her chest.

Nkite quickly gathered her thoughts and got up, helping Gron do the same. 'We rest for a while. Find your loved ones and rest. We'll be safe in here for now.'

'But what about the heli-fighters?' asked one voice in the dark. 'There's a river running through this mountain, they will know to check the other side, we have to keep moving!'

Nkite frowned. 'There are dozens of rivers running through the mountain, it'll take the Crimson Empire a while to work out which one we are in so we rest and then soon we shall make our way to the base.'

The man paused for a moment and then answered back, frustration naked in his tone. 'I'm not listening to you, Nkite. Your shields we supposed to protect us.'

'And they did,' Gron said leaping to her defence.

'Tell that to my brother,' came the response.

'I am so sorry, but we are all casualties of war. We must stick together,' came another voice.

'Very poetic,' came another dissenting voice.

'People please!' pleaded Gron.

Arguments broke out among some of the dwellers whilst others did their best to shut them down.

'Nkite, please?' asked Gron.

The girl gave a withering look to her old friend and stood up.

'Listen!' she cried, stopping the majority of the heated exchanges immediately. 'You can fight amongst yourselves all you like but it isn't going to help us. If you don't want to listen to me, fine. If you don't want to follow the plan, the one we all voted on if we were ever attacked, also fine. If you want to blame me for anyone's death and it makes you feel better be my guest. But the one thing we cannot do is despair. We are alive and when we reach the heart of the mountain, we can send an SOS to the Sapphire Regime and they will help us. Now if you do not agree, and you think that allying yourself to me for any longer is intolerable then go, find your way. I won't worry about you. You'll be doing me a favour, but for now, we have all just lost our homes and some of us have lost loved ones in the process. We need time to gather and if you don't want to, go find the other end of this river and leave.'

The dwellers were silent. The grieving man who had started the argument was the first to break the awkwardness.

'I don't need you to excuse me, I go on my own accord...anyone else?' a few people walked over to be with him. Nkite could hear their feet shuffle over the rocks.

'Good luck then,' she called out and with that, she heard their footsteps grow further and further away.

Gron sighed. 'Right, does anybody need medical attention?'

A mumble replaced the silence.

Nkite left him to it and walked off to be by herself as she heard her old friend ask for children to be seen first. She retired into a little cave mouth on her own and collapsed on her haunches. Hugging her knees tightly she let her shoulders drop and she descended into an uncontrollable sob. Gron looked back, his heart full of sadness. Now that Bakal was gone, he knew that people would look to Nkite for leadership. Knowing the toll that the war was beginning to have on her, he worried for Nkite and as he set about his work with others who were kind enough to volunteer to help, Nkite just let the pain flow out of her.

X

Now that the Venus II looked like it had been battered and damaged by battle, it sailed closer to the mainframe without raising as much fanfare as it usually would. In the years they had been travelling together the Venus II and its occupants had become infamous across the galaxy. There was notoriety that came with Captain Random and his friends being in the area sometimes to such an extent that whole countries, nay, even planets had been named after them. In fact, one such planet that they had saved from extinction when they helped redirect a flaming meteorite away from it was so grateful it even renamed itself. So now, when the peoples of the universe attend carefully to their A-Z of the Fadrigo cluster in the Margalonian system, they would have to scratch out the planet named Hardrafamagorian and simply replace it with the name, Jake, instead.

Even so, just to be on the safe side, the crew of the Venus II were still cloaked as they sailed closer to the rendezvous point. Inside the cockpit, Random and Skateboard were at their usual pilot and co-pilot seats whilst Anji and Jake stood behind them.

'I've been looking down on that planet for a while now and I keep little flashes,' said Anji. 'What's causing it? Bad weather?'

'Fighting,' came Random's one-worded response.

'It's so bad that you can see the battle from space?' asked Jake.

'It's so bad there is a security mainframe defending the rest of the galaxy from what's going on down there,' replied Random.

Jake gulped. 'Great.' He looked down at himself. His body still had not fought off the effects of the water from the fountain of youth. Inside he was growing more and more worried that he would not recover in time to be of any use to his friends in what lay head. Yet instead of worrying them, he decided to keep it to himself for the time being.

'Incoming transmission, sir,' said Skateboard.

'Punching it through,' replied Random, who leaned forward to flick a switch on the dashboard.

The image of a green-scaled reptile flashed onto the viewscreen. 'Captain Random, I am Commander Serridian of the Rodasian Security Mainframe.'

'Commander, good to meet you, I trust that our mutual acquaintance has been in contact?' replied Random. Anji watched as Random conversed with such natural flourish and style that she often wondered why he didn't always talk like this.

In moments where he had been required to be diplomatic, or was meeting a new life form for the first time, Random would switch on the charm and really surprise her with his eloquence. Pity he couldn't just be himself, she thought.

'I have, Captain, yes but I'm afraid the plan has changed.'

Random's face sank. 'Well, not with us, schmuck!'

Anji raised her eyebrows. So much for the eloquent tone.

'I'm afraid that there is the possibility that our message was intercepted by someone.'

'What, someone managed to hack you?' asked Jake. 'Considering you're a security mainframe that's pretty rubbish.'

'Skateboard can you verify this?' asked Random.

'I'm afraid that due to confidentiality I am unable to allow your AI robot access to our systems. I'm sorry, Captain.'

Random was dumbfounded. It had taken him a lot of effort to come back to Rodas. It was a place that deep down in his heart he knew he had to save but wanted to be further away from it than anything else in the universe.

He thought back to the Oracle of Fate, the strange being who had set him on the path back to his destiny and cursed her. 'I bet you're having a right laugh, Oracle,' he said below his breath, knowing that he was probably being watched by her at this very moment.

'This does not mean that I cannot assist in your landing on the planet, Captain, I merely cannot meet with you in person, nor can you come here.'

'What can you do then?' asked Anji.

'I can give you a code. Once you have loaded it into your ship's computer, it will mean that your ship will be impervious to the effects of the mainframe,' replied Commander Serridian.

'Meaning?' asked Jake.

'We can come and go as we please, sir,' Skateboard answered. 'But that's potentially very dangerous, isn't it Commander?'

'Yes,' said Serridian, who had suddenly adopted an even more serious tone. 'Once you land on Rodas your ship could be picked up by the Crimson Empire of Sapphire Regime. Even under cloaking you might be captured. For centuries the mainframe has contained the horror of the atrocities on Rodas.

If the Venus II falls into the wrong hands – any hands apart from your own – the code can be replicated and the war will spread throughout the galaxy.

I am risking not only my command but my life in giving you this message...potentially the future and safety of everyone in this star system, Ursa-17, and beyond.'

'So how are you going to give it to us if you say that your messages are being compromised?' asked Random. Skateboard's diodes whirred as he searched for an answer.

'I think I may have the answer, sir. Commander, you can send the information to me. If ship-to-ship communication is being compromised then sending it directly to me should be safe. My firewalls are tighter than a Space Seal freighter hull.'

Commander Serridian nodded. 'That is a wise suggestion but I am currently scrambling this message through my personal computer so I can always tell you the code now.'

'If it's all the same, sir, I trust my method more. Would you care to oblige?'

The Commander nodded then out of shot he began to tap away at something. 'Bagari tells me that you are the ones who can put a stop to all of this once and for all. I don't doubt her, this isn't the first time that I have placed my life and career in her hands. I hope she is right.'

'She is,' replied Anji.

'You should see our track record,' said Jake.

'I know...I come from the planet...Jake,' the Commander hesitated before finding his planet's new name. 'Call me old fashioned but I preferred what it was called before. No offence.'

'Hold on, there's a planet named after me?' chirped Jake.

'Not now, Jake,' said Random. 'Skateboard?'

'I am processing the code now sir,' said the AI robot, who then used his connection with the Venus II to process the code.

'Protect the code with your lives,' warned Commander Serridian.

'We will, thanks Commander,' said Random. 'Give our regards to the Admiral when you see her next. Oh, and tell her that if she suggests staging a planned trashing of my ship again for no good reason it's coming out of her wallet, not mine!'

Serridian smirked. 'Good luck, Captain.'

The viewscreen went blank.

'Right, are we ready?' asked Skateboard.

'Nope,' said Random.

'Nah-ah,' replied Anji.

'A whole planet, named after me!' said the still-startled Jake.

'But that's never stopped us before,' said Random. 'Take us in somewhere quiet Skateboard, please. We don't want to be captured instantly again.'

'Again, sir?'

'We always seem to be captured as soon as we land anywhere, it's the best way to find out what's going on!' said Anji.

'Not this time. We don't know what we might come up against when we get there. It's best to stay undercover for as long as we can on Rodas,' Random looked deadly serious.

'Understood, we'll go and get ready, come on Captain Planet, let's go find those laser cutters we use as guns all the time,' said Anji as she picked Jake up off the floor and led him out of the cockpit.

'I've found a suitable landing site, sir. Not much activity but not far away from any Rodasians' either,' said Skateboard.

'Wait, Skateboard,' Random paused for a moment. 'How do you feel about going home? Honestly?'

'I cannot lie, sir.'

Random smiled. 'I asked as I know I'll get a straight answer from you. I mean we are home and yet...I can't think of anywhere else I'd rather be further from.'

'I feel exactly the same, sir.'

Random bit his lip. 'I can't help but feel like we've made a bad decision coming back.'

'Not a bad decision, sir, only the right one,' said Skateboard.

Random pondered for a second. Skateboard was right. He is always right. There were many innocent people they were about to try and save. 'This whole planet needs salvation. Are we really the ones to deliver it?'

'Aren't we always?' Skateboard hoped that his words would fire his friend up.

Random smiled. 'Okay, but before we go, I think you and I had better have a Plan B...'

Random imparted his plan to his oldest friend. The AI robot poured over every detail, taking in every piece of information that he was given and storing them as tightly as he would the code the Commander had given him. However, it was the first part of the plan that made him wary.

'You're sure about that?' asked Skateboard.

'You and the Venus need to be kept safe and out of the picture, you heard what the Commander said.'

'But, Anji and Jake and you... you'll be alone down there.'

'Not for long, not if you follow the plan.'

Skateboard's diodes sighed. 'It'll take time.'

'Then as soon as we are down on the planet's surface you start with the plan.'

'But I thought it was Plan B, sir?'

Random sighed. 'It was but I realised when Serridian was telling us about the code that this probably would be safer for everyone.'

'Except you three. Are you sure that you want to risk their lives too?' asked Skateboard.

'Absolutely not, but I know they won't take no for an answer, as do you,' replied Random.

'Do we tell them the plan?' asked Skateboard.

'No, keep it private for now. I'll tell them if I need to when we are on Rodas,' said Random. 'Do we have a deal?'

Skateboard sighed. 'Reluctantly, sir.'

'Good, well then, Skateboard. What are we waiting for?'

Random picked up his steering column and the Venus lurched in space, spinning in a graceful spiral before settling on the coordinates set by Skateboard.

'Next stop,' said Random. 'Rodas.'

XI

The dead, cold fingertips of Kalor Maloso passed over the giant viewer map. He was waiting impatiently for news on the bombings that his army was carrying out. He tapped the bony, fleshless digits on the map and then finally thumbed it with all his might, sending a tiny fleck of glass somersaulting through the air.

He strode over to his communication terminal, still as strong as ever but feeling slightly weaker from his latest ordeal. 'Commander, report!'

'The enemy troops are continuing to retreat. We have levelled many pillars of the old capital,' came a trembling voice through the speaker.'

'Are there many survivors?' asked Maloso.

The Commander hesitated. 'I have seen reports that some from a river-dwelling managed to escape inside Mount Dschali. The heli-fighter unit leader told me that they opened fire on refugees and sealed them in.'

'Send troops inside the mountain to flush them out, Commander. There can be no survivors this time.'

'As you wish, my Lord.'

'Oh, and Commander?'

'Yes, my Lord?'

'Have the unit leader and his team killed for their incompetence.'

The Commander was silent for a few moments. 'As you wish.'

The communications link clicked off and Kalor Maloso was alone in the silent darkness again. He walked over to his main view window and basked in the glory of his work below him. The fire that raged kept him alive and perked up his spirit. 'The time is so nearly upon us,' he said to himself.

Suddenly, he noticed the security mainframe shimmer in the distance. Maloso frowned. He picked up a pair of binoculars that sat close by and fixed them in that direction. There was nothing that his old eyes could see other than more fighting and far-off explosions, so nothing other than the norm.

He replaced the binoculars and turned from the window and made for his chair.

He placed his hand on his chin and was lost in a sea of thought.

XII

A barren, desolate wilderness greeted the eyes of the travellers as their spaceship settled down on the sand dunes of the decimated world. The landing gear let out a whine - groaning under the stress and strain of hundreds of tons worth of titanium and seda metal that crunched the legs of the Venus II further into the ground like a mallet hitting a tent peg into place.

Its battle-worn colours and bleak, dense appearance blended in well with its surroundings on this occasion but given any other landscape and it would have attracted all manner of attention had the cloaking device not been firmly switched on.

In fact, given the huge exterior, that's what the Venus II normally did. But on this occasion, there was no fanfare. As the dust snaked and roared around the bottom of the ship, it began to settle on the stabilising pads that the Venus II stood on.

The only sound that could be heard now was the faint vibration of the inner door mechanism whirring away. All of a sudden, there was a mighty hiss from the hydraulics and the door began to slowly drop down from the belly of the ship.

Footsteps could also be heard clattering down the metal gangway.

Well, if there was anybody around to hear it, but the spot they had picked to land upon was indeed as Skateboard had assured, deserted.

The shadows of three bodies illuminated the gangway – exposed by the bright, white lights from inside the spaceship. The first figure, Random's, took a deep breath as he stood at the front of the pack. 'Let's go,' he said and made his way heavily down the bottom of the ramp.

He bent down and touched the sand with his gloved fingers, feeling the coarse grains fall through the gaps between his digits. Sniffing, he shot a look back to his two companions. Jake stood on the ramp scratching his blonde hair, whilst observing the calm that surrounded them all.

Anji played nervously with her bag that swung irritatingly on her right shoulder. After several seconds of awkward silence, she decided to speak.

'So, we made it then?'

The first person looked away, knowing the answer but not wanting to dignify his friend with a response.

'Yes,' he eventually croaked. 'Yes, we made it.'

'It's not what I expected,' cried the blonde-haired boy.

He looked up at the strange fluorescent moon.

Even though the moon was as bright as anything he had ever seen, the horizon still looked as dark as a harsh winter night back on Earth.

'I was expecting huge towers high in the sky and flying cars. What happened here?'

'The war to end all wars,' exclaimed the leader of the party as he straightened his legs and stood up. He could make out a faint outline of the once, great citadel in the far distance. 'Yet, it still rages. For centuries my home planet has been a battlefield. Millions upon millions have died and it was my responsibility to stop the fighting.'

Anji tore forward and put a reassuring hand on the shoulder of her companion.

'None of this is your fault, Random!' she insisted.

Random turned towards her and gave a glimmer of a smile from his dour expression. For all of the adventures both he and these two-earth people had experienced, all the fun and laughs and the ever so slightly dangerous places they had visited in the quest to get back to this world, he knew he had made a terrible decision bringing them here.

'Anji, you will never know what suffering I have caused. It's time I made up for it.'

'How?' Jake asked Random.

'By making sure that this is the final day. I have to put it right, Jake. It is my destiny.'

Jake was worried. He had never seen Random so serious, so morose and so determined before.

Was this really the same boy that had whooped and cheered his way down a thousand-foot rainbow on the planet Spectronia? Or the same spiky-haired, funny costumed-wearing guy who had used a discarded feather to tickle his way out of the prison tombs of Catacombe 62? Gulping hard, he took Anji's hands and followed his friend towards the unfriendly outline of what looked like a city.

Together, these three had been through so much.

It had been their choice to leave their planet behind and join this funny-looking boy who fell from the stars and since they didn't have a home to go back to anyway, it didn't matter to them if they ever made it back.

But at the same time, both Jake and Anji didn't want to get hurt. So far, they had endured many bumps and bruises on the planet hop back to Random's home world, but this time, there was a full-scale war staring them in the face. And why had Random allowed himself to be talked into bringing them into the hornet's nest?

If I had a dad, he'd never have let me come, Jake thought to himself as he trawled along the sand, which had entered a hole in his favourite pair of trainers and was causing more than a little irritation to his left foot.

A pang of guilt about Anji and Jake's accompanying him to Rodas sparked in his chest. He remembered what Skateboard had said to him in the cockpit earlier, about endangering his friend's lives.

'Remember way back when? Back when we first met, I had no intention of letting you come with me,' Random said as he walked, the chilling night air carrying his sentence back into the direction of his two friends. 'I just wanted to forget about my responsibilities, run away and never come back here. But you two, you two showed me how to be a better person and for that I thank you, but after we assess the situation and analyse what our next move should be I am taking you back to the Venus and locking the door. Do you understand?'

Jake and Anji nodded as they clambered through the soft sand.

'And what if you don't come back?' Anji's lips were beginning to feel sore as the wind continued to blow the sand in her face.

'Then Skateboard will pilot the ship to wherever you want and you can live your lives out however and wherever you like.'

'But you are coming back, aren't you?' Jake craned his neck to see if he could make out Random's face in the gloom.

Random felt terrible. Although he had the physiognomy of a boy just a couple of years older than his counterparts, well, when Jake recovered from his accident, he was in fact a far more advanced being than they were.

He was not as susceptible to illness and disease as humans were but right now, he had a throbbing feeling in his chest that he had never felt before. The most human of emotions.

Fear.

The trio jumped as Random's wrist communicator crackled into life. Over the wind, he could just make out a metallic voice.

'Sir, I must warn you that my sensors have picked up hostile life forms in your vicinity. It would be wise to come back to the ship as soon as possible.'

Random strained to be heard as he continued to walk.

'How many of them?'

Fifteen, Sir. They appear to be on land hawkers, roughly 80 clicks away.'

'Okay, no problem. We are getting close to the edge of the citadel now. I will report back to you when we get there. Await my instruction please Skateboard,' Random ordered before clicking a switch on his communicator and returning to the task in hand.

Random sighed for so long it was heard by future generations. 'Come on, we are nearly there.'

The trio got down on their hands and knees as they negotiated the slight curve on the ground that licked up into the sky. 'Stupid bag!' Anji grunted as she swiped it over her shoulder, almost knocking Jake out in the process.

After a few minutes of crawling in the dirt, they heard something they had not heard before.

The wind had died down and all they could hear now was the sound of explosions, screams of pain and terror and the very occasional whizz of hyper jet fighters and laser fire.

Random's heart was thumping so loud that he thought he could hear it over the sound of destruction.

'Right, that's it. Back to the Venus now, both of you!'

'We are not going anywhere,' Anji protested. 'We are staying by your side and that is final.'

'What? Are you mad!' Jake shouted. 'Can you not hear that down there!? Let's go while we still have the chance!'

'I'm staying.'

'Oh yeah? Well, I'm going!'

The boys' protests were interrupted by an explosion so loud it made the ground tremor for almost a minute.

'...On second thoughts, I'd better protect you, Anji!' Jake declared, despite cowering and holding onto the legs of his friend. She shot him an unimpressed glance.

'Stay low now, we have to get to the edge,' Random implored.

The three youngsters crawled their way closer and closer, the pitch-black landscape was giving away to a blood-red horizon, like a doomed sunrise. Slowly, they pulled themselves up to eye level and saw one of the most indescribable scenes of devastation it had ever been their misfortune to witness.

'Anji...Jake,' Random stuttered. 'This is the citadel of the planet of Rodas. My home...'

XIII

The sheer scale of the conflict took Anji's breath away. She looked on as peculiar, waspish vehicles swarmed what must have once been a magnificent city and rained fire down upon it. She had always understood why Random had no desire to come home. There was so little of it left.

'Right,' he said, shaking her thoughts from her mind, 'What's the plan, Random?'

Random was staring blankly towards the citadel. He remembered it well from the only day he had ever spent on this hell hole but its splendour was now just a rotting husk.

'We have to find the Sapphire Regime,' he replied.

'Who are they?' asked Jake.

'About as close as you can get to the good guys on this planet,' said Random. 'The Crimson Empire are the aggressors. The Oracle told me that it was the Empire whose plans would bring about the destruction of Rodas. We need to find out what they have planned.'

Jake pondered for a second. 'So why don't we just go straight to the Crimson Empire then? Do some spying?'

'Let's just say that we wouldn't fit in,' said Random.

'Story of my life,' Anji retorted. 'But seriously, Jake's got a point.'

'The Crimson Empire are the red-skinned inhabitants of Rodas. The Sapphire Regime are blue. See what I mean?'

'I getcha. So where do you fit in?' asked Jake.

'I don't,' replied Random. He scouted the area for a safe passageway down onto the surface. The sounds of war filled the air and the three friends were having to shout to make themselves heard so he pointed in the direction he wanted them to move instead of continuing to holler.

'What?' said Jake unhelpfully.

'Down there!' said Random as he rolled his eyes.

A screech of sound started to loom close to them. Random peered through the smoke and felt alarmed as the land hawkers that Skateboard had warned them about were now almost on top of them.

'Quick!' he cried as he pulled both his friends down into the mud. Anji screamed as a formation of the unimaginably sharp-looking craft was suddenly on top of them in the blink of an eye.

'Get down there you two and hide, I'll see you in a minute now go!' ordered Random. Anji and Jake didn't argue and began to make their way down the steep decline to the ground surface.

Random pulled his hood up over his face and stood before the fifteen land hawkers that had now stopped in front of him. The horrible-looking things had long, rusty daggers on the end of them and the masked men who piloted them revved their engines to intimidate the hooded figure who stood before them. But Random was far from intimidated.

'Are you with the Sapphire Regime?' asked Random. 'I request to speak with your leader.'

The head land hawker sped towards him full pelt.

'So, that's a no then,' Random said to himself. The rest of the land hawker crew also took off in Random's direction.

Random crouched down and prepared himself for the fight. With breathtaking accuracy, he jumped over the daggers at the right moment and leap high over the head of the lead land hawker and landed on the seat behind him. Before his attacker even had time to register where Random had gone, he found himself flying through the air before landing with a sickening thump against the ground and losing consciousness.

His land hawker, now under Random's control, spun around to face the rest of them.

'Come on then fellas, let's get this over with,' cried Random, who squeezed the right handlebar and sped on towards them, relieved that he had luckily found the right one and he hadn't rather embarrassingly squeezed on the brake instead.

Not far away, Skateboard sat watching the fight on his monitor, completely helpless. Long ago, the biomolecular capabilities of the Venus II had scanned all four of its regular inhabitants and Skateboard could keep an eye on them when they left the ship. It had sounded unethical when he had told them, but in reality, it was to ensure their health wasn't compromised by the alien atmosphere or that they weren't about to succumb to something which would make them poorly. But in the safety of the cockpit, it was the AI robot who felt ill as he noticed that Random was outnumbered while Jake and Anji were left open to danger.

He was powerless, unable to help, and forbidden to get involved. Plus, he had another mission, one that he and Random had agreed on and one that would take him away from Rodas for some time. He had to leave soon otherwise time would really be his enemy, let alone the Crimson Empire. With a heavy heart, he decided he would have to tear himself away from the danger and do what he had been told. Sighing loudly, he set the controls of the Venus II to a new destination, where he wouldn't be able to step in and help his friends or keep them from danger.

The Venus II's landing gear groaned as its engines roared and sent it flying upwards into the air. Still cloaked and invisible, Skateboard knew even if he had wanted to stay that the ship couldn't. If its security mainframe dodging code was ever found out, the consequences could be catastrophic. Instead, he consulted the navigation computer and inputted coordinates. He took one last look out of the viewscreen and saw down below the tiny figure of Random, who appeared to be making light work of the fight that he was currently winning. As the smoke and smog of destruction began to bleed into the dark starry space and the mainframe also honed into view, Skateboard implemented the code again and the Venus II tore away from Rodas and into the vacuum of space once more.

The computer started to bleep and Skateboard, his mind still on the planet far below, was brought sharply back into focus on the mission in hand. He scanned the readings and followed the navigation computer's instructions. With some minor adjustments to the ship's speed output, he sent a wireless command to the computer and threw the Venus II into hyperdrive and in doing so, brought himself closer to his first intended destination.

Spectronia.

XIV

'Don't look back, Jake just, keep moving!' screamed Anji as she slid and stumbled her way down the muddy embankment to the ground. She had spotted Jake lagging behind, clearly more concerned about how Random was getting on. She'd wanted to stay behind to help but she knew better than to become embroiled in a physical fight when Random was more than capable of handling them himself.

'Sorry, Anj, I think he's winning anyway,' said Jake.

'I can't believe what we're seeing here,' said Anji. 'It's awful. How can anyone live like this?' she looked around her as they continued their descent. 'The sky seems to be on fire. I can't tell where it begins and where it ends.'

'Terrible, isn't it?' said Jake. 'By the way, I noticed the calendar on your wall earlier. Do you know what today is back on Earth?'

'Really Jake? While we are in a war zone trying not to fall down a slippery bank you want to discuss my calendar?'

'Yeah, I want to take your mind off it all,' shouted Jake over a nearby explosion which nearly knocked the two teenagers off their balance.

When she had brought it with her on their latest
visit back from their home world, it had bemused
Jake. Then he began to understand that a link
back home, no matter how tenuous, was perfectly
understandable, especially after the years they
had been out having adventures in the big wide
cosmos.

'Go on then, enlighten me,' she gave in. It was
sweet of Jake to want to take her mind off their
predicament she had thought. It would be rude
of her not to humour him.

'July 13th. We'd be graduating from school
around now.'

Anji stopped in her tracks, her footing losing a
little bit of traction in the process. 'Really?'

'You'd circled the date. Had you been back to
our school?'

Anji sighed. 'What was left of it.' She
remembered the day that it had burnt to the
ground and the part that she and Jake had its
demise. Then she remembered Jemima Wright,
the school bully and the surprising reunion she
had unexpectedly had with her. She shook the
thought of it all from her mind, wanting to forget
again. 'We'd have finished our exams now.'

'And had our prom. Remember our promise,
Anj?' Jake said nervously.

Back on Earth, just before their lives had

changed forever, the pair had made a promise to one another that they would attend prom together if they were still single when the time arose. It had been a promise that had got them through some tough times over the years, especially on the rainbow planet Spectronia where Jake had been buried alive by a crazed archaeologist and Anji had managed to help him keep it together while he awaited rescue over a communication line.

'I mean, I know I have the body of a child right now but I had never forgotten-' he continued.

'Jake, I don't mean to sound mean or anything but this doesn't feel like the time or the place that we should be talking about this.' Anji interrupted.

Jake sighed. She had a point, especially as all hell was raining down around them. Here they were, surrounded by all manner of death and destruction and he was asking her to remember that they had promised each other a date! He started to shirk. Maybe she had forgotten? Maybe her feelings had changed? Maybe it was because the fountain of youth had robbed him momentarily of his strapping good looks and to her, he looked like a toddler. Either way, he tried not to take it too personally and fell silent again.

'I mean, we can always talk about it lat-'

Jake was unable to finish his sentence because just at that moment his balance gave way and he found himself slip-sliding into the filthy mud. As he cursed and continued to tumble, his momentum also took Anji down with him and the pair began to hurtle towards the harsh-looking ground. Before long they came to a grateful stop at the foot of the embankment in a tangle of limbs and swear words.

'For goodness' sake, Jake! You muppet!' said Anji as she tried to pick herself up. Her hair and clothes were caked in thick sludgy mud and she could feel her plait being weighed down by the filth she and her clumsy friend had just rolled around in.

'It's not my fault!' spat Jake, clearly annoyed. He hated it when Anji blamed him for things. Granted it had been him who had caused this incident but had she taken the entire weight of him when they fell on the hard floor? Had she grazed the palms on her hands trying to stop her before the slippery mud became hard gravel? Highly unlikely on both accounts since he'd done his best to stop her from coming to any harm by trying to keep his body under hers so that he took the brunt. 'Okay, it is but I didn't mean it.'

'You never do!' said Anji as she picked herself up.

'That bank was slippery. What was I supposed to do, fly down?'

'In a way we did!' said Anji.

'Well at least we're safe,' said Jake, unaware that his words were famous and if they weren't too careful, last.

A bright light shone on their faces. They both strained their eyes through the lights but all they could see were the outlines of a number of what looked like soldiers pointing guns at them.

Anji and Jake involuntarily put their hands up.

'You and your big mouth,' said Anji.

*

High above them, Random has just knocked the fifteenth member of the land hawker gang unconscious.

He hadn't needed to end on such a flourish as to triple somersault in mid-air whilst performing a roundhouse kick into the face of two of his attackers simultaneously but as he glided to the floor with the grace of a ballerina, it had certainly made him feel better.

He looked around him.

All of the dangerously sharp bikes had crashed into the dirt. Some were even on fire and the gang were all lying in a state of unconsciousness.

As Random dusted his hands, admiring his work, he wanted to say something cool as the cherry on the cake. Then, breathing through the dusty foggy air, he noticed out of the corner of his eye that down at the bottom of the precipice, his friends were being held at gunpoint and it would be rather a waste of time if he did. Especially as he didn't have anything particularly cool to say.

At the speed of light, he tore down the embankment, missing the trail of slippery mud that had entrapped his friends and hurled himself in front of a rather startled Anji and Jake.

'Woah. Woah, before you kill my friends there's something vitally important that you should know,' he cried, throwing his hands above his head just like the other two.

Through the legion of soldiers that stood before them, one moved out of the straight line.

'You. Come closer,' they implored, a strong booming voice emitting through. Random did as he was told. Although he was more than capable of taking this lot down much in the same vein as he had the land hawker gang, it wasn't in his – or his best friends – interests for him to do so. For now, he was at the mercy of these mysterious people.

The soldier took their left hand off the barrel of

their laser rifle and pressed a button on the side of their helmet. His visor retracted neatly into the roof of his helmet and continued to recede backwards until it was like he hadn't been wearing a helmet at all.

Random peered through the gloom at the soldier's features. The man's hair was thick and dark and slicked back but it was his face that held his more prominent features. His chiselled jaw and long straight nose were all that remained of what had possibly once been a fairly handsome face. Everything else spoke volumes of the ravages of war that this stranger had witnessed. The scars, overlaying and protruding each other made a cobweb of flesh that had grown back in all the wrong places. But crucially, for Random at least, it was the pigmentation of his skin that would prove the difference between friend and foe.

Luckily for them, the stranger's face was blue.

'You're face it's-' the soldier gulped.

'Purple,' replied Random.

'It can't be,' said the soldier in hushed tones.

The soldiers all stood blankly in identical pure black outfits and began to shift uneasily. Their helmets had reminded Anji and Jake of the same one motorcyclists wore back on Earth, only much cooler to look at and just as sleek and dark as the rest of their outfits. Their guns were still trained on the trio but their aim was beginning to waver.

'But you're a fairy tale, a myth,' said the soldier.

'Some fairy tales are true,' said Random.

The soldier shook his head and snapped back at his staff. 'Keep your eyes on them.' He looked back at Random and the other two. All three looked nothing like he had ever seen. A white boy, a dark-skinned girl and a purple boy. None of which looked as though they belonged on Rodas and yet in one case he knew that one did.

'Tell me quickly,' he barked. 'You said that there is something important that we should know.'

'Yes,' said Random. 'We make much better hostages than we do corpses.'

The soldier turned back to his battalion. 'We're taking them with us, I want three soldiers on each of them at all times, do you understand?'

'Where are you taking us?' asked Anji, suddenly able to shake the mild terror she was experiencing from her mind.

'Underground. We can't let you out of our sight,' said the soldier.

'Takten, the mission cannot deviate,' said one anonymous soldier to the scar-faced man.

'I know, that's why we are taking them with us,' he replied.

'They could slow us down. Distract us even from the rescue,' stressed the soldier.

'Sorry, Mr Takten, is it? Did you say rescue?' enquired Random.

'I am not at liberty to discuss our concerns with you. Yes, Djanga. They must come with us,' said Takten, 'Now quick, we must get inside the tunnels.'

The soldier, whose name Random, Anji and Jake now knew was Djanga took one look at them and then hurried over to them. 'You heard him, get moving.'

'Where?' asked Jake. 'And can we take our arms down now?'

'You heard the man now move forward,' said Djanga, who failed to answer the second part, much to the annoyance of the already harangued Jake and Anji.

The soldiers surrounded the three travellers who began to march quickly towards a nearby mountainside roughly two hundred yards away from the mud slip. As the bombs and explosions continued to rain around them, Jake risked the wrath of the soldiers by putting the palms of his hands over his ears to protect himself. Despite years of listening to all kinds of music as loud as technically possible, he was hoping to protect what little he had of his hearing left.

Before long they reached the mountain side and Takten produced what looked like a magic wand, only it was as thick as a broom handle and pressed a button on it. A door suddenly shimmered into existence in the rocks.

'A secret tunnel, nice!' gasped Anji.

'In here, quick!' cried Takten and before they knew it, Random and his friends had been pushed through the door and suddenly they were in a brightly lit corridor inside the mountain.

Takten counted his soldiers through and then produced the wand again and as the door shimmered away again shutting the harsh realities of war outside, he pushed his way to the front of the pack.

'Djanga, how far to the group's location?'

Djanga peered at a monitor on the back of his wrist. 'We're six hundred metres away.'

'Better get moving then. Come on.'

'Can somebody please tell us what the zark is going on? We might be your prisoners but you could do us the common decency to tell us where we are going?' Random was clearly a little ticked off. Jake on the other hand was just happy to be safe.

'I can't tell you anything,' said Takten. 'Now come on.'

'Takten. I am here of my own free will. All those stories I'm sure that you have heard of me, they are all true. If I had wanted to apprehend you, I would have done by now, believe me. I'm not the enemy of the Sapphire Regime. I want to help

you. I know how the war is going and I don't like
the look of the future on Rodas anymore than
you do. Now if you let me and my friend's help
then we will be more than happy to, but we
won't be herded like cattle by you or by
anybody.'

Takten took no time to reach for his laser rifle,
but Random was one step ahead and had already
placed his hand upon it firmly. His soldiers all
turned their weapons on Random, who was
staring intently into Takten's stoic eyes. Anji's
heart jumped up into her mouth whilst Jake let
out a rather embarrassing yelp of surprise.

Takten tried to counter Random's strength by
pushing against his hand but it was to no avail.

'How dare you make an example of me in front
of my men.'

'I'm sorry but I have to know where you are
taking us.'

'Why, are you scared?' Takten's words felt like
barbed wire to Random.

'Of course not,' he replied.

'Are you sure? You don't know what people
think of you here, do you?'

'I can imagine,' said Random.

'No, I don't think you do. But I'm telling you
now your reputation will be further tarnished if
you don't let us complete our mission.'

'And what's that then?'

'We have people trapped inside this mountain who if we don't reach them soon will be slaughtered by members of the Crimson Empire. We already think of you as a coward so how do you think their families will feel when I tell them that you stopped us from doing our duty in saving them?' despite Random's physical advantage it was Takten who truly held the upper hand.

'That's all I wanted to know,' said Random.

'Come on mate,' said Jake. 'Please, we've only just arrived. Let's not get killed already, eh?'

Random stared into Takten's eyes. 'What better way to prove you wrong than to help?'

Takten laughed. 'You'll have to do more than that to redeem yourself, Random.' He spat Random's name out in a volley of disdain. Random snapped his hand back and released Takten who with dignity straightened himself up. 'At ease men, save your ammunition for the red faces. We don't want it wasted on him. Now come on!'

They made it down the corridor, leaving Random, Anji and Jake no time to collect their thoughts.

'I take it they want us to help then?' asked Anji.

'I gathered that too,' said Random as they followed hurriedly.

'So, from that frank exchange that you're not too popular on this planet?' said Jake trying to break the tension.

'That's mildly put,' said Random. 'Now come on, we've got people to save.'

XV

Nkite had known that there would be more trouble the moment she heard a communicator buzzing through the crowd of recuperating river dwellers. She had got up from her position sitting on the rock and helping Gron tend to a little girl's head wound and made her way through the crowd of people all huddled in the narrow corridor in the mountain.

'Let me through please,' she demanded, obtaining a few curt looks from the people she barged past before reaching the person with the communicator. It was a young man, whose blue skin was pale and clammy. He shot a look of panic at Nkite, who instantly hurled her frame against him and after pulling the startled man up against the wall, clasped a hand around his throat.

'Spying on us are you!' she spat.

The river dwellers were all regarding Nkite with watching eyes. 'Nkite, let him go,' said one man, who tried to come between them and was rather surprised at the struggle to wrestle Nkite's claw away. 'Nkite leave it, you don't understand,' he said as the man Nkite was attacking was finally detached from her vice-like grip and fell back.

He coughed vigorously, his communicator still buzzing for attention.

Nkite held both he and the man who had stopped her in condemnation. 'He's a spy, he's led them to us!'

'I have not!' coughed the attacked man. 'Bakal...she...'

'She had friends inside the Sapphire Regime,' said the other man, who took over from his friend who was clearly struggling to find his breath again. 'She tasked us with communicators to alert the Regime when we are in trouble and things got worse.'

Nkite's breathing steadied. She bought the story. Bakal was indeed well connected still to the army to so why wouldn't she have agents along the riverfront in the chance that they were ever in danger? 'So why wasn't I informed?' she said.

'You're a loose cannon,' said the man hoarsely, still rubbing his throat. 'Bakal didn't trust you.'

'She trusted me enough to take over if she was killed!' screamed Nkite. 'She trusted me to keep going back into the war. What did you guys do, huh? You ran away like cowards!'

The other man stepped in again and confronted Nkite face-to-face. 'And if we don't start running again soon, we'll all be dead!'

Nkite looked shocked.

'The Crimson Empire. They have found us.'

'How?' demanded Nkite.

'One of our agents was a part of the group that broke off,' said the man who Nkite had attacked. 'He sent a signal before...' he broke off, visibly upset by the reality of what had happened to someone Nkite assumed had been a friend once.

'Look, Nkite, Bakal had her reasons to not tell you, we all have secrets to keep, but now is not the time to debate. We have to move.'

'Where?' asked Nkite, who was feeling her command slipping through her fingers. Bakal had kept her in the dark. She was on the back foot and these guys seemed to know what to do better than her. Some leader she made...

'We have a rendezvous point with Commander Takten, not far from here, but we have to move quickly. He and his battalion are on their way but so are the Crimson-'

A rally of laser fire shot all around them, sending some of the river dwellers falling to the ground, dead on impact. Nkite gazed in horror as she among others ran for what little cover they could find.

'Get back to the opening!' she hollered as more bodies fell around her. As the river dwellers panicked and tried to make their way back to where they had entered the mountain, she felt a sudden burning sensation graze the top of her left shoulder, the pain of which sent her falling to the floor on top of what was now the corpse of a fallen comrade. The fall saved her from certain death and as she remained lying in the dirt with those who had been killed, she witnessed pandemonium all around her.

At the other end of the corridor, there was nothing but a murderous outline of soldiers mercilessly gunning down all who lay in the line of fire.

The Sapphire Regime were too late. The Crimson Empire had already found them...

XVI

Random's ultra-sensitive hearing had picked up on the sound of gunfire long before Takten and his men had.

'They've found them!' he shouted before taking off with immense speed, tearing towards the sound. 'Quickly!' shouted Takten as the battalion shot off behind him. He turned back to Anji and Jake, aware that they were unarmed. 'You two, try and find cover!' Anji and Jake also picked up the pace. They both felt their hearts beating hard against their ribcages, fear beginning to set in with the scenario they found themselves in. In all the years they had fought for good in the universe alongside Random they had never killed. Now they were racing headlong into a bloody gun battle, unarmed, where people were being shot dead where they stood. Anji began to fret.

She couldn't kill. Never. But in the chaos, they found themselves in there was a very real possibility that she and Jake would have to take up arms and fight.

And no matter how much she pushed the thought to the back of her mind, it wouldn't budge. Suddenly, for the very first time, she regretted not listening to Random.

As the cries of people in terror and deafening laser fire filled the corridor, she started to wish they had never come to Rodas at all.

Random burst into the corridor and immediately smashed his fists into the back of two unsuspecting soldier's helmets, cracking the metal-like frames like eggs and sending them sprawling forward into their counterparts, which in turn sent a volley of laser fire into the roof of the rocky corridor. As debris rained down, Random's super speed and all-out aggression sent more crimson soldiers all which ways, and for perhaps the first time in a long time, he was showing them no mercy. Slowly, the sound of gunfire was replaced by the screams of the Crimson Empire battalion. Nkite, holding her injured shoulder and on the verge of blackout from the pain, opened her eyes and witnessed a figure in the far distance moving with such blistering speed and power, she knew instantly who their saviour was. Then she began to think she was hallucinating or dead already. As the laser fire ceased, she saw the figure smash the final two standing soldiers together and then witnessed them fall lifelessly to the floor like ragdolls.

As Takten and his men rounded the corner, they saw Random surrounded by dozens of motionless bodies.

The battalion leader pushed his way forward. Random stood there, panting, his face contorted with anger.

'You could let us have some of the fun,' muttered Takten before turning his attention where it was needed most. 'You,' he pointed at his men, 'Search for survivors quick. We've got to get them out of these tunnels fast.'

Anji and Jake rounded the corner. Jake spotted the bodies first and felt instantly nauseous. Anji did her best to blot out the death all around them and they both went over to Random, who was still standing taut, his fists clenched, staring down at what was left of the Crimson Empire soldiers.

'Random? Random, it's okay its-' Anji cautiously put her hand upon Random's arm which seemed to diffuse him immediately.

'Anji,' he whispered. 'I didn't hold back. I couldn't.' He started to look at his battered hands.

Anji gave him a little smile. 'You saved them, that's all that matters.'

'Yeah, and let's face it they deserved it! I'm going to go and help those people down there,' said Jake as he made off towards the river dwellers.

'This is why I ran away. This is why I didn't want you here. Not only for your protection but...I didn't want you to see me like this,' his hands were covered in the debris of battle.

'You're fighting for good. Never forget that,' she said. He gave her a look of immense sadness but before they had time to talk any further, they heard Jake from further down the corridor.

'Hey, this one's still alive!' he shouted. He was horrified by what he had been forced to walk through. This was the first time he had seen so many people dead. They had been lucky on their adventures up until this point. Most of their do-good actions hadn't involved conflict as bloody as this but now the war was staring him right in the face and he was unable to blink away the nightmare. But amongst the fallen had lay a girl, her shoulder bleeding and she looked in a bad way. Hearing her groan, he knelt down next to her.

'Hey, are you alright?'

Nkite opened her eyes. Through her double vision, she could make out the young, white face and shaggy blonde hair that drooped down over her. She shot Jake a confused look.

'Does it look like it?' she moaned.

'Well now you come to mention it, no, but are you hit anywhere else except your shoulder?'

'That's more like it,' she bluffed, failing to mention the atrocities she had witnessed today had also left her with a broken heart. She struggled to her feet and Jake gingerly helped. 'Woah, easy, take it easy Miss?'

'Nkite. Who are you?'

'I'm Jake.'

As Jake pulled Nkite up to her full height, he noticed Random and Anji standing next to them.

'You're with him,' said Nkite without question.

'Well, yeah.'

'Then I want no part of your help,' she yanked herself away painfully, wincing and stumbling a little as she did so.

'That's no way to say thank you,' said Jake.

It was completely the wrong thing to say. Nkite's eyes welled up. She gritted her teeth and strode right up to Random's face.

'Why would I say thank you to the man who could have put an end to this long ago? You see these bodies all around us?' she gestured to the waste of life at their feet.

'We got here as soon as we could,' said Random in defence, his face burning with shame.

'You should never have left in the first place! Thank you...you should fall down at our feet and beg for our forgiveness never mind ask for thanks!' Pools of tears fell from the corners of Nkite's eyes. All the years of hope had been shattered into a million pieces thanks to the horrors she had endured today. All of it for nothing. So many of her people were gone and it wasn't the soldiers who has pulled the trigger on them in the corridors or the pilots who had capsized their boat in the river or set fire to their homes that were to blame. They could have been dealt with so many years ago if Random hadn't fled Rodas at the earliest opportunity. Her dreams of peace and prosperity were gone. All that she had now was sorrow.

'My people need me,' she whispered. Saying nothing more she gingerly made her way towards the survivors who were being tended to by Takten's men at the other end of the corridor. For the first time the noise of people crying, screams of pain and the hum of talk filled the bloody air. Anji and Jake stood stunned at Nkite's defiance.

'Well how do you like that?' said an indignant Jake. He began to feel anger bubble to the surface as if Nkite's words had unlocked his perception and the devastation surrounding them had finally gotten to him. 'After all that you just did. I mean honestly. She'd be dead if it wasn't for-'

'Jake, leave it,' interrupted Anji. Random stood there silent, his cheeks wet with remorse.

As the trio walked away towards the throng of river dwellers that were looking shocked and stunned as they recuperated from their ordeal, one of the Crimson Empire soldiers began to stir from amid the pile of his stricken colleagues. His entire body was wracked with a burning agony, not surprising considering minutes earlier it had been hurled at the wall with a force that would break any man over and over. As he slowly regained consciousness, he was also aware that this burning agony was also the fire in which his life was slowly starting to fall away. He had to report back. Although his vision inside the helmet was impaired, he could make out the purple one who had attacked him. He knew exactly who he was. He knew that he had to let his master know that Random was finally back on Rodas.

Suddenly his attention was diverted by the muffled sounds of soldiers talking. Considering how his battalion had been decimated he was fairly certain that the voices were not those of his comrades. In fact, if any like him were still alive, lying twisted and broken in the pile of corpses with him, he'd wish nothing but death upon them like he was now yearning for himself.

To be captured and tortured would mean no way back to the Crimson Empire, even if they were to recover and escape.

To be incarcerated was a weakness that Kalor Maloso would never tolerate.

But as he listened intently to the words of the Sapphire Regime officers, he was relieved to hear that they had no intention of taking prisoners. No, an instant shot from a blaster rifle to any who were still alive was to be the order.

The injured soldier knew that he had to move quickly and quickly he did. It took all of his energy to reach for the distress signal on his wrist and activate it. That'd let the command know that they had perished and that for the Crimson Empire, their worst enemy was here and ready to annihilate them. With a little smile, he winced as a bolt of laser fire shot right through his head and he died with a smile on his face, the executor failing to realise what he had just done.

*

As Kalor Maloso was preparing himself in the chamber the distress signal reached him. An intermittent beeping rang around his dark room before a voice fizzed over his speaker system.

'My Lord, I-'

'Save your breath, Colonel, I am well aware of the situation,' Maloso butted in. 'In fact, I have the answer to all our problems. Take a battalion to the mountainside and bring Random here.'

The Colonel seemed hesitant. 'He may not come willingly.'

'I believe he will,' said Maloso.

'As you wish, sir,' said the Colonel before the sound of both his voice and the distress signal faded away into the darkness.

Maloso looked down at the chamber he was reclining in, patting it graciously. 'For so long you have sustained me now...it's time to sustain Rodas...'

He heard a raucous thumping from below his chamber.

He smiled.

From time to time, the things he had long trapped down there tended to do that.

Whether they were hungry or just disgruntled at their situation, he tended to give the abominations what they wanted so they would be silent and still for a long time.

For so long he hid the unmentionables in the dark beneath his feet.

Now, they appeared to be stirring, almost like they knew what he was about to do.

Maloso pressed a button on the side of the chamber and the door hissed slowly shut, a hot vapour swirling all around him.

He input the command into the computer and took a deep breath as a multitude of sharp-looking needles and horrific spiky implements snaked menacingly out of the top of the chamber and shot deep within his body.

He tried not to scream but the operation that the machine was carrying out on him was excruciating and beneath the swirling clouds of smoke and steamy vapour a truly horrendous experiment was taking shape.

He could feel the implements pulling and tearing at his body, ripping him piece by piece. As he suffered the torment, he remembered how many times he had done this before and how this time, it would be more worth it than anything else he had ever had to endure. This would be the last time he had promised himself that, but this time the machine had more of him, so much more of him than before.

As the banging from beneath the floor of the room became harder and more urgent, Maloso couldn't hold back his agony anymore and a shriek of terrifying proportions echoed over the sounds of the banging and the machine operating.

Outside the room lay a thick metal door and two guards in ceremonial crimson robes. The stead-fast issue of Maloso's personal guards were notoriously ruthless and hard-nosed but even they were shaking a little in their boots as the piercing shriek of pain penetrated their armoured helmets.

They had never heard Maloso like this before and although they had been briefed, along with the high command of the Crimson Empire, on the details of his master plan, to hear it being carried out meant that there was no going back.

From this moment on, Kalor Maloso, and Rodas, were never going to be the same again and as the cries of pain reached a horrible velocity, the entire planet of Rodas was about to shake in the aftermath of what the terrible man had done...

XVII

'The Crimson Empire has entered a new phase of warfare,' said Takten to his audience. As the soldiers cleared up the mess that their ambush had caused and patched up the survivors, he took the time to explain to Random, Anji, Jake, Nkite, Djanga and Gron the latest on the war effort. He had wanted to get them all out as quickly as possible before a further attack, which he knew was oncoming, but while his troops were working as hard as they could evacuate the mountain, he felt it was time to open up about how badly the Sapphire Regime were fairing – especially after seeing Random's powers first-hand. 'For years now we have been suffering losses. Our battlegrounds have fallen and we have been driven back, forced to live like rats underground.'

'So that explains these tunnels then?' said Anji. 'I had wondered.'

'The tunnels were built by our forefathers as a solution to trench warfare but before long they were abandoned and instead rebels from both sides would use them.'

'Rebels from both sides?' asked Nkite.

'It's true. I was a soldier when they were dug,' said Gron, who was perched with the others on one of the giant boulders that were scattered around the place. 'There were whispers among the ranks so when I deserted, I came down here, long before I found the river.'

'And you lived with people from the other side?' asked Jake.

'Just as it should be,' continued Gron. 'Much like the river people. We learnt to live together in harmony. Shunning the war outside.'

'Ignoring reality,' spat Takten.

'You can't blame them,' said Jake. 'I mean, we've only been here five minutes and we've already seen enough.'

'How did you get here?' asked Nkite.

'The craft that he stole, surely?' said Takten pointing his gun at Random, who was sitting arms folded with a concentrated look on his face.

'Well, if you must know, I was kidnapped before I stole it if that makes it any better,' he responded.

'But why? Did you not know why you were created?' asked Nkite.

'I did, yes, I'm ashamed to say. And why did I run? The obvious reason. I was scared,' Random said honestly.

'Scared of fighting?' said Takten, angered by the cowardice of the man before him.

'Sacred of sacrifice,' said Random, who got up from the boulder and started to pace about the corridor. 'I did not ask to be created. I was brought into this world for one reason and one reason only.'

'And you chose to escape,' said Nkite. 'Don't you think that's what we all want? None of us asked to be brought into this world either and like you, we didn't have a choice.'

Random sighed. 'You don't understand.'

'Then tell us!' shouted Nkite.

'Hey, hey give him a chance,' said Jake.

Anji noticed the look of sorrow in Random's eye. 'Understand what, Random?'

Random looked at his friends. 'The rebels Takten spoke of. They created me. Took elements of both their sides and made me in a laboratory. Only it went wrong. A heli-fighter crashed in the lab at the moment of my creation. It killed two people. A scientist and a rebel soldier. My parents. They extracted the best elements of their characters and installed them into one single compound. Me. After the crash, my first memory is of opening the chamber door and seeing their dead bodies just lying there on the floor. It was hell all around me. But I had their voices in my head. Somehow, they were communicating with me, talking to me, guiding me towards my sole purpose. But I was a boy, nothing but a child, unaware of the powers I had been given but fully aware of my terrible responsibility. If you were a child, given the chance to escape a terrible future wouldn't you take it?'

'I did,' replied Nkite. 'But I ran back into the fire, and I've been running back in ever since.'

'As have I,' said Random.

'It's true,' Anji said. 'The first thing Random did was save our world.'

'Yeah, then we joined him and saved one called Genocia,' chirped Jake. 'It had a terrible monster living under-'

'And so on, and so on,' said Random, talking over Jake's enthusiastic retelling. 'All the while knowing that I had to fulfil my destiny. Now I think about it, I wasn't running away from Rodas. I was running back.'

'It's a shame your epiphany didn't come sooner,' said Takten. 'The Crimson Empire's numbers have been growing stronger. There are so many in number and none of our intel knows how. Meanwhile, the Sapphire Regime is becoming an endangered race.'

'All this fighting, all this heartache, for what? I mean, what started it?' asked Anji.

'The old saying goes that the elders couldn't make the colour purple,' said Gron.

'What?!' spluttered Jake. 'That's insane!'

'It's true, apparently,' said Nkite. 'Almost too silly to make it real.'

'And yet it is,' confirmed Random.

'But you're red and blue on this planet. That's what makes purple!' said Anji, who nearly fell off her boulder she was so flabbergasted at the ridiculousness of it all.

'We know that now but we didn't know then. Rodas was a different planet in the old times,' said Gron.

'Is that why you're so special, Random? Because you are purple?' asked Jake.

'I'm the best of both worlds, even if I say so myself, now it's time to stop talking and time to prove it.' He went over to Nkite and placed his hand on her shoulder. 'Nkite, I am so sorry for all the hurt I have caused you and your people but I promise you I will make it up to you now.'

Nkite looked at him quizzically. 'What are you going to do?'

Random straightened himself up and turned to Takten. 'Takten, this war must end now and I can make it so.'

He looked at him with equal bemusement. 'How?'

'Kalor Maloso seems to have found a way to keep regenerating his army, correct? The Crimson Empire is playing dirtier to win this war than before, right?'

'Right,' replied Anji and Jake in unison.

'Then it's obvious. Maloso is fiddling with the books! He's doing something to make his Empire stronger and harder to beat which means...'

'He's bringing soldiers back from the dead?' asked Jake.

'A little far-fetched Jake, try again,' said Random.

'He's cloning his soldiers?' asked Anji, leaving Jake to shoot her an annoyed look as that was literally what he was about to say.

'Well, let's see shall we,' said Random. He marched through the corridor, past river dwellers who looked on at him in bewilderment and awe as the others followed him. He came to a stop at the pile of dead Crimson Empire soldiers and bent down to examine them. He felt along one of the corpse's helmets and found a release catch which suddenly snapped open, revealing the horrifying face of an open-eyed dead man. He pushed the catch button on another and turned the body over. Despite the ravages of war being etched across both dead faces, they looked otherwise identical. He did the same again to another corpse, leaving the on-lookers open-mouthed.

'Now either by a million to one chance I've just uncovered a family of triplets in this troop or the cloning idea is the correct one,' confirmed

Random as he got back to his feet. 'Honestly, Takten, doesn't the Sapphire Regime check the deceased?

Takten was dumbfounded and a little anxious. 'How, how is he doing that?'

'Easy. This planet has always had the technology. Think about it. If they can create someone like me in a giant test tube then why can't they clone? The Crimson Empire must have discovered this technology and hoarded it for themselves, away from prying eyes. But there's more. The security mainframe is worried that they cannot keep the war contained so there's something else going on here. I just don't know what,' said Random as he put his fingers to his lips to think and then thought against it after touching dead bodies.

'So how do we stop them?' asked Nkite.

'Not you, Nkite. Me,' replied Random.

'How?' asked Takten.

'I need to get inside the Crimson Empire's base. Find out what's really happening here.'

'That's impossible, it'll be suicide,' said Takten.

'Not if I'm the one that Maloso wants all along,' said Random.

'You're giving yourself up?!' cried Anji.

'It's the only way,' replied Random.

'Now hang on a minute!' said Jake. 'You can't do that, you'll be killed.'

'Not if I can help it,' said Random.

'And can you?' asked Anji.

'I don't know yet,' was Random's less than convincing response.

'Random you can't,' she protested.

'I can, I will and I must,' said Random stoically. 'Take a look around you, Anji. Look at these people. This is just a snapshot of centuries of torment and pain. Rodas has suffered long enough. It's time it was saved.'

'Well, you can't go in alone,' said Jake.

'Don't make me repeat myself, Jake,' warned Random.

'Look, if this Maloso bloke is half as bad as you say he is then you need help,' he replied.

'Oh always, and since I learnt long ago that there is no telling either of you to stay out of danger then I need both of you to do as exactly as I say,' said Random as he draped his arms over both his friend's shoulders. 'Now Jake, if you want to get your hands dirty, I need someone to pose as a guard. We can tell Moloso that I came willingly. Then when you are inside the base you can pass intel back to Mr Takten here.'

'Highly unlikely, I'm coming with you,' said Takten. 'You'll need more than one guard to convince the Crimson Empire that your intentions are true. If my men can escort these people back to our base then we can send the report directly to Sapphire HQ.'

'That's a great idea. You'll both have to wear a disguise. I'm sorry to ask you of this but I think you'll have to wear these men's suits to disguise yourselves,' said Random.

'Dead man's boots, lovely,' gulped Jake. 'But hang on, these won't fit me, I'm still growing after that fountain of youth business, remember?'

'Random walked up to Jake and measured himself next to him. 'You're almost back to normal, Jake. In fact, I'd say you've gained half a foot in the last hour, hadn't you noticed?'

Jake felt his body and stood up on his tiptoes. 'Oh yeah, well, there has been a lot going on I suppose.'

'You can't let him have all the fun,' said Anji. 'What about me?' Anji was smarting. So, it was fine for Jake to help Random in his dangerous mission but her? Is that what Random had in mind? Surely not? He knew her better than that. He knew what she could bring to the table.

'Of course not, I wouldn't leave you out of the fun now, would I? Okay, Anji, and Nkite, we'll report the information back to you. You need to get the river dwellers back to Sapphire HQ. Takten, can you give them a map to show them the way?' Random declared.

Anji drew a sigh of relief. That'd be a dangerous mission, for sure. Just what she was looking for!

'Yes, and Djanga knows the way, but Random, who said that you were giving the orders? I am in charge here. I'd appreciate it if you remembered that,' said Takten.

'Do you have a better plan?' replied Random.

Takten stayed silent. No, he didn't.

'Good man,' said Random.

'Is that it?' asked Anji.

'No. Whilst waiting for Jake's information, you will also need to wait for Skateboard. He'll send you a signal when he is back on Rodas.'

'Wait, what? Skateboard's gone?' gasped Anji.

'Not for long, he will be back soon. Take this device. It'll track him to you,' Random handed Anji a small little disc and placed it in the palm of her hand.

'What happens when we've got the information we require? Asked Takten.

'You get the hell out of there. Don't wait for me. Hopefully, I won't be far behind you. I'll try to disable the Crimson Empire from inside and then the Sapphire Regime can attack. You've all been in the dark for too long, it's time to emerge from the shadows,' said Random.

'Excuse me, young man, but what can I do,' asked Gron. Random put a reassuring arm around him.

'Help get your people to safety. No one else should die today. Not on our watch and not on yours, eh, peeps?'

Anji, Nkite and Gron nodded, a slight smile returning to the lips of the two Rodasian's faces. Nkite felt a warmth return in her heart. For all that she hated Random right now, he was giving her hope that she started to think was gone.

'Right, there'll be more Crimson Empire soldiers on the way so we have to act fast but we can do it. All of us. We can stop the war today and we will. So, let's get to work!' said Random as he sprung off down the corridor.

A roar came from a band of soldiers and river dwellers who had overheard everything. An optimism was growing, the tide possibly turning. The Rodasians had been beaten and broken but they could mend and they could emerge triumphant. As everyone went about their jobs, Takten instructed his men to fall in to outline the plan, a smile spread across Random's face.

He could do it. They could do it and if all went to his plan the worst part of his destiny wouldn't have to happen.

The war had raged for thousands of years. It had claimed the lives of billions upon billions of innocent people, of people coerced into a futile, race-driven war that should never have been allowed to escalate.

Random and his friends were about to draw a line in the sand.

The Battle for Rodas was about to begin...

...just as soon as Jake found a Crimson Empire
uniform with boots in a size 8...

Book Two

REDEMPTION

I

'I have heard your pleas for help, Skateboard, but I must say that I am not convinced.'

Skateboard stood alone, back in a place he had been banished from some time ago. From the data in his memory bank, there was very little to differentiate the incredible gold splendour of the throne room on Spectronia from how it had looked when he and his friends had last been on the planet. It had been a few years back that they had crash landed upon its spectacularly colourful plains and been tricked into helping a group of sadistic archaeologists to find an incredibly powerful element. It was called the Zedron Flux and its very name caused a cache of files to corrupt in Skateboard's motherboard every time he thought of it.

The Flux itself was harmless until it was used. Torn between letting a race of gods called the Osirans from destroying Spectronia to obtain it and putting his life at risk, Random had activated the element and committed a terrible atrocity in the process. He had saved Spectronia and its inhabitants but he had wiped out a race of beings. Skateboard knew that Random's guilt over the event was something he had yet to come to terms with fully, indeed if he ever would recover from it, and the Flux's energy had almost killed him too. And after all of that, the Flux was taken into hiding again, just as the man who had it in his possession realised it was not safe to hide in this world and Random and his friends were banished from Spectronia for life by the Queen of the planet, Solenia.

It was with great surprise when they were formulating their plan that Random had requested Skateboard visit Spectronia for help first. Indeed, the great ruler who was sitting before him, resplendent in her throne and flanked by her aid and a multitude of Valkyrie guards who had escorted him from the Venus II upon landing, was thinking just the same as the AI robot.

She had listened to him plead his case for help and yet Solenia knew that it would take more than just the word of a robot to convince her to take action. Although moments before her world had been visited once again by the Venus II and one of its occupants, she too had been wrestling with an internal dilemma. Spectronia had always been a peaceful planet and Solenia had led her people into battle against the Osirans – a battle that had it not been for Random's sacrifice – would have seen her planet obliterated. Although she had banished the outsiders, she had also taken a large number of casualties as a black mark against her own name. As she was their ruler, she made herself an exception and made a vow to attend every funeral, and every memorial and swore that she and her people would never intervene again, so long as trouble evaded Spectronia. Indeed, it had taken some strong words, on more than one occasion, from her oldest and more trusted aid, Proctor, to finally convince her to awake from her inactivity. She hadn't expected to have to make good on her U-turn immediately, especially potentially doing so to help the only people who she'd ever had to banish from her world!

'In many ways,' she continued, 'I sympathise with your predicament. But I must give your request some careful consideration. What you ask would require me to sacrifice men and women under my rule. I have learnt from experiencing the cold loneliness of power and what it can do to my people when I make the wrong decision. I am wary not to make one so hastily that could cost the lives of so many.'

'With respect, your majesty,' said Skateboard in a calm tone. 'Every second many who know not of such a benevolent ruler are killed in the crossfire of a futile war. Men, women, children. Too many in number to tally those that have been lost. Lives have been ruined for generation upon generation and if it isn't stopped soon the war will spill out across the cosmos.

It could even reach here. Rodas is only fifteen million light years away from Spectronia. Its disease could spread if we don't act now. My friends and I can stop it but we need as many allies as possible.'

'Your Majesty,' said Proctor, 'I have heard of the problems on Rodas. Indeed, the stories of a planet torn apart by a war against races were something your father was briefed upon long ago. I believe you are also aware. It's far from a fairy tale. I humbly suggest that you consider what you have been asked.'

'I am very aware, Proctor and do not need a history lesson now,' said Solenia. She turned back to Skateboard. 'The business of another planet, no matter how appalling its predicament, is not one of concern for us. Even if you say the war is on the brink of expanding across the stars there are many planets in this system with the might to withstand any trouble before it lands at our door. Why have you not asked any of them for help?'

'It is a good question, your Majesty,' replied Skateboard, 'and one I have no answer for except that we have little time to act. As we speak Random, Anji and Jake are trapped on Rodas behind a barrier that intelligence tells us is on the verge of collapse. We only have time to call upon allies. Random saved your world, no matter the aftermath. All that he asks is that you help him return the favour.'

'A favour that involves death,' said Solenia. She mused for a moment. Random had saved their world. Spectronia still hung in the sky because of the sacrifice he made. She had been surprised to hear that he was still alive. Seeing him lying in the dirt barely moving after the Flux had done its work had given her little cause to believe he would live. And now he was asking her for help, despite being banished from coming back. But if she didn't, would it make her and Spectronia seem weak? To shy behind planets in their way had been far from a noble suggestion now she thought of it.

'How would we get there?' she asked.

Skateboard felt a glimmer of hope ignite inside of him. Finally, Solenia was asking logistical questions so she must have some interest in helping, he thought. 'Do you not have any form of craft to transport you?'

'We have none. We have never left this planet,' said Proctor, who immediately felt a glare from Solenia.

'You seem eager,' she muttered. 'How much room do you have on your vessel?'

Skateboard pondered for a moment. 'Given the average height and build of your Valkyries I would say that we could make use of the engine rooms and gather a hundred inside the ship. It wouldn't be a comfortable trip for many, but it wouldn't be a long one either.'

'And our dosas?'

'Oh,' said Skateboard. 'You'd take horses too?'

The dosas were the Spectronian's trusty steeds, much like the horses Skateboard had seen back on Earth.

'What else would my Valkyries ride into battle on?'

Skateboard was flummoxed. 'An excellent point. Well, I suppose we could fit them on but it would be a tight squeeze…' he said before starting to panic about the mess they would cause on the ship.

'And do you plan to visit any other planets to ask for help? Why was Spectronia your first port of call?' asked Solenia.

'Well, you are the planet we owe it to the most,' said Skateboard, who was lying a little about the planet being the closest to Rodas on his list.

'Proctor, I am well aware of what you think about all of this so I need not ask,' said Solenia.

'Your Majesty-'

'It's okay, Proctor. I understand the plight of Rodas. I understand that despite the robot's banishment still applying he has broken our laws, but I admire his courage and also sympathise with the cause,' she huffed, remembering a conversation she and Proctor had been having before Skateboard's arrival.

'Very well. Skateboard, your banishment is rescinded forthwith. I shall assemble my best fighters and we shall join your cause.'

Skateboard's diodes breathed a heavy sigh of relief. 'Thank you so much, your Majesty,' he bowed as much as his rigid metal framework would allow.

'Proctor, summon the Valkyries. We leave immediately. You are in charge until we get home,' Solenia strode up from her throne and down the steps to stand by Skateboard's side. She patted him gently. 'It's time Spectronia came out of the shadows and wrote its name in the stars.'

'Very good, your Majesty,' said Proctor, with a concerned look on his face. Solenia noticed this and gave him a reassuring smile.

'It's okay, Proctor. We're coming home alive. Walk with me,' she instructed Skateboard. 'We must ready ourselves with haste. Tell me of the other recruits who will help in this cause.'

'We have links with the Space Seals. They are aware of the situation. I updated our contact on the way here. She is putting a case towards the fleet to repel any potential break out from outside the security mainframe.'

'Anyone else?' asked Solenia, as the pair walked through a throne room which had suddenly became a hive of activity.

'Yes, your Majesty. We just need to make a quick trip to Genocia before we return to Rodas. We have friends there who should also be able to help.'

'So far you have a hundred of us, three people on the ground, a contact trying to convince a fleet and some friends on a world I have never heard of before who might help. My confidence wanes by the second,' said Solenia.

'Fear not, your Majesty. All will fall into place.'

'It better, because if it doesn't and if we make it out of this battle alive then I'll consider doing more than reinstating your banishment, is that clear?'

'Yes, your Majesty,' said Skateboard, who added the personal threat of execution to his ever-growing list of things that were worrying him.

'Good, now that's settled, you'd better show me where you have parked,' said Solenia as she strode off in front of Skateboard, whose concerns about Rodas, death, his friends, keeping promises and huge heaps of poo from the Valkyries horses, which he had just remembered were called dosas, had really started to put him off his stride. Meekly, he followed, hoping, praying, that all would fall into place.

II

The room smelt like a foul barbeque. It had been a while since Kalor Maloso's cries had been heard by his guards and so, despite the order for them not to enter under any circumstances, they were duty-bound to protect their leader.

The room was awash with thick smoke and white vapour. It was also as hot as a sauna in July. The first guard, his experience of his Lord's previous exposure to the chamber immediately made for it. Despite not seeing very clearly, he remembered its general whereabouts and the second guard followed, newer to the job and not as familiar with the gruesome place as her superior.

'My Lord?' asked the first guard.

As they approached the chamber, great tentacles of instruments, dripping in unspeakable fluids seems to be slowly snaking back into the chamber's housing. A tube high above them seemed to gurgle incessantly like a loud drain. The banging from below the floor had subsided. The room was an eerie hell hole.

As the guards peered inside the chamber interior, a terrible demonic skeleton screamed in their faces, sending them reeling to the floor and shrieking in horror. The skeleton, its blood red eyes piercing the smoky gloom like headlamps in the dark looked menacingly at them and terrified the second guard to such an extent that she emptied the contents of her bladder instantly.

'GET OUT!!!' the demon shrieked.

Both guards scrambled across the floor and left the room in such terror that upon shutting the door they both collapsed to the ground. The shrieking continued and their hearts beat so rapidly they could almost hear them as loudly as the screams coming from the room.

'W-w-was that?' stuttered the second guard.

The first guard did nothing else but nod, and faint.

Kalor Maloso started to calm down. He staggered out of the chamber and slowly and painfully made his way over to a control centre at the side of the room. Still grunting and moaning in agony, his bony fingers reached for the controls and before long, the gurgling in the pipes above began to intensify and in return, so did the incessant banging from under the floorboards.

Slowly the cries of agony were replaced with a guttural laugh. With a final press of a button, Kalor Maloso threw himself to the floor and laughed even harder. The pipes rattled loudly; the floorboards shook.

The war on Rodas was about to get much, much worse.

III

Random shirked a little as the handcuffs clasped against his wrists and secured tightly around them.

'Do they have to be so tight?' he complained to Takten, whose expression of annoyance was noted by Random. He scanned his face and decided it might be best to get his question out in the open. 'You don't like me either do you?'

'What that girl said in the cave wasn't wrong,' said Takten, referring to Nkite's outburst minutes earlier. 'Just because I am a soldier it doesn't mean I don't feel.'

'You've lost people?' asked Random.

Takten nodded as he worked on his laser rifle and began packing his uniform away in a bag as he stood before Random wearing the commandeered suit of his sworn enemy. 'Friends. Family. Comrades. You name it.'

'Takten, I really am sorry for what I have done.'

'I don't want to hear it,' he spat, but upon looking up and seeing the remorse in Random's eyes, the battle-hardened exterior softened a little. 'What you forget Random is that being here now won't bring back anybody who has passed.'

'But it will stop more from falling. You're right I can't bring them back but I can make sure that tomorrow is a better day for Rodas.'

Takten snorted. 'Has anyone ever told you what a messiah complex you have?'

Random shook his head. 'I'm serious. What I am about to do will bring an end to this war.'

'You haven't exactly said what you're planning to do. Once we get in and get the information we need, then what?'

'For very good reason,' said Random. He looked behind him, scanning the area for any prying eyes. The river dwellers were in the process of moving out and Jake had taken himself off beyond a rock somewhere to get dressed. He couldn't see Anji anywhere but just to be on the safe side took Takten by the arm and led him aside. 'My friends. I want them to be as safe as possible. If I tell them too much then I can't guarantee that they will follow through with my instructions.'

'So?' asked Takten.

'They could put themselves in more harms way.'

'Then why bring them here in the first place?' asked Takten.

'I tried to leave them behind but in the end I know that I needed them,' whispered Random. 'Besides, if I tell them that what I am about to do might result in my death then it might end up also resulting in theirs and I couldn't live with that...especially if I was dead...anyway,' Random said, his mind running off in different directions when it was struggling to remain focussed. 'So I want you to look after Jake and get him out of there in the slightest hint of trouble. Don't wait for me because...I might not be coming back,' he finished, with a solemn look on his face.

Takten understood. Some of his men had risen through the ranks with him. As time had gone on, he and Djanga had become inseparable. If his friend were staring down the barrel then Takten could guarantee he would throw his own body in the firing line before the trigger had been pulled.

'I understand. We might live like barbarians at times in this war Random but trust and loyalty are still commodities that make us feel like Kings. I will protect your friend.'

Random smiled. 'Good man!' His face changed to one of puzzlement. 'Now, where have Jake and Anji got to?'

*

Jake was perched awkwardly on the side of a boulder. Having snaked the Crimson Empire suit over his clothes he had tried hard to forget that it had been taken off a corpse earlier. Now he was cursing the boots.

'I'm sure Random said these were a size 8,' he muttered as he threw one of the heavy boots to the ground, the other perched hopelessly on the end of his toes.

'Hey,' came a familiar voice.

'Anj, help us out here. This suit is all baggy and the boots might as well belong to a toy doll!'

'Can't you ask for some better ones?' she asked.

'I'm not going back into the corpse pile,' said Jake. 'Wow. There's a sentence I never thought I would say.'

Anji's face gave a wry smile and she sat down next to him.

'Look, Jake, about earlier. I... I remembered the date.'

Jake's frustrations seemed to melt away for a brief moment. 'Oh?'

'Y'see I... god why is this so awkward?' she said quietly.

'Because it's me that you are talking to and that my real name is King Awkard?' replied Jake.

'Jake, I love you-'

Jake's heart started thumping out of control. She said it. She actually said those words. He'd longed to hear them for so many years. Sure, his hormones had led him astray over the years but his real feeling for Anji had always been there, no matter how much he had tried to hide them.

'-but,' she continued.

'No, no need to continue I heard the first bit and that'll do me,' he said hastily. 'I guess it's time I said the same-'

'Jake please,' she said, putting his hand in hers. 'I love you so much, more than anyone else in my life. I've never said it so explicitly before because, well, I hoped that I wouldn't have to until now. You've been my best friend for so long and when we made that promise, back at the pond on Earth, I often wondered what we'd be like all grown up and I wanted to still have you in my life. And look, I still do,' she smiled a smile that made Jake's heart sing. 'But as time has gone by, I've changed. We've changed.'

Jake started to develop a sickening feeling in his stomach. 'What do you mean, Anj?'

'I'm sorry. I guess that the feelings I thought I would have developed leading up to prom...I just, don't love you in that way.'

'Anj, you're confusing me,' said Jake, the mask of bravado slipping. 'What are you saying? That you love me as a friend?'

Anji started to feel tears trickle down her cheeks. 'I thought that's how we both felt?'

Jake was stunned. 'Yes, so did I but...I guess,' he sniffed, wiping back his own falling tears, 'I guess there was a piece of me that was holding out for more.'

'Jake.'

'Never mind,' he looked away, unable to look his old friend in the eye.

The two old friends sat perched together on the boulder much in the same way that they had all those years ago as children. But for the first time there now felt like there was a chasm between them. Jake felt so stupid. No, he felt betrayed.

'When I was in the sand...buried alive, you only mentioned the prom to keep me-'

'I never meant to hurt you, please don't let us fall out over this, not now,' Anji pleaded. She hadn't realised it but she was squeezing his hand, which Jake quickly snapped away from her.

Nkite had watched the exchange. For a while, she had wanted to give them space but when she heard Takten's cry of instruction, she knew that she would have to step in. She walked up to the pair and she cleared her throat.

'Hello,' she said softly. 'I'm sorry to interrupt you both but Commander Takten has given the order to move out,' she said. Random and Takten also appeared.

'Right,' said Random, instantly noticing that his two friends were emotional. 'Everything okay?'

'Yeah,' sniffed Anji, wiping her face.

'Always,' lied Jake.

'Good,' said Random, who with his handcuffs firmly on beckoned them both up for a big warm hug. 'Look, we'll get through this.'

Neither Anji nor Jake smiled, with Jake looking the other way so that he didn't have to look at his old friend.

Random relinquished first, still detecting that something wasn't right with the pair but also thinking that this was neither the time nor the place to discuss it. 'Oh Jake, what's wrong with the suit?'

'Damn thing won't fit,' he said resigned.

Nkite took one look at the baggy, ill-fitting onesie and knew instantly, as did Takten, but hopped in before he had the chance to speak.

'Just press this,' she said, pushing a small button on his wrist communicator. The suit suddenly shrink-wrapped around Jake's body and also gave him extra dimensions he knew he didn't have. He looked down. He now had abs! Where had his flabby tummy gone? He also flexed his arms. He had bulging biceps!

'Wow!' he said, finally cheered up.

'It's a feature on the suits. Supposed to keep the soldiers in peak condition even if they aren't without them,' she confirmed.

'How did you know about this?' asked Takten.

Nkite flashed him a cheeky grin. 'You don't have to be a soldier to know this kind of stuff.'

'Thanks!' said Jake. 'Blimey, I'll never want to take it off now!'

Anji watched him, her eyes still sad. She had to admit to herself that he looked quite the part.

'Right, are we all set? Take care of each other,' said Random to Nkite and Anji. 'We'll see you at the rendezvous.'

Anji gave him a smile and Random walked off, followed by Takten and Jake.

'Jake,' she called after him but received no response. She sighed. This couldn't be the last time she's seeing them both. Not like this.

Nkite rubbed her arm affectionately. 'Hey,' she said.

'Sorry, right let's go,' said Anji.

'It's not the right time to be falling out with your friends,' said Nkite, not sure if she was saying the right thing or not.

Anji gave her a withering look.

They pushed their way gently through the crowd, meeting Djanga as they reached the front. Anji looked around and just witnessed the shadows of Random and Jake melt away into the darkness down another path in the mountain.

'Right girls,' said Djanga, who turned to his battalion. 'Move out!'

As Djanga barked the order his men, who were stationed at the front and back of the crowd, started on their trip. Anji looked down at the ground in sadness.

Nkite, who was helping Gron along the way, also held out her hand and took Anji's in her grasp.

'We can talk about it if you like?' she offered.

'Sorry Nkite but I've just met you and I don't feel comfort-'

'Okay, just it's going to be a long walk that's all.'

The river dwellers started signing in unison behind them. Anji was taken aback by the sheer beauty and sadness in their words. It was an old song, from the early days of the war, one which united both Crimson and Sapphire races in the group. Its lyrics were about hope, about seeing the morning again at the end of a stormy night. The river dwellers had been taught down the ages these precious words but only vowed to sing them when times looked like they were going to be brighter again. Now that they were being led to safety, and after hearing Random's words, they had so much cause for optimism.

The purple one had returned. He was going to lead Rodas to salvation.

Even Gron had started to join in, weeping as every syllable left his lips. Djanga and his men remained stoic. Anji bit her lip, really trying hard not to cry again.

Nkite clicked her tongue. 'Zarks. Well, if you change your mind...I hate singing.'

IV

'What I don't get, Benaya is why we have been asked to do this when the forces have been at it for ages.'

Delilah was moaning again. It was something her long-suffering sister had grown used to. Sadly, as Benaya herself didn't have a voice it wasn't like she could ever argue back, well, unless she deployed her well-used sign language signal for her to quit it. Ever since they had been children growing up on the planet Genocia together, she had been the one who had been unfortunate to share a room with her sister. Not like their older sibling Titu, who was lucky enough to have his own space.

She had often wondered why she had been cursed with the luck of being the youngest in her family and lumbered with the awkward middle child.

To be fair to Delilah, on this occasion at least, she did have a point. In the years that had passed since they met the mysterious Captain Random, his two human friends and his metal robot counterpart, they had continued to fight the good fight. As teenagers they had been enslaved in the mines far below the planet's surface, not that they were hardened criminals.

It was the way of the planet and as time went on, more and more people who were imprisoned with them were sent to something called "the soul destroyer" and they were never seen again.

When Random and Jake had been imprisoned with them, the sisters had helped to blow open a planet-wide conspiracy and bring down the government. After they had gone, the now free and pardoned duo were recruited by the factions that had made up the new government to carry out missions. These missions could range from arresting sympathisers to the old ways to hunting down and stunning the mutated remnants of the days of nuclear fallout in the outside wastelands of the planet. The mutts, as they were called, had been shunned by the government as a dirty secret to the pollution that had been caused under their long reign. Now that the planet was healing, the new regime had found a way to rehabilitate the mutts and partially restore them to how they were before they were affected by the fallout. But the air was still dirty and the atmosphere was still dangerous and as the chemicals in the fallout changed people through their respiratory systems, Delilah and Benaya were wearing a protective piece of equipment called a rebreather, which recycled the air that they breathed instantly, meaning no need for expensive and heavy oxygen tanks.

Through the thick dangerous fog, Benaya could only just make out her sister's shaved head a few feet in front of her. She shrugged, squinting through her face mask and breathing steadily into her rebreather. The pair continued to move through the smog with nothing to guide their way but torches mounted onto their laser rifles. They were set to stun, of course. They were not killers. These mutts would be called in and taken back by a follow-up party, who as far as they were aware, were on their way.

Suddenly Delilah stopped in her tracks. Her location system began to emit a beeping sound. Then another. And another. They raised their weapons and prepared for a scrap.

'Get behind me, Benaya. This isn't going to be easy.'

Benaya sighed. It never was.

The mutts were starting to surround them. One by one they emerged like terrifying zombies through the thick fog. Delilah readied her gun. 'On my mark. Wait until they are close enough.'

The sisters stood back-to-back, ready, waiting. The mutts tore through the mist, just metres away. Delilah and Benaya opened fire, turning in a circle using their weapons with pin-point accuracy. Within moments, two dozen mutts lay unconscious on the ground.

Delilah smiled. 'Nice shooting, sis.'

She put her weapon down and reached for her
communicator. 'Longboat, this is Red Fox, we
have completed our mission. You are free to pick
us up now.' A familiar voice fizzed back over the
intercom. 'Good job as always, Delilah.' Benaya
looked pleasantly surprised at her sister, who
smiled back.

'Yana! You sly old thing.'

'Good to hear from you again, you two.' The
voice over the communicator was that of an old
ally. Yana had met the sisters through Random
after she and her fellow freedom fighters, Rader
and Dail had saved Anji from being sent to the
mines. They had been unable to rescue Random
and Jake and Yana, who had infiltrated the Grand
Chamber of Genocia and acted undercover, had
been discovering more and more of the corrupt
and horrifying truth about how the planet was
run. After the uprising, and as the dust settled on
the planet, Yana had been enlisted to work for the
new government as one of the new cabinet
ministers. It had been a steep career change for
her, one which had always seen her taking a
more active role in life, but one that she had
accepted on the proviso that her old friends
worked with her to make the planet a better
home for all of them. But Delilah and Benaya, for
all of her hinting and probing, had always been
hard to recruit for the jobs that she was in charge
of.

'But...why couldn't you just do the job yourself?' asked Delilah.

'What good would our recruitment drive be without testing out potential employees first?'

Delilah tutted. 'Yana, we're freelancers. We don't want to work for the new Government full-time, we've spoken about this before. We are just fine where we are.'

'Trust me on this one and stand by,' Yana replied. 'We will pick you and the mutts up in a few minutes.'

'So, you've been monitoring us all along? You could have given us a lift,' said Delilah.

'Will make it up to you, I promise. A good day's work for you girls. 36 mutts collected.'

Delilah's face dropped. '36?'

Benaya stared in shock. The tracking system had been quietly beeping to itself for the last few seconds. Without warning, more mutts tore through the toxic cloud and knocked Delilah to the ground, sending her rifle clean out of her hand and the communicator far from her reach. Whatever Yana was shouting was inaudible over the screams and the shots being fired by Benaya. The bounty hunter managed to take out a few of the mutts but she too was overpowered. The duo was surrounded and held down by the terrifying hoard.

Struggle as they might, they were powerless to escape. As the mutts raised their crude instruments of death over their prisoners, a terrible roar of engines ripped over their heads, scaring them away.

The mutts left Delilah and Benaya and scattered back into the fog. Whatever had just saved them came in to land very close. Benaya picked herself up and helped her sister to her feet. It was a ship that had saved them. But who?

The sisters gingerly made their way towards it. The ship had a very distinct outline but its features were obstructed by the dust and dirt it had landed in. A ramp started to lower and a figure began to descend. As they peered through the fog, they cried out with surprise when they saw who it was.

'Skateboard!'

'Miss Delilah. Miss Benaya, I need you to come with me.'

'How did you know where to find us?'

'There isn't time now. Please, we need your help!'

Delilah's smile turned into a frown of concern. 'What's the matter? What's happened?'

Benaya signed. Where were Random and the other two?

'They are in danger. Terrible, terrible danger. And they need your help.'

'But how?'

'We really do not have time to talk now. I can explain on the way.'

Another ship roared past. 'That's Yana. She can help too. She owes us a favour.'

'I am counting on it, miss. We need all the help we can muster.'

Benaya and Delilah shot a concerned glance between themselves.

'Listen to me, the fate of our friends may well rest in our hands. We need to get back to them as soon as possible. There is no time to waste. Will you come?'

The new ship, which was bulkier and had landed with much less stealth than the Venus II settled on the hard ground very close to them. The bulkhead hissed open and the familiar face of Yana was the first to venture out into the open, her rebreather obscuring her face. Skateboard saw her and the armed guards who were trailing her out of the ship. She looked older, as did Benaya and Delilah, but Skateboard wouldn't have said as much. It had been a number of years since he had last seen them and even in a time of great peril, he wouldn't forget his manners and mention a thing like that.

'Miss Yana,' he said.

Yana and her guard approached the gangway. 'Skateboard. It's good to see you again.'

'And you. I'm afraid I have very little time. Our friends are trapped on a planet that is at war. He has asked me to recruit our old allies to help us win. Will you all do so?'

'You want us to rescue them?' asked Delilah. She looked at Benaya unconvinced.

'Yes...I hope that if all goes to plan there will be no need to fight,' said Skateboard.

'Well, that's a shame,' said Yana. 'This desk job is so boring; I could do with a good fight. How many people do you need?'

'As many as who are willing,' said Skateboard.

Benaya walked up the gangway, having already made her mind up. She turned to Delilah and smiled.

Delilah rolled her eyes. 'Fine,' she sighed, 'but if you get me killed, you'll never hear the last of it. Yana?'

Yana looked at them. 'Okay, I might be able to rustle up some support from our armed forces. Where is this war?'

'Rodas,' replied Skateboard.

Yana's face fell. 'Ah, that's going to be tricky then.'

'How come?' asked Delilah.

'The civil war on Rodas has raged for centuries. Many planets have signed treaties not to intervene, even in a state of intergalactic emergency. Genocia signed the treaty a long time ago.'

'I see,' said Skateboard. 'It's okay, I understand.'

'Well, I didn't say that I wouldn't help. Only I can't give you an armada,' said Yana. She turned to her guards. 'Rader, Dail? Continue with our operation here and tell the Prime Minister that I'm going to be late home.'

Skateboard was surprised that he hadn't recognised them.

'But Yana, we'll come with you!' said Rader.

'I'm sorry boys but I need you to take over in my absence,' Yana replied.

'But what should we tell the PM? You'll be dismissed if they find out!' said Dail.

'Tell them I've gone off-world for a bit, and make sure they don't find out why. This is to go no further, do you both hear me?' she ordered to her old friends.

'But telling the PM that you've gone off-world will get you dismissed anyway,' said Rader.

'That's true. Oh well, I didn't enjoy the desk job anyway. Besides you both deserve a promotion,' she winked. 'I'll be fine, I'll be back before you both know it.'

She leaned in and hugged her old friends. As Rader and Dail pulled away, they waved to the three familiar faces and went off to continue their work, rather reluctantly.

As they faded from view, Yana turned towards Skateboard. 'Right, I hope you've got somewhere I can change.'

Skateboard observed her attire. She was wearing a formal business suit and high heels.

'Yes, there should be something a little more practical in the wardrobe. I'm sure that Miss Anji won't mind you borrowing a garment or two.'

'What about weapons?' asked Delilah.

'Oh,' said Yana, patting her top pocket. 'Don't worry about that. I work in politics, remember? I always carry something to cover my back.'

Benaya smiled.

'Very well,' said Skateboard. 'Let's go. We've got very little time.'

The foursome made their way up the runway.

Benaya smelt a less-than-desirable scent emitting from the Venus II the closer they got to the entrance.

'Ugh, what is that smell?' asked Delilah.

'Oh yes, well you may want to hold your noses, there's about a hundred animals on board.'

'What is this,' coughed Yana, the stench sticking in her throat. 'A rescue mission or a zoo?'

'If you would lower your tone, please, Yana, there is a Queen on board,' said Skateboard.

Delilah, Benaya and Yana all looked at each other as the gangway receded into the belly of the ship and the Venus II prepared itself for take-off. Whatever they had just signed up for, they were sure that it was going to be memorable!

V

Whilst Random had been marched out of the mountain by Jake and Commander Takten, something hideous was starting to emerge from the shadows.

Deep within the bowels of the Crimson Empire's massive headquarters lay a vast room from which Kalor Maloso's master plan was starting to converge. As technicians stood around the huge area, monitoring a catalogue of readouts that to the untrained eye would mean nothing more than utter gibberish.

Along the top gantry of what was more like a processing plant than anything else, guards strode up and down, their heavy boots clanging loudly overhead what were thousands upon thousands of steel grey vats.

Inside each of them, a hideous gurgling and churning of matter drowned out all other sounds that were struggling to be heard.

Outside each vat stood a group of lab-coated scientists, who were also monitoring the readings on the side of the vats. They wore ear protectors, not because of the deafening sounds, but because of the terrible screams of pain and agony that were groaning from within each of the tall and thick steel drums.

On each vat was a progress bar of some sort which was flowing steadily to the top of its limit line like liquid filling a cup to the brim. Steadily every single vat inside the processing plant was moving ever closer and whatever concoction that was being brewed within them would be complete.

The process was alarmingly quick. As soon as the materials had been transferred down to the plant the machines had got to work. Now, mere minutes later, they were ready.

A loud ping emitted from every single vat at the same time like a factory of microwaves all spontaneously springing to life. The screaming stopped. A scientist in front of each of these huge vats took their readouts.

High up on the gantry, a General stood eagerly awaiting the fruits of the technician's labours. He peered with huge interest and witnessed a hive of activity as the heavy industry noise – and the screams from within the vats – died down. A hissing sound replaced them, aggravating the General's already aggressive tinnitus. From his left, he became aware of one of his soldiers marching up to him.

'Lieutenant,' he said without tearing his gaze from the action far below.

'General,' came the reply. The Lieutenant also looked over. 'How many has he requested this time?'

'250,000.'

The Lieutenant shuddered. 'It must have nearly killed him.'

The General turned to her. 'He's been dead for centuries. But now, in his final gift to our cause, we'll be triumphant. Are the heli-fighters ready?'

'Yes, General. We have recalled as many as we could, all except those currently on the front line. The aircraft carriers have all fallen back. In total, we have five hundred of them ready to do as our Lord commands.'

'Good, this first batch shall take the crafts and head for the security mainframe.'

'Is that what has been ordered, General?' said the Lieutenant, barely able to believe what she had just been told.

'It's our Lord's wish. The others shall wipe out what little pockets of the Sapphire Regime remain on this planet. As for us, we shall join our new soldiers up in the air. The security mainframe won't be able to repel our firepower this time.' The General felt so excited inside. He rarely smiled and yet he couldn't wipe his sinister grin off his face.

'We've been unable to before, the security mainframe has always repelled any attacks. Why should it work this time?'

'Two reasons,' said the General. 'One, we've never centred such a fierce attack on the containment field before and two, because we have the code to turn it off. An insider in the mainframe gave it to us. Well, he took some persuading. We were looking after his family after all. They also gave it to the purple one.'

The Lieutenant gasped. 'He's back?'

'Yes, and the trap is set. Today we win this war. There will be no other outcome.'

A loud groaning from far below interrupted their discussion. As the General and the Lieutenant looked down, every single vat appeared to be cracking open. A heavy steel door was peeling itself open allowing a cloud of smoke and gas hissing into the processing plant. The activity from the scientists and technicians became frantic as slowly red-coloured figures began to appear from within the vats.

The Lieutenant smiled. She had never seen so many soldiers being created at once before.

One by one the thousands upon thousands of newly created lives fell in like the obedient soldiers they were and marched neatly out of the processing plant. The metal doors all snapped back shut again and in the blink of an eye, the process began again.

'Good, they understand what they must do. It's amazing what those tech boys can do isn't it?' purred the General. 'You'd better return to your post Lieutenant, and inform your superiors. The new blood is on its way.'

*

'What a mess,' said Jake as he and Takten marched Random off out of the mountain.

'How far to Maloso?' asked Random.

'A fairway. We shall need to commandeer a heli-fighter,' replied Takten.

'Where are we going to find one of them?' asked Jake.

The trio dropped to the floor as not far above their heads a couple of aircraft were playing out the climax of a dogfight, culminating in the heli-fighter being chased through the sky and crashing into the side of the mountain.

'I mean in one piece?' finished Jake.

Takten shot him an annoyed look. 'We'll find on the way. Heli-fighters have to land for their engines to charge.'

As Takten finished his sentence, he spotted one such heli-fighter doing just that, landing roughly a hundred metres from the spot where they were crouching in.

'Speaking of which...' said Takten as he gestured for Jake and Random to follow him.

'Wait, we'd better stay out of view,' said Random.

'Why?' asked Jake.

'We don't know which side that heli-fighter belongs to,' replied Random.

'It's a Crimson Empire ship. They are the only ones who have heli-fighters with that livery on their doors, but you're right, we can't have any questions being asked until we are on the inside. Wait here.' Takten leapt to his feet and made for the heli-fighter.

'Won't he need some help?' asked Jake.

'I get the feeling he can handle it. Anyway, it gives us a chance to have a chat.'

Jake shuffled a bit. 'What about?'

'You and Anji. Are you both okay.'

Jake sighed. 'We're about to infiltrate the base of what sounds like the evilest people we've ever faced and you want to talk about this?'

'Jake, I don't know what is about to happen. I want to know that everything is alright between my best friends in case...'

'...in case of what?'

Random stopped himself from saying any more. 'I just want to know if I can help.'

Jake looked down at his feet. He tried his best to blot out the sound of war all around them. Then he wished he hadn't.

'It's just...before we met you Anj and I...we...made a pact. That pact has got me through some tough times. Now...I'm so stupid.'

'Jake, I know we all take a jibe at one another but I can assure you I don't think that you are stupid and I know for a fact that Anji doesn't either. She cares for you; I can promise you that. And whatever this promise was to you I'm sure that it pales in comparison to how you both feel about each other. I mean come on, your best friends. This will pass.'

'I hope so,' said Jake. 'Cheers Random.'

'Look, whatever you feel now it'll pass. Your friendship is more important than one fallout. Especially to me.' Random smiled.

Jake smiled back. 'Hey, random question, but why isn't anybody shooting at us? Two people in the middle of a war field. How come they aren't shooting at us?'

'I think they are too preoccupied. In fact, is it me or is it all getting quieter?' asked Random.

'I'm not sure, maybe we're just getting used to it?' Jake spotted a waving figure standing in the distance next to the heli-fighter. 'Hey, I think Takten has done it!'

Random got up. 'Come on.' The two friends made their way gingerly across the rocky terrain. When they reached Takten, the soldier was beckoning them quickly onto the heli-fighter, helping the shackled Random up the short ladder inside the craft.

Jake took a look around the ship.

It was cramped, with enough room for two people to carry out the piloting duties and another bank of two seats at computers that looked more like tactical positions, given the radar emitting through the dark ship.

'What did you do with the people on board?' asked Jake.

'You don't want to know,' replied Takten. 'You'd better sit with me upfront. Random, you stay in here. And belt up, I haven't flown one of these since the academy.'

'I can give it a go,' said Jake.

'Better leave it to the soldier,' said Random, who hinted at the seat belts on the seat he has chosen. 'Would you mind?'

Jake helped Random into his chair and made his way into the cockpit, immediately spotting the blood stains on the wing mirror in front of him.

'I hope that's on the outside,' he quipped uneasily as Takten chose not to reply.

'Off we go. By the way, it's more than likely that we'll be shot at as soon as we are in the air. You'll have to man the cannons.'

Jake took a look around and familiarised himself with the controls. He glanced upon a bank of buttons and a steering wheel with what looked like a crude gun and sighter on top of it. 'Gotcha.'

'Have you fired a gun before?' asked Takten as the engines began to fire up. He checked a readout on the dashboard and was relieved that the batteries were not as flat as he thought they'd be.

'A bit,' replied Jake.

'That'll do,' said Takten. 'We have enough fuel to get to the Crimson Empire's headquarters. Hold on...it's going to be a bumpy ride.'

Jake gulped as the heli-fighter shot off up into the air vertically and then sailed off into the murky, bloody fog of battle up ahead.

VI

Admiral Bagari reclined in the leather chair in her office and poured herself a glass of whisky. As she replaced the bottle back in the cabinet under her desk, she picked the glass up to her lips and took a short and sharp swig. She moved over to a bank of buttons that sat on top of her desk and pressed one, requesting the person who answered to make sure that she was not disturbed. As she released the button, she returned her gaze to the huge window and pondered out into space.

Bagari had received a call from Skateboard. In the encoded message he had notified her that he had recruited some old friends to help in the fight on Rodas and had also asked for her involvement too. It was a request that she hadn't responded to and yet it was one she had to turn down. The Space Seals Corp was almost as old as the war on Rodas and as such, was sworn centuries back not to interfere in the conflict on that planet. It was a promise that had been signed in triplicate and it was wrapped up in so much red tape that it was almost impossible to undo.

Yet whilst she was duty-bound to refuse, she didn't want to. Although she loathed calling Random and his counterparts friends, they were strong allies and had done much to help her keep the universe safe. The terrible encounter with Stratos. The wormholes opening up across the universe threatened to bring destruction, she had worked with them and in doing so she had been bumped up the ranks in the fleet. Indeed, The Stargazer was now the flagship battle freighter and she was in charge and she was bestowed that responsibility in no small part thanks to her involvement with Random.

Now here she was, in his hour of need and she was unable to do anything else other than to help him get behind enemy lines. She dreaded to think what the Admiralty would do to her if they ever found out. A demotion, a dressing down in front of peers and a loss of her command. She knew the rules and by God, she didn't want to break them.

But that didn't stop her wanting to call her peers together and try to convince them to take part but she knew they would refuse. Only if the mainframe was breached would there be a call for help for the Space Seals to step in and in a weird, very dangerous way, she kind of wanted that to happen.

She knew very well the atrocities that had taken place on that awful, shunned planet. But she wanted to see action, she wanted to help out an end to suffering.

After all, that's why she joined the Space Seals in the first place. She looked out at the stars. She knew most of them. It was part of the training when she enlisted in the academy to know them but she'd already known so many off by heart. As a little girl, she and her father would gaze nightly through the telescope in his observatory back at home and he would tell her of all the places he had been and where he still wanted to go. It used to make Bagari feel a little sad that she couldn't go with him but she would when she was older, she'd told herself. She'd enlist, just like he did, and sail the stars of the galaxy.

She tried not to think of the rest of her childhood. A locked door stopped her dead in her tracks. Instead, she thought of Rodas and thought of Random. She picked out a cluster of distant stars. It was Ursa-17 – the galaxy that contained Rodas. She could be there in a matter of hours...

Suddenly her train of thought was interrupted by a beeping sound coming from a small monitor that was rising out of her desk.

Admiral Bagari stared at the screen. It was a personal message that had bypassed her official channels. Sighing she accepted the call and a familiar face appeared.

'Commander Serridian,' she said almost with a hint of surprise.

'Admiral...it's good to see you.'

The Admiral had a smile on her lips when she saw her old friend on the screen. It had slowly started to fade when she saw the distress on Serridian's face.

'Why am I getting the feeling that this isn't going to be a happy catch-up?' Bagari said.

'I'm sorry, Vanessa. I'm so, so sorry.'

'What have you done?'

A few minutes later Bagari burst out of her office and made her way down one of the long corridors of her ship. She ignored everybody who she passed, each one of them stopping in their tracks and saluting her with the respect she had earned. Before long she had made it to the command bridge.

'Ensign. Put me through to the Admiralty now!' she barked.

'Yes, Admiral,' came the reply. Bagari's face was like thunder. Serridian. How could he do it? He should have come straight to her. They trusted each other implicitly. Their friendship had gone back to their academy days. She'd been present on the day he had got married to his wife.

Hell, she'd introduced them! She was friends with both of them.

How had he got himself tied up in such a mess? How had his family ended up getting stuck on Rodas?

It wasn't the way that she had wanted to get involved in the fight but it was just the thing that would get the Space Seals over to Rodas to help, just as she had been itching to do.

A number of people flashed up on the big screen that Bagari was standing in front of. Ignoring their unanimous calls for answers as to why they were having a sudden conference, Bagari could waste no time.

'The security mainframe surrounding the planet Rodas has been compromised. We have to go there now.'

The Admiralty fell silent. The oldest looking of the group, a thin stick-like man, spoke first.

'How have you come by this information?'

'I have been informed of a soldier working on the mainframe who has been blackmailed into giving away the shutdown code. Their deception had been notified to the mainframe high command but they are unable to change the code. There is also an attack being mounted on the mainframe, one far greater than any it has ever withstood before. We have to support the mainframe. If the war reaches the other planets in Ursa-17, or further, the consequences will be dire.'

'We will debate this news,' said another Admiral.

'There is no time,' replied Bagari. 'The Stargazer and three other battle freighters are within range. We will be there in no time at all.'

'This is too delicate a political decision for us to make on the spot,' said the old Admiral.

'Then let me take the decision for us and I'll pay the consequences if all fails,' said Bagari.

The Admiralty and the crew of the Stargazer looked at each other unnerved.

'You would lose your command,' said an octopus-like-looking Admiral.

'What's a command if you can't do anything right with it?' replied Bagari.

'You will go down for this,' said the old Admiral.

'The galaxy will go down if we don't act. I'm not debating this any further. The battle on Rodas is nearing its end. The war of an entire galaxy is on the brink. We have to go...even if no one else is coming with us.'

'What must your crew think?' asked a female Admiral.

'They can think what they like. Any disagreement with my decision will be noted in my log and I'll make sure that they will not be punished.' Bagari had barely blinked.

'We have to go now. Whether you like it or not the Space Seals must do what we were set up to do. Protect and serve.'

The Admiralty fell silent again. The older man spoke first.

'We shall discuss this. For now, the Stargazer along with the Phoenix and the Lancet will go to Rodas. Do not intervene unless provoked or it is indeed necessary. Make contact with the mainframe high command and make sure that you have all the facts before engaging. Is that understood?'

'Crystal. I hope to see you all soon. Bagari out.' The screen snapped off and returned to the impressive starscape outside the battle freighter. She immediately marched to her chair as the command bridge hummed with activity.

'Red alert. Full speed ahead to Rodas now. All hands on deck. Prepare for battle.'

VII

By an open window that overlooked the chaos of Rodas down below, Serridian was as white as a ghost. He'd let them down. He'd let them all down. There was no way that he could go on. The guilt was tearing him apart and the worst part was that it had all been for nothing.

He peered down at the electronic read-out on his tablet again. He still couldn't believe the message that it displayed.

Serridian had been conned.

He felt sick. So, they hadn't been kidnapped after all? His family were safe. When he had been informed, just earlier that day that a terrorist group, sympathising with the Crimson Empire had captured his family on his home planet, he hadn't thought to check its validity. Stupidly he had believed it. Why had he been chosen? Was someone in the Crimson Empire looking into his file and having seen a weakness there? Whatever had happened he had caused a massive security breach and now the rest of the universe was going to pay for it.

If only his wife had picked up the phone when he called home.

He would never have sent the code on the encrypted line to the anonymous "caller" if she hadn't been out at the time but he had panicked. He'd been so foolish. He'd betrayed everyone he knew and loved and worse of all he may have condemned Rodas to a bloody end.

He returned his gaze to the view window. Out of the corner of his eye, he could see the rhymical throbbing electric charge that bolted all through the mainframe. It was like a massive metal netting containing everything that was bad and evil about Rodas inside. Serridian had been consigned to the mainframe as an Ensign when he graduated from the Space Seals and he along with 500,000 other lifeforms from around the galaxy dedicated nine months a year of their lives to stay and maintain it, making sure that it would never be compromised. Even now he could see a distant wave of heli-fighters breaking through the clouds, the usual flashes and bangs of conflict that flashed through a hazy dust-like fog. Then he saw more. Then more. Second, by second it looked as though the fleet was growing and heading straight for the mainframe. Serridian shivered and dropped his tablet, the screen smashing as shards of glass collided with the hard floor. He scrambled for the intercom, the loud din of the engines and blades of the heli-fighters getting louder and louder as they grew closer.

Suddenly an alarm klaxon broke the tense air in Serridian's living quarters.

All along the mainframe red lights began to flicker off and on in unison. The mainframe had withstood attempts on it before but they had never seen a number attacking such as this. Serridian saw the advancing heli-fighters. This wasn't a small battalion of crimson attackers. This was thousands.

His hands shaking, he reached for the intercom and clicked the recording button as the shadow of the heli-fighters began to blot out the bright neon sun.

'This is Commander Serridian of Rodasian security mainframe section 1401, I'm sorry...I'm just...the mainframe code has been compromised. I didn't...I was tricked. I have taken the liberty of contacting the Space Seals for help...forgive me, I know the protocol but I take full responsibility. Serridian out.'

His voice trembling with fear, he sent the message to his superior, priority urgent, hoping that they would find the time to hear it. Praying, even, that his old friend Vanessa Bagari would get there in time.

He reached for his intercom, now only too aware that his large window was completely swamped by the vision of a number of heli-fighters poised to shoot. Serridian sweated profusely, a cold fear gripping him. He scrambled to send another, final message.

'My love...we are under attack; I may not get another chance so I just wanted to say-'

Serridian's words were drowned out by the horrific sound of laser fire. With the security shield down, the sound of the klaxon suddenly fell mute in his ears as the heli-fighters opened fire. Frozen to the spot, Serridian watched as the glass on his window shattered before long, despite being reinforced against attack it was no match without a protective layer. His room, along with so many others exploded, a huge fireball engulfing everything within. Those manning the defence systems returned fire with equal venom but it was too late to save the likes of Serridian.

His final message would remain unsent. His final act had given the Crimson Empire a dangerous advantage.

*

It wasn't the incessant singing that was ringing in Djanga's mind. It also wasn't the fact that they were making next to no progress in getting anywhere near HQ. There wasn't the thought of the impending ambush at any moment either which was worrying him. He was pretty certain that his men could withstand it.

He knew that they were being hunted. The Crimson Empire were too omnipresent, always lurking in plain sight and in the shadows, for them not to be hot on their scent, especially after those who had been killed by him and his men upon rescuing the river dwellers. As he and the other marched on, far too slowly for his liking, it was none of these thoughts or sounds which were making him start to worry.

It was the noise that he could hear high above them, through layer upon layer of rock, that was making him uneasy. Despite their relative safety inside the mountain, there was a hum, a soft, distant hum which he had picked up not long after they had started their trip. It was a miracle he had any hearing left, let alone hearing that was good enough for him to pick up on something he had originally thought might be shell shock. He'd carried it with him for years, ever since his days as a Private on the front line protecting the boundary of his city, Kalasias. But as their journey had continued the sound of humming had grown ever so slightly louder. Looking side-to-side with his troops, he had wondered if he was going a bit mad, a common occupational hazard in his line of work. He'd started to realise that they had picked up on it too. Cautiously, he nodded and they readied their guns.

Behind them, Anji and Nkite had been having a ball. For the last few hours, they had been nattering away, getting to know one another.

Gron, who stood arm in arm with them, smiled to himself, not uttering a word, delighted that his young friend was making acquaintance and smiling again.

'...and then he fell in it!' chuckled Anji, concluding her story.

Nkite snorted. 'Into the fountain of youth!?'

'Yes!' they both burst out in laughter.

'He's a funny one, your friend,' said Nkite.

'Yeah, you can say that again,' said Anji, her laugh dying down, her eyes lost in thought. Suddenly she was miles away.

'You speak about him a lot,' said Nkite, noticing her new friend's sudden change in mood.

'We've had a lot of adventures together. It'd be rude of me to leave him out,' said Anji.

'Well, you don't seem to speak as much about Random.'

Anji realised she hadn't. 'He's different.'

'Tell me about it. When I was a child, I remember being lost. Alone. We were being evacuated from our home. My Mother and Father, we got separated. I was so scared but then I looked up and I saw this incredible sight. A blast of colour, a colour I had never seen before. I'd seen the coming together of two explosions simultaneously and in that moment, I had hope. Guess who it was who gave me that hope.'

Anji didn't have to think twice. 'Random.'

'It was rumoured back then that something was coming to save us, to stop the war. I never thought I'd bear witness to it.'

'So, you don't hate Random then?' asked Anji.

'He inspired me. Set me on a path. I have helped save so many people thanks to what I saw that night. The things I used to do. I once lured some soldiers into a church and shot them with purple paint. You should have seen their faces. It was like I had shot them with some deadly virus!'

'Paint! Like a paint gun?'

'Kind of,' replied Nkite. 'I'd seen how that purple colour had been made. For centuries people have talked about it being the real reason why we went to war in the first place. Red and blue. In that explosion, in my paintball concoctions, I saw peace, a world in which we could both live together. You know why?'

Anji shook her head.

Nkite continued. 'It was us and them. The Crimson Empire and the Sapphire Regime come together in harmony, repelling evil. That's what your friend Random had always represented to me. To so many. And so, we waited for him to return.'

'And now that he is here, the war will end,' said Gron. 'I can feel it in my old bones.'

'For so long I had had so much hope in my heart but today...having met him, I am not so sure anymore,' said Nkite.

'They do say don't meet your heroes,' joked Anji.

'Why do they say that? And who is "they?"' asked a bemused Gron.

Anji was lost for words momentarily. She'd forgotten that her way of speaking could sometimes be lost on those who were not from her part of the galaxy. The translation programme that had installed itself in her mind the moment she had stepped onto the Venus II back in the day made it easy to forget that wherever she went she was speaking a completely alien language.

'Look. I've seen Random do the most amazing things. I've seen him fight for so many people.'

'Then why is it only now that he has chosen to come back to fight for his own?' asked Nkite.

'I don't think that I should speak on his behalf. Please do believe me when I tell you that he has struggled with his conscience ever since he left.'

Nkite looked at the ground and kicked the dirt. 'Tell that to the people he hasn't saved.'

'I wish I could. Trust me. He'll find a way. He always does.' Anji smiled.

'I'll believe it when I see it with my own eyes,' she muttered.

'You will, Nkite. I don't doubt it. You'll see the streak of hope in the sky high above Rodas once again,' Gron smiled.

'You'll have to forgive my young friend, Anji, she's had a tough time of late.'

'Haven't you all,' said Anji who then broke into a friendly smile, 'it's fine, I get it. I can't comprehend the kind of lives you've all had but I've had my tough moments too.'

'How did you get through them?' asked Nkite with an inquisitive look in her eyes.

'I had my friends,' replied Anji.

'Then wouldn't it be better to keep your friends close than to drive them away?' said Nkite.

Anji knew exactly what she was referring to. She'd been probing her about Jake for most of the journey. 'Look, it's complicated.'

Gron and Nkite fell silent for a moment, knowing to leave the subject there, so they were then shocked that Anji began blurting out to them.

'It's just I've known him for so long that any feeling I used to have might have become quite...brotherly. We've been through a lot, and when we were young, we made a promise that we'd be together for prom, and if we were home right now, we'd probably have had it, but I'm not sure we'd have gone together, probably not. I mean who knows who we'd have gone with?

He's managed to get the hots for girls all over the cosmos but I've never once been so blatant. I mean, who does he think he is? He's not the only one who can have feelings for others, is he? I'm not saying I have feelings for anyone, well, not right now, well, I'm not sure, there's this thing that happened...sorry, I'm babbling, aren't I?'

Nkite and Gron looked stunned. 'Maybe,' said Nkite.

'Sorry. I've got a lot going on in my head,' sighed Anji. 'At the end of the day, I have such a good relationship with Jake. I don't want anything to break it.'

'Then young girl, may I suggest when he comes back to you that you tell him that. It sounds like you have such a special bond,' said Gron.

'If he does make it back,' said Nkite.

Anji started to panic a little.

'That doesn't really help,' said Gron, before Anji had the chance to say something potentially worse. She fumed. There she was, doing her best to console a stranger she'd only just met and that's what she comes back with?

'Sorry. I don't really have time to talk about boys,' said Nkite.

'It's okay, honestly you're not missing out on much!' said Anji who was starting to regain her good mood. But deep down she really was starting to worry. What if things didn't go to plan? What if she never saw Jake again? Soon she was having trouble thinking about it anymore because of a loud hum that started to interrupt her train of thought.

'Stop!' came the cry from Djanga.

The soldiers protecting the hoard of river dwellers all barked out the same order. They all readied their guns as those that they were trying to protect started to sound panicked.

'Sargeant Djanga to HQ, come in please,' said Djanga into his wrist communicator. A horrendous concoction of noise burst through the tiny speaker. Anji's heart started to beat faster.

'Djanga. This is SRHQ. We are under attack. Repeat we are under attack,' came the cry from the other end of the communicator. It kept fizzing and popping in and out like the connection was slowly breaking. 'The Crimson Empire. There are too many of them. We are trying to hold them back but we've never seen...'

'Hello? HQ come in!' yelled Djanga.

'...thousands breaking through our embankments. Protect the refugees and fall back to Hawk 159. That's an order...need every man and woman who can fig-'

The comlink died.

'That humming sound, what is it?' asked Anji. It was now so loud it was as though they were all standing on an airfield.

'Heli-fighters.'

'How can we hear them? We must be hundreds of feet away from them,' said Nkite.

Suddenly it sounded like a bomb had gone off far away. The corridor started to shake and tiny bits of rock and dust fell down upon them all.

'They are bombarding the mountain!' said Djanga.

'Captain, Hawk 159 how far away would you say that we are from there?' asked Djanga to the soldier standing next to him.

'It's almost directly above us,' he said consulting his map.

'Oh, my zark,' cursed Djanga. 'We have to get to the surface now.'

'If we do that, we'll all be killed!' cried Anji.

'If we stay here, we will be buried alive!' said Djanga.

'I don't understand, we should be well protected even by a heavy bombardment. We shouldn't be at risk,' said Nkite.

'That's the trouble. It's not just a heavy bombardment it's a number of artilleries I've never seen before.'

'How do you know?' asked Anji.

'Listen to it! It shouldn't be possible but those engines are so great in number-'

Another shock of bombs sent the group sprawling to the ground, and some of them started to scream and panic. Anji could hear babies and children begin to cry.

'Is there anywhere safe we can take them?' she asked.

'No,' said Djanga chillingly.

'Then where's the next best place!?' said Anji in an angry yell.

Djanga grabbed the map from his Captain and gave it to Anji. On it was a lime green luminous digital read-out of the mountain and its surrounding flat, ground level and underground level areas.

'Take them here,' said Djanga pointing at what Anji looked like a nearby exit from the mountain. 'It's just far enough away for now.'

'And what will you do?' asked Nkite.

Djanga cocked his gun. 'Try and hold them off. You two are in charge. Go there and don't move unless you have to. Clear?'

'Crystal,' said Anji.

'You'd better take these,' said Djanga, who reached down into two handgun holsters on both of his thighs. He handed them to Anji and Nkite. 'Now go!'

Another explosion high up above rocked the mountain. Anji fell to the floor and was helped back up by Gron, who had somehow wedged himself beside a rock for stability.

'Right men, Hawk 159, let's go! Move!' said Djanga.

He and the rest of the Sapphire Regime soldiers who were supposed to lead the river dwellers to safety tore themselves away from those they were tasked to protect.

Anji watched as the soldiers left their view. She breathed heavily. She looked at the sea of terrified people in front of her. So many men and women, children and babies both red and blue looked back at her, fear flooding from their faces.

She looked at Nkite, who looked equally as fearful. Anji looked at her trembling hand and the gun that had been forced into it. She took a deep breath and pocketed it.

'Right,' she said taking a look at the map. The exit wasn't far away, she reckoned, and she steeled herself for the task ahead. 'Let's get out of here!'

VIII

As they flew high above the devastated ground far below, the occupants of the commandeered heli-fighter were shocked by the lack of opposition they had come across. Surely the soldiers Takten had dispatched would have been discovered by now? Hadn't they raised the alarm? As time wore on and their journey continued without incident, they soon realised why it was all too easy.

As they neared Kalor Maloso's base, a shadow had begun to form over the cockpit from outside. Random, having been stowed in the cramped mid-section had noticed it too. He tried to get up from his seat but fell back.

'Jake, could you unfasten me please?'

Jake was too preoccupied gapping at what was causing the shadow.

'Jake?' Random called again.

'Random you'd better see this,' said Takten, who was also staring in disbelief at what he was seeing.

'Fine, if no one else will do it,' Random said to himself. He clenched his body until it went rigid and with his strength, broke the clasp on his seat belt and moved to join the other two in the cockpit.

When he got there, he too was astonished.

'Zarks...' he said quietly.

The three men watched as they witnessed the huge swarm of heli-fighters shooting at the security mainframe.

'How many of them are there?' asked Jake, not taking his eyes off the action unfolding above them.

'Too many to count,' replied Takten. 'This is bad.'

Random regarded the lasers which looked like they were coming from the mainframe itself. 'At least it looks like they are fighting back.'

'It's not enough,' said Takten grimly.

'But that mainframe stretches across the planet, surely it will stay intact?' asked Jake.

'Not with a force that large concentrating on one specific spot,' said Random. 'What use would a net be if there's a massive hole in it.'

'They're trying to break out of the planet,' said Takten. 'I've never seen so many enemy heli-fighters before.'

'Then where have they come from?' asked Jake.

'I don't know, but it's time I found out,' said Random.

'You mean us?' replied Takten.

'No. I'm sorry but the plan has changed,' said Random firmly.

Takten was about to protest when he intercepted an incoming transmission through the communication channel. He stared at the readout. 'Oh, my zarks.'

'What?' asked Jake who was straining to see the read-out.

'There's an imminent attack on Hawk 159.'

'Is that as bad as it sounds?' asked Random.

'It's a stronghold for the Sapphire Regime. What's worse it's the final barrier before our base, and it's close to the mountain we left the refugees in.'

Jake's stomach lurched. 'Anji,' he said to Random. 'We have to help them.'

'They might not know that they are under attack, I don't have access to my channels in here,' said Takten.

'Then that settles it, the plan changes. Takten, how far to Maloso's base?' asked Random.

'We're almost on top of it, just over the ridge, but Random-'

'It won't be as heavily guarded as we thought. You two drop me off and go back to Hawk 159.'

'But Random-' Jake said.

'Don't argue with me, Anji may need your help. Even if they haven't made it out of the mountain yet they could be ambushed by this attack. Now please, don't argue you two.
When I give the order, Takten opens the door,' Random said as he strode towards it.

'So, I'm wearing a dead man's suit for nothing?' said Jake, feeling disgusted in himself and not for the first time wanting nothing more at that moment than a really hot shower.

'Plans change,' said Random. 'I'm sorry Jake. Hopefully, this will be the last time we have to make any.'

'Shall I let you out?' said Jake brandishing the key.

'You mean he's going to jump?' said Takten in astonishment. 'We're two thousand miles above ground level.'

'Yeah, he can handle it,' said Jake brushing his concern away.

Random looked at Jake and broke his handcuffs off with ease.

'Oh, well that was pointless then,' said Jake tossing the key away.

'Ready, Random?' asked Takten.

'Ready,' confirmed Random, who was bracing himself in the doorway.

'Good luck,' said Jake.

'And to you two,' said Random. He gave his friend a smile. 'See you soon.'

'Now,' said Takten. The door burst open and Random was sucked out instantly.

The cabin alarms started to sound, warning of depressurisation, prompting Takten to close them. The howl of the inrushing air ceased almost as quickly as it had started.

'Does he usually do things like that?' asked Takten.

'It's weirder when he doesn't,' replied Jake.

Random hurtled through the air, his eyes firmly fixed below. Fixed, and watering like mad considering he was falling at a very fast velocity. He ignored the roar of the rushing air past him as he formed his body into an arrow shape, intent on penetrating the base below.

Kalor Maloso's base – the Crimson Empire's HQ – was massive. A dirty, turgid rusty red, it didn't look tall from Random's vantage point but it was monstrous in scale. The base itself had been built into the blood-red rock of a mountainside, a common thing to find on Rodas, it seemed. It looked old, battle-worn. Random noticed that some parts of it looked newer and less battle scorched by laser fire.

As he tumbled ever closer, he began to brace himself.

Then, as he counted down the seconds in his head, something he had been doing since he had chosen the more direct route to his location, he pulled on a cord at his side.

Suddenly, a parachute exploded out of a bag on his back and sent him hurtling upwards in the air, a moment that to Random felt like his organs had all shot out his body and then rearranged themselves again as the parachute sent him sailing below.

Whilst Jake and Takten had been talking, Random had noticed a parachute pack hanging up by the side of the door on the heli-fighter, so he took the opportunity to nab it while they were not looking and hopefully look as cool as could be in leaving them via the door as they were flying.

After all, he had thought to himself whilst quickly constructing the idea in his head, it might be the last time he would be able to do something so heroic in front of his friend.

As he sailed down, he surveyed the base and looked for a way in. He noticed what looked like an observation part of the complex which was jutting out of the base and deduced that this was probably the area where Maloso ran his operations.

If he was right, the war would end a lot quicker.

If he was wrong, he'd have to get his hands dirty whilst finding Maloso.

Having found a possible route in he looked up.

His parachute obscured his view of the attack on the mainframe but everywhere else around him was silent. It was like the Crimson Empire had focused itself on two main targets. Then he thought of his friends. Clearly, Anji was going to be in trouble so sending Jake back to help her would help them make up.

He'd always known how close they both were. It didn't take a genius to have seen the connection the pair had, especially after so many years with them at his side. They'd never had a fight before and although Random didn't know all of the ins and outs, as he sailed down safely onto the roof of the base and tore his parachute pack off his back, he tried his best to shake his concern for them out of his mind.

Random walked up to the mountainside and looked for an opening into the base. He found none. He put his hands cautiously against the rockface, searching for a hidden entrance or something that would trip a release mechanism to allow him entrance.

He found none. Random huffed. He heard the distant gunfire high up above and noticed that the battle was starting to be lost by the security mainframe. More and more fires blinked into existence in the sky as piece by piece more of the netting that had contained the chaos of war for so many centuries was starting to tear further and further apart.

Random grit his teeth. Had Skateboard failed to convince Bagari to fight? There didn't seem to be any sign of the Space Seals anywhere. There wasn't any way of him knowing, either, whether his robot friend had been successful in recruiting their old friends to help.

He started to clench his fists and then, the all-too-familiar voices started to talk to Random again.

'What are you waiting for?' asked the female voice.

'Back up,' replied Random, still staring helplessly at the battle.

'It's down to you, Random. It's always been down to you. This was your burden. No one else's,' said the male voice.

'Okay, just shut up a second will you? All my life I've had your voice in my head. Taunting me. Polluting my mind with the idea that I am the only one who can stop all of this. But how can I? I know I've done some incredible things but this is beyond me.'

'You doubt yourself at the moment of destiny,' said the female voice calmly.

Random felt a tear drop down his cheek. 'Will I see them again? My friends?'

The voices stayed silent almost as though they knew that this wasn't the moment to install false hope.

Random sighed heavily. 'Okay, no more interruptions now. You're right. It's time I did something on my own. No friends to help. No help is on its way in any sense. Just me, Maloso and the fate of Rodas. No pressure...' he muttered the last part to himself. He gazed at the floor. There appeared to be a trap door leading into the base.

He looked down, wiping away dirt and grime off what looked like a small handle and a window that was smeared and ancient. He tried the handle, which felt rusty and stiff, and slowly managed to open it. Unable to see through the window he had no idea what awaited him inside.

'The easy way in?' he said as he swung his legs over the opening and dropped himself through. As soon as his boots clanged onto the metal floor seven feet below the opening, what had been a dark corridor suddenly turned into a red flashing, loud klaxon shouting chaos. Under the klaxon, a dozen or so guns clicked into life and as he straightened himself up, Random spotted the red sighter lights on his body. He stood up and faced the gun-toting soldiers down. He clenched his fists, ready for the fight.

'The hard way.'

IX

'Behind you!'

Anji's warning was picked up instantly by Nkite, who twirled in the air and fired a shot that burnt straight into the chest of a Crimson Empire soldier. The blast sent him reeling back, knocking one of his comrades to the floor as Nkite reloaded her pistol. Anji bent back down under the rock and allowed herself a chance to look back at those that she was helping to save.

'Anyone else got a gun?' she cried. Some of the river dwellers, men and women who were able to fight had instantly leapt to the group's defence the moment they had been ambushed at the exit of the mountain. Nkite had been telling Anji and Gron how their path to freedom had been too easy. Upon opening the exit door, and suffering a shot to the shoulder which still flooded her mind with pain every time she shot at her enemies, she knew that she had been right.

The Crimson Empire had been waiting for them all along. This was going to be a sport for them. Nkite took out a couple more soldiers as did some of the river dwellers.

'Anji, fire!' she yelled. 'Come on!'

Anji knew she had to. It was kill or be killed.

Gron did his best to keep his head down and put a protective arm around a young child who was crying uncontrollably. Many others were sobbing tears of terror as the group were slowly being driven back into the mountain. It wasn't any good. Step-by-step more and more soldiers were starting to push their way past the small firepower that Nkite was leading.

Anji fired her pistol and managed to miss a soldier by roughly a foot.

'What are you doing?' snapped Nkite.

Anji knew exactly. She couldn't do it. She knew she had to but she couldn't bring herself to shoot and kill someone, even though they were wanting to kill her! She was trying to aim her shots in places where they would be wounded. Eventually, she felt the gun wrestled from her hand by someone.

It was Nkite and she was furious.

'Whose side are you on?' she bit as she ducked down beneath the rock to keep out of harm's way.

'I'm sorry,' said Anji. 'I can't kill them.'

'You're no leader, get out of the way then!'

Anji wanted to punch Nkite in the face but this wasn't the time nor the place. Plus, she knew deep down she was right. Anji slumped back down the rock towards the cowering river dwellers as Nkite returned a volley of fire.

Anji found Gron. He knew immediately why she had fallen back to be with him and the others but Anji felt no judging looks from the old man burning in her direction. He understood. This wasn't her fight. But Anji felt remorse still. She was so torn but she wasn't a killer. She took the map out of her pocket and inspected it hurriedly.

Upon closer inspection, there was what looked like a smaller exit quite close by.

'We can get through here!' she yelled.

'It's too close to the exit up there, we'll perish,' said Gron.

'It's worth a chance!' said Anji.

Gron nodded. They had no other option. They could keep going backwards but to what avail? If they kept falling back, they would eventually be pincered and trapped still inside the mountain. They needed help...fast.

Jake and Takten were nearly at Hawk 159 but still too far away to help. In the distance, they could see a battle taking place on the ground. The scales were imbalanced in the favour of one side by five to one, Takten estimated, and he could see his men were losing badly. To the left of them was a breakaway group of soldiers who appeared to be firing on what Jake could make out as an opening in the mountainside. He could also make out that they were slowly making their way inside.

'Anji! Hey, they are firing on Anji and the refugees!' he cried.

'Dirty red faces,' he spat.

'Woah,' replied Jake, 'that's not on.'

'Look at what they are doing! They are wiping out my battalion! We have to help them!'

Jake took a moment to compose himself. He would have to be the sensible one in the cockpit.

They were screwed, he thought.

'Commander, there are innocent people trapped in that mountainside. They are unarmed. We've got to help them first.'

'I'm the soldier, we'll do what I say!'

Jake huffed. 'Fine, one heli-fighter against thousands of soldiers who can swat us down like a fly or one heli-fighter against a few dozen soldiers attacking unarmed civilians. What's it to be, soldier?'

Takten shot Jake a look of venom. 'There're red faces in the mountain too. Who's to say that they won't turn on our kind.'

'Where's all of this coming from all of a sudden?' asked Jake, disgusted by what he was hearing.

'They do nothing but murder us and you expect me to take pity?'

Jake was getting angry. 'On people who have turned their back on fighting and who are now probably being killed unarmed yes! I know you've fought for a long time but please park your prejudices for a few minutes and help them! There's nothing you can do for your men but you can still save others. Please Takten, please?'

Jake's tone had softened as his rant had concluded. Takten took one more rueful look at his comrades. He'd been in charge of them for a few years and had got to know them all. The men and women, their stories of what had led them to fight in his battalion. They'd lost people along the way and everyone had hurt and made the glory of winning the war that more distant a goal. But deep-down Takten knew that the teenager was right.

'Take the wheel,' he grunted. Jake looked at him quizzically and jumped to attention when Takten barked the same words at him again. 'Okay,' he replied, swapping seats as the heli-fighter buffeted shortly as the pilots were changing over. He had experience flying the Venus II and some other light spacecraft in his time and familiarising himself with the controls briefly he felt confident.

'Taking us in,' he said and as he hit the throttle the little heli-fighters engines groaned as they hit maximum speed.

Takten's face was one of tortured angst as he placed himself at the controls of the guns.

He was going to make sure he wiped out every stinking Crimson Empire soldier within his sighter and every single death was going to be for every one of his soldiers who were currently being slaughtered.

'We're in range in five...four...three...two...' Jake counted down as their position got closer and closer to the mountain.

Suddenly a burst of laser fire exploded from underneath the bowels of the heli-fighter. Takten had pressed down on his trigger a second early, sending masses of rock and debris from the ground flying up into the air, creating a slight dust cloud for the heli-fighter to fly through. A number of the soldiers at the back of the hoard that were breaking their way into the mountainside turned their attention suddenly on the craft that was attacking them from above but it was too late. Takten's marksman skills were exemplary. A big number of Crimson Empire soldiers cried out in agony as they were mowed down and fell to the ground. As Jake brought the heli-fighter around for another attack, Takten continued laying down his fire, taking out more and more of his enemies in the process. Some returned fire but they were no match for the heli-fighter, even if a few lasers burrowed into the hull of the ship, it wasn't enough to bring them down.

Takten smiled at everybody that fell lifelessly into the ground.

'This is for you, team.'

Inside the mountain, Nkite was starting to lose focus. The pain was just too much. She started to wane and a couple of her shots buried themselves in the floor. One of the river dwellers noticed that she was in trouble and went to her side. As he did, Anji returned to the front line with the map to tell Nkite that they had a chance of another escape route and she was distressed when she saw that the young girl had fallen unconscious.

'We've got to fall back,' cried out the river dweller.

'Then do it!' cried our Anji.

Moments later, they noticed that the sound of the laser fire was starting to die down. Before long, it became apparent that there were not many Crimson Empire soldiers firing on them anymore. After a time, there were only a few left after some had run away. Then there were none.

Silence fell inside the mountain.

Nkite began to stir. Her face was sweating profusely. She wiped her brow with her good arm and tried to pick herself up.

'Did we?' she muttered and Anji shook her head. Bravely, she nervously moved closer towards the opening. As she did, she could hear nearby more laser fire but there didn't appear to be any as close as it had been. As she did her best to step over the throngs of dead soldiers lying at her feet, she squinted as the daylight outside became even brighter. Somewhere close she could hear an engine, one that sounded like it was on its last legs. Tentatively she peered through the mountainside opening.

Their attackers were all dead.

'Hello Anj,' said a familiar voice.

Anji looked in the direction the voice had come from and she instantly forgot about the war, about the danger outside of the mountain and ran towards the calling voice. The figure who had called out started running towards her too. There was a second figure, gun-wielding and limping slightly as they walked away from what was now a smoking crashed heli-fighter.

Jake held his arms out to Anji and pulled her in, hugging her tighter than he had ever held her. He kissed her hard on her shoulder and pulled away, holding her head in his hands. She was crying, and so was he.

'You're okay!' he said. 'We did it. We saved you!'

'Jake, I'm so sorry,' said Anji.

Behind them, the river dwellers, led by a gingerly moving Nkite who was being supported as she walked, moved out of the mountain.

'Stay inside for now, there is a battle taking place nearby!' cried our Takten.

'What happened?' asked Nkite.

'We happened,' said Jake proudly. He looked at Takten who was in no mood to celebrate.

'I'll radio for backup,' he said as he limped past Nkite and into the mountain.

'What's up with him?' asked Anji.

'His battalion is outnumbered. I've seen it, Anj. It's awful.'

'Did you do this?' asked Nkite, who was pointing at the throng of dead Crimson Empire soldiers scattered around them.

'Well, he did, I drove...then crashed...I've never landed a heli-fighter before, still haven't technically,' said Jake.

'Let's get back inside, and tend to your wound,' said Gron, who beckoned Nkite in. She shot Jake a smile of thanks and let herself be led away.

It was just Anji and Jake now.

'Jake I-'

'Let's not fall out ever again, yeah?' Jake interrupted.

Anji smiled. 'You read my mind.'

Jake took her hand. 'Let's get undercover.'

'Where's Random?' asked Anji as they followed the others.

'He's at the Crimson Empire base.'

'We must help him!' cried Anji.

'I know. While we think of what to do, shall we talk?'

Anji nodded. 'Of course.'

The friends walked arm-in-arm, doing their best to blinker out the horror surrounding them, and just trying to be happy that through everything that was happening at least they could take some consolation that they were together.

X

As he fired another round of lasers into a wall of broken and twisted mainframe, the General beamed a smile that was so sinister it made evil look good. For years he had wanted to do this. To lead the attack, and once he was absolutely sure that they were going to win, it was going to make all of his previous achievements look like nothing. As he watched as the security officers on board the mainframe who to him were returning fire in a frenzy, he pin-pointed his sights on one person he could see through the damaged windows where they were standing. With glee, he opened fire and watched as the window shattered and exploded into tiny shards of fire. Some of the occupants of the defence post tumbled out of what was now a room ablaze and he laughed to himself as he saw someone hurl themselves out of what had been the window. As the General saw them plummet to their death, he noticed something else. There was a shard of black sky poking out beyond the mainframe. It was incredible to the General. A black abyss with scattered twinkling stars. He whooped and cheered and made for his radio.

'All units. We've almost broken through, keep going!'

He spun his heli-fighter to one side, evading enemy fire with ease. Despite the overwhelming numbers the Crimson Empire had on their side they were taking heavy casualties. In a normal attack, one of those the General had been on countless times and lost, they would have been obliterated, even if they had made some progress in their attack. After every campaign against the mainframe those that were keeping the war contained on Rodas always seemed to repair any damage quickly – and redouble their artillery also. But on this occasion, it wasn't going to be. The Crimson Empire had them. The number of ships was far too many for even the countless guns of the mainframe to handle.

The General turned to the officer who was sitting beside him in the cockpit. 'Tactical,' he asked. 'How much longer until the mainframe is fully breached?'

The officer, a young woman whose battle-scarred features were concealed by the standard issue helmet they were all required to wear, punched some instructions into her computer. 'Estimate roughly three minutes, sir.'

'Let's make it one,' he purred grabbing for the trigger again and squeezing it with all the want and abandon of a naughty child with a water pistol in summertime. 'Prepare to enter the code. I can't wait to see the entire thing shut down...'

The heli-fighter's incredible force looked like an army of flying ants in the sky and they were crawling all over the security mainframe. Inside, the people who had worked so hard for so long to maintain order and repel the attacks against them were starting to lose hope.

In a command chair, a man named Phillips sat watching the battle through gritted teeth. Like his opposite number, the General, he too was a seasoned campaigner but nothing had prepared him for anything like this. As soon as the attack had begun, he had sounded battle stations, unaware that the code had been cracked by the Crimson Empire and that they were about to fail in their lifelong mission. 'Report!' he yelled as a bank of computers near him started to spark threateningly.

In front of him, dozens of people hurried around their post, sending messages to the front line and to anyone who might be able to help. But he knew that the situation was hopeless. Down below, intel has kept them up-to-speed with the terrible surge of the Crimson Empire.

He knew that the Sapphire Regime had been driven so far back and were now in such small numbers they were practically extinct. Phillips had sat there, revolted at the detail of how Kalor Maloso's master plan had played out.

The blue side of Rodas was now on the verge of extinction and somehow, he'd swelled the number of his army to an astonishing size and they no one seemed to have any idea how he had done it.

To his immediate right, the computers that had been sparking and hissing suddenly gave out and exploded across the room, sending him and the others in the room sprawling to the floor. Phillips picked himself up, a sharp pain shooting up through his thigh. He took a quick look down and noticed that a piece of shrapnel had embedded itself deep inside. As blood started to gush from the fresh wound, he refused the help of one of his officers and pulled himself back up into the chair.

It was forbidden to ask for help from outside. He looked at the chaos around him. The officers he knew lying wounded or worse at his feet. The mainframe he had sworn to protect went up in smoke. The impossible size of the fleet of the Crimson Empire was about to crush his previously impenetrable mainframe. As he started to black out from the pain, he had one thing firmly focused on his mind.

To hell with forbidden. They needed help.

As the hole in the mainframe was blown even bigger, he opened an outside channel.

'This is...Admiral Phillips of the Rodasian Security...Mainframe...We've-'

'We hear you loud and clear, Admiral,' came a female voice crackling over the speaker system.

Phillips looked aghast as a volley of heavy artillery pierced through the newly made hole in the mainframe and took out a dozen or so unsuspecting heli-fighters. Seconds later another bombardment took out more and again and then again.

The General looked on with rage burning under his skin as a cascade of ships that were unfamiliar to him burst into the planet's atmosphere and opened fire on his fleet. He reached for his communicator again. 'Maintain your fire on the mainframe!'

'Sir!' cried the soldier sitting at tactical. 'There's something else coming through!'

They watched on as a huge battle freighter sailed through the hole and began opening fire on the fleet. The General took note of the massive gun turrets that were firing relentlessly. 'Attack the freighter!'

Admiral Bagari stared in disbelief at what the Stargazer had flown into. 'Seal the hole in the mainframe. We have to protect it at all costs. Tactical, maintain your firepower. Give them all we can.'

'Aye, Admiral,' came the call. She watched on as her officers worked as fast as they could to repel the barrage of heli-fighters. The crew lurched as the Orbtial groaned to a halt, the vast bulk of the huge battle freighter having sealed the breach.

Bagari watched as a group of heli-fighters separated from the swarm and began to approach the Stargazer. 'Have we got the intel on the number of ships attacking the mainframe?' she asked.

'There are 21,976 of them. Falling all the time. They have minimal shields. Not enough to defend against our weapons,' said the Tactical officer.

'These are small crafts,' replied Bagari. 'But to stop just under 22,000 of them is a big ask. We need backup. How far away is the rest of the fleet?'

The comm officer pressed several buttons on her command post. '14 minutes away, Admiral.'

Bagari gritted her teeth. The Stargazer could hold her own but she knew they could be in trouble if they couldn't get there any sooner.

'Send a call out to the fleet. Tell them to step on it,' said Bagari.

'Yes, Admiral.'

The crew of the Stargazer looked on the viewscreen as a hoard of heli-fighters opened fire. The battle freighter lurched slightly.

'Divert auxiliary power to shields, everything except life support and weaponry,' said Bagari. She witnessed a crossfire of relentless red laser fire hitting the heli-fighters and picking them off one by one and seeing them sear out of the picture in a blaze of fire. Still, they attacked.

'Admiral, they are changing the code to the mainframe!' said one of the officers working on the long bank of instruments stretched out before Bagari.

'How can you tell?' asked Bagari.

'We've been granted access by the security mainframe; they want our help in resetting the code.'

'Do it!' Bagari yelled as the Stargazer was hit with more enemy fire.

'I can't. I'm locked out,' panicked the young officer. He received a message on his read-out screen. 'The mainframe is too!'

Bagari started to feel the panic hit her like a wave. In all her years in charge of the Stargazer, they had been in situations just as lethal but now the entire security of the planet was about to be compromised – and there was nothing they could do to stop it.

'Don't worry, Admiral, I believe I can help.'

A familiar old voice broke through over the intercom.

Bagari allowed herself a smile.

'You took your time,' she joked.

'We're barely any later than yourselves,' came the calm robotic voice. 'Now, might I ask you to move over a little so that we can squeeze through please?'

Bagari nodded at the helm. The battle freighter lurched again, still giving it everything it had and yet barely making a dent in the sheer volume of enemy vessels.

'Thank you, kindly,' said the voice again.

The helm and tactical officers gave each other a quizzical look. Suddenly, a battered, damaged ship, which until recently was the envy of the universe in the good-looking ship's department exploded across the viewscreen, firing upon the heli-fighters as it tore into the planet's atmosphere.

'Good to have you with us, Admiral,' said the robotic voice again.

'You too Skateboard, now any luck with the code?' replied Bagari.

'Oh, I changed it a few seconds ago. Sorry, I got slightly distracted. I managed to lock out the Crimson Empire's hacking attempts and send them a spike. You shouldn't worry about them trying to do that again.'

'Incredible,' said Bagari. 'You'd better get out of here; we'll hold the fort.'

'Agreed. The situation is looking dire on the planet's surface. We shall locate Anji and Jake and set about with our plan.'

'Best of luck to you all,' said Bagari. 'Stargazer out.'

The comm-link fell silent. Bagari watched as the Venus II suddenly became invisible. It had managed to pick off several heli-fighters and manoeuvre past any deadly attacks from enemy fighters before Skateboard had deployed its cloaking device.

'Let's just hope they are all okay,' she said to herself before turning to the matter at hand.

'Tactical, keep firing,' she anchored herself to her command chair. 'This is going to get bumpy.'

XI

Random pelted as fast as he could down one of the many identical corridors in the Crimson Empire's headquarters. Around every corner he had thought he was coming nearer and nearer to Kalor Maloso and yet the soldiers were continuing to drive him back.

But he wasn't going to let them.

As he bounced off the walls and ceiling with impeccable agility and prowess, he dismantled the soldier's guns with ease and brought everybody to their knees. The word was spreading rapidly around the base that he was there. It had left some of the most hardened amongst Kalor Maloso's troops quaking in their boots.

Some of them remembered the night that Random got away.

When the purple explosion was seen planet-wide across Rodas, it was the moment that had made the Crimson Empire shudder with fear.

It also accelerated the plans they had for total planetary domination.

Yet despite the inspiration, they knew that one-day Random would come back and the being who was created to stop them would return.

Now he was here and there was no chance of any of them putting an end to him. He was just too quick. Too strong.

It was up to Maloso now.

Random pushed aside a laser-like spear and snapped it in one swift movement. He punched the soldier who had been holding it firmly in their chest and sent them sprawling across the floor. Random was panting but didn't look tired from his exertions. He strode across what looked like a cargo hall but he had no awareness of the space of the room, only the instinct to duck and weave past the enemy shots from high above on a gantry.

He picked up what looked like a discarded piece of sheet metal and threw it high above his head.

The metal sheered through the gantry, causing it to groan and buckle. The soldiers who had been firing down upon him started to scramble to escape the gantry but before they could, the split caused it to fall inwards.

Some held on for dear life, others fell from the great height to their ends but Random didn't look behind him.

The attack on his person seemed to be dying down. As he made his way down another corridor, he grew tired of searching for Maloso and instead of incapacitating another of his attackers, he moved at the speed of light right up to the face of his latest obstacle and snapped their arm behind their back, disarming them instantly.

'Please, no!' was the pathetic cry in response to Random's brutal action.

'No more games. Take me to him.'

*

Anji sat looking out of the mountain exit into what looked like a harsh red sandstorm. Over the discontent of the people, she was trying to help, she could hear the sound of gunfire fresh as the morning sun in her ears. Rodas really was a hell hole and she was doubting their efforts to help.

It hadn't been long after reuniting with Jake that he and Takten had decided to scout the battle taking place just over the ridge. Accompanied by a few of the more keen and able river dwellers, they had taken off again in the direction of danger, leaving Anji alone in her thoughts and the people she had somehow helped to keep safe regathering themselves but she couldn't help but feel alone despite being surrounded by over a hundred other souls.

Random was in the hornet's nest, Skateboard was missing and she had almost lost Jake, her one constant in the crazy adventures they had got themselves into ever since they were kids.

She had noticed Nkite's looks of disappointment too and they hadn't been helping her mood. Sure, she couldn't fire on someone, even if they were trying to kill her. After all that she had been through, didn't that say more about her character than Nkite ever could? Even now she could feel her disapproving gaze as Gron finished patching her up.

Gron had also clocked his young friend's annoyance. 'She didn't do anything wrong; you know?'

'She said she'd help,' replied Nkite.

'And so, she has. We're all still alive. If it wasn't for you and her, I doubt that would have been the outcome.'

Nkite groaned.

'Nkite. I know today has been a bad one but you really mustn't take it out on her.'

'Talking about me, are you?' said Anji.

Gron sighed. 'I meant no ill.'

Anji moved to join them. She smiled. 'I know. Could we have a minute please?'

Gron nodded and gave a look to Nkite. The girl snorted and looked the other way as Anji sided up next to her.

'Look. I'm not a killer. I never have been and I never will.'

'Then what use are you to us?' said Nkite.

'Nkite we're trying to save lives here not take them.' Anji gave the girl a sympathetic look. 'I know. It's hard.'

Nkite laughed. 'It's much worse than that. All we've ever known is death and killing.'

'You also know compassion. Take Gron for example. I've only known him for five minutes and he's one of the kindest people I've ever encountered. And there's you. When we were trying to escape the caves, you were telling me about why you fight, why it kept you going. At not one moment in your stories did I think that you were all about killing. Nkite, you have saved so many people. Just look at them,' she gestured to the river dwellers. Nkite watched as they went about passing around food rations. She saw mothers and fathers cradling their children. She saw every one of them putting on a brave face.

'They are doing what they can,' said Nkite.

Anji tried not to tut. 'Nkite they are alive. I can see hope in their eyes. I can still see it in yours.'

'Really? All I can feel is doubt. We are marooned. Cut off from the people who were supposed to help and why? Because they themselves are trapped.'

'Who knows? When Jake and Takten get back, they might tell us differently. Maybe the Sapphire Regime are fighting back!'

'The air feels colder now,' whispered Nkite. 'I'm
sorry I was angry at you. In a way I envy you.
You stood in the face of danger and said no. That
was once me. Until today. Now I am not sure
what that makes me.'

Anji placed a caring hand on Nkite's own. 'It
makes you a hero. In a world of chaos, you are a
shining light, Nkite. So are these people. Look at
them. Red and blue together. There's no fighting
here, even after everything that they have been
through. This is what Rodas should be. As long
as people like you are around it is what Rodas
WILL be.'

Nkite allowed herself a little smile.

'Anyway,' said Anji, changing the subject,
'how's the shoulder?'

'It'll heal,' Nkite said wincing as she moved it a
little. 'I'll take on board your words Anji if you
promise to take on board mine.'

'Go on then,' smiled Anji.

'Never stoop to our level. Even in the bleakest
hour, don't change who you are.'

Anji nodded. 'I promise.'

Gron had been checking up on some of his
people but noticed that the two girls were getting
on much better now. He allowed himself a smile
and realised that today, despite all the horror
they had collectively been through, he probably
smiled more than he had done in a long while.

He walked into the open space outside of the mountain and looked out into the barren wilderness. He could feel the coarseness of the dirt on the ground being whipped up into the air.

'A storm is coming,' he yelled back as the wind grew louder.

'Hopefully, it'll pass,' said Anji. 'They always do.'

'Wait,' said Nkite who spotted something in the distance.

Anji and Gron met her gaze and tried to look out for what she had spotted. Slowly, a few faint outlines of what looked like people started to bleed into view. It looked like they were running. One of them was yelling something indistinctly.

'It's Jake!' cried Anji.

'What's he saying?' asked Gron.

Nkite's face hardened and she grabbed her gun from her holster. 'We don't need to hear it to know.'

It was Jake. He was pelting it back towards them at a speed that Anji had never seen before. His pace was almost fast! As they got closer, they could see that the others with him were firing shots at something behind them as the blue glow from their lasers disappeared into the gloom. A string of red lasers seemed to be following Jake and the others and they desperately zig-zagged to avoid them.

'Get back!' came the now barely audible cry from Jake.

'Oh my god...' said Anji.

Through the sandstorm, the terrifying sight of what appeared to be hundreds of Crimson Empire troops bled into view over the ridge and they were running to.

Jake, Takten and two of the river dwellers who had accompanied them finally made it into the cavemouth. Jake collapsed exhausted into Anji's arms.

'Anyone who can fight with me, the rest of you fall back!' cried out Nkite.

'The Sapphire Regime?' asked Anji.

Jake was unable to reply and was gasping for air.

'Crushed,' said Takten. 'All gone.'

'What?' asked Anji. 'What about Djanga?'

'I told you,' shouted Takten crossly, 'they are gone!'

The volume of the distressed river dwellers rang around the mountain cave.

'Please!' said Anji as she dropped Jake on the floor, winding him, 'Move back!'

'Anji, go with them,' said Nkite, who with her good arm was helping Jake back to his feet.

'I'm staying here,' replied Anji.

They took cover as shots were fired at them, sending debris all over the place.

'Return fire!' yelled Takten. The rebels did as they were instructed. Jake pulled Anji behind a rock and picked up his gun and started to fire blankly into the onrushing hoard.

Takten's face was awash with tears. His whole regiment was dead. He'd seen their lifeless bodies with his own eyes. He couldn't save them. Now they were sitting ducks. No way out. If they retreated back into the mountain, they were only delaying the inevitable. By firing back now at least they were putting up a fight.

The Sapphire Regime's HQ. Its smouldering ruin was burnt into his memory. The place he had gone to train to become a soldier, unlike so many others in his intake, willingly, was the place that had made him a soldier. No, not just a soldier. A man. It was gone. He knew not what had happened to them or just how many of the Sapphire Regime still existed but he didn't hold out much hope that many had got out alive.

As he stared unblinkingly into the onslaught, he started to notice a light up above. It tripped his concentration. Soon the other rebels also stopped fighting.

Jake trained his eyes on the intruder on the battlefield and a wide smile beamed across his face. 'Anj!!!' he exclaimed.

Anji took one look up and grabbed Jake's arm. 'Skateboard!'

The light was so much more than just a light. It was hope for all of them. A familiar sight blew through the dust and opened fire on the Crimson Empire, taking out so many soldiers in one swoop.

It was the Venus II.

The gantry lowered from the belly of the ship out of which sprung what looked like an army of fantastic multi-coloured horses. Upon their back rode an equally impressive array of people whose skin was also all the colours of the rainbow in bright gold armour and from the spears that each of them was wielding shot lightning bolts which also helped in the ambush.

'Anj, aren't they?'

'Dosas, yeah Jake,' replied Anji, who was just as stunned as her friend was. 'So that's where Skateboard has been!'

The Crimson Empire was stunned by the counterattack, almost as much as Nkite and the other river dwellers were. As the Venus II hovered close to the ground, the sound of its engine adding to the orchestra of laser fire, galloping hooves and the winds of war, a few more people bounded down the gantry and into the cave mouth.

Anji and Jake were astonished to see who they were as they jumped over the same rocks that they, along with Nkite, Takten and the fighting river dwellers were sheltering behind.

'Hold on, you're-'

'Let's leave it until later, Jake,' said Yana, who spoke whilst simultaneously firing her weapon and landing one of her shots firmly in the helmet of a Crimson Empire soldier, which broke open like an egg.

'Delilah! Benaya!'

'Like she said Jake, later!' yelled Delilah.

'Yeah...' blinked Jake. Back to the matter at hand.

On board the Venus II, Skateboard was alone but in contact with his friends. He had fitted Solenia, Yana, Delilah and Benaya with earpieces which allowed them all to stay in contact. 'Solenia, we have to drive the troops away from the mountain. I'll lay down a spray of fire, could you mop up, so to speak?'

'On it,' came the curt reply.

'I'll reapply the cloaking device and protect the Valkyries,' he announced. After doing just that, the Venus II became invisible again. Before that some of the Crimson Empire troops had shot at the ship, leaving minimal damage but a shield system that had been weakened a little. It had been necessary to forgo the cloaking device to lower the gantry – it had been a design flaw for the Venus II that Skateboard had known about but never got around to fixing.

Also, as the Venus II had been designed on Rodas as a galaxy-class fighter ship in the first place, he had the capability to deal with pretty much any enemy hostility. It was the first time he had ever used it, and normally he was against violence, but this was Rodas, there was an entire planet, nay galaxy to save, and he would deal with his morality chip at a later date.

For now, he had to do, no, they all had to do what they were doing, and that was winning.

XII

Kalor Maloso sat in his chair, overseeing his master plan and the magnificence of it all. High above, his ships were fighting to open the security mainframe, something that they had never been able to do until now. Across the barren wilderness that had once been the proud citadel of Rodas and the brilliant architecture that until recently had once been the rotten ruins of the cities and dwellings that were now nothing but dust. He had levelled Rodas into the dirt and his forces were now using it to cull in vast numbers what remained of the Sapphire Regime. All the time the soundtrack to his chaos was screaming out over the intercom system. But it wasn't the noise from the battle outside he was purring too. He'd cut himself off from those he had full power over.

The room was cold now. He could feel a chill weaving its way through his bones. He pulled his robe up around what was left of him but he knew it wouldn't keep out the chill of what awaited him.

Like children leaving home, he'd decided to leave his forces to it. The millions of soldiers he had at his disposal knew their orders and followed them implicitly.

He'd brought about conquest for the Crimson Empire, he could see it as clear as day all around him. As he had observed, what was left of his enemies was all but gone.

All that was left now was the final confrontation, he had to be strong for that. The end was in sight.

The noise of people shouting, firing off weapons and fighting and screaming that played out over his speaker systems was what was happening within his very own base. Maloso smiled. He wouldn't have long to wait now.

He rested his eyes as he continued to wait and played out his victories in his head. Before his mind's eye, all the glorious echoes of the past came to life in front of him. The bombing of the Alixier, the end of the resistance, the time he had personally pulled the limbs from his opposite number in the Sapphire Regime and watched the horror on their face as they had bled to death before him. What glorious memories to accompany him into the darkness.

In that moment the doors to the room split open, the combination of wood and metal splintering and bending in a show of great strength. His personal triumphs folded themselves neatly back in his memories and he opened his eyes and looked at the person who had broken in and disturbed his peace.

The person in question he had been waiting to see again for so long and as he gazed down at them, his chair at a higher vantage point than the entrance to the room, he noticed the dazed, almost lifeless forms of his personal guards, dangling from the grip of the intruder like two rag dolls, and smiled a benevolent grin.

'Ah Random,' he sneered. 'What's taken you so long?'

*

On the ground, the section unit leader who had led the attack on the Sapphire Regime was lying in the mud. All around his broken frame, he could see more of his troops being brought to their knees.

These people, he thought. Who were they? They were not of red or blue colour? These were aliens who had involved themselves in a war in which he felt they had no business. As he coughed violently for the third time since an electric spear had pierced his stomach just a minute earlier, he reached for his intercom. The main battalion had to know about this.

His breakaway section, who had spotted that they were being spied on and were pulled away from the fun of the battle with their enemies, had been lured into a trap, he was certain of it.

Now, as he flipped the communication link open, it was time to turn the tide back in their favour again.

Were there more of these outsiders? What about the attack on the mainframe, was that going to plan? He had to know. As a taste of copper filled his lungs and made him choke even more, he began to call for his superior when out of nowhere, a pretty woman on a multi-coloured horse drove another spear into his flesh, this time plunging him in the chest. The link was open, but no message made its way back to HQ. They wouldn't have heard it anyway. There was no one manning the communications link now. Not since someone had got inside the Crimson Empire base and torn it to shreds...

Solenia pulled her spear out of the soldier's chest and spun her horse around. The attacking faction was almost vanquished. She looked around her. She saw a few casualties among her own number but then after some quick mental arithmetic, relaxed in the knowledge that none of her Valkyries had been killed.

With the enemy now in full retreat, she raised her spear high above her head and cheered victoriously. The Valkyries followed in their Queen's triumph.

'I don't want to spoil your moment, your Majesty, but we have far from won. Suggest we return to the mountainside. We can discuss there our next move and please, we must hurry before they attack again, in greater force.' Skateboard's instruction was a sound one, she thought and she led her army back across the battlefield as she heard the roar of the invisible Venus II's engines high above her.

Jake and Anji emerged from their hiding place and hugged each other before turning to their old friends and embracing them enthusiastically.

'What the hell are you guys doing here?' asked Jake.

'These are friends of yours?' asked Nkite, who along with her comrades had finished their mini-celebration.

'Old, old friends!' confirmed Anji. 'And look at you Yana, you're wearing a suit now!'

'Skateboard found us,' replied Delilah. 'He told us that you needed some help. Considering what you did for Genocia it was the least that we could do to lend a hand.'

As she spoke the roar of the Venus II's engine grew louder as Skateboard hovered the ship above the mountain opening, allowing the hundred or so dosas into the cave underneath. Upon entering the cave two Valkyries dismounted their dosas, who behaved impeccably unlike the horses Anji had seen back in her time on Earth and they helped Solenia off her steed.

'Blimey, Solenia, you too? When I see him, I'll have to tell Skateboard that if I'm ever in a hostage situation...again...I want him to do the talking!'

Benaya stood aghast at the dosas. They were the most elegant creatures she had ever seen. She turned to Delilah and signed to her that if they survived this, she wanted one for her next birthday.

'I believe that you should address me as Your Majesty before saying anything else to me, young Jake.'

Jake blushed and bowed. Anji followed suit whilst Yana, Delilah and Benaya felt that after hours of being cooped up on a small spaceship with the Queen, they were more than well acquainted to bow or curtsy again. Even if she'd requested them to do it and had refused to speak to them until she did.

'Oh yes, and, er, sorry your Majesty, about the Flux and all while we are at it,' said Jake apologetically.

'Thank you. Yes, I must concede that he is a worthy speaker, make no mistake.'

The gangway hydraulics hissed as Skateboard walked out from the Venus II. Anji and Jake threw themselves at him and hugged him so tightly that he thought they were going to buckle his metalwork.

'Skateboard, it's so good to see you! So that's where you go to? You went back to find old friends?' asked Anji, so happy to see him she could feel tears erupting in the corners of her eyes.

'Indeed, miss Anji. I'm so sorry it took us so long.'

'So, whose plan was this?' asked Jake.

'It was Captain Randoms. I fear that he is not with you?'

'He's in the Crimson Empire's base,' said a forlorn-looking Takten. He was sitting at the foot of a large rock staring into the ground. Nkite had noticed that he had been like that since the battle had been won and felt for him and all that he had lost. 'I took him there myself.'

'Then there is no time to waste. We need to implement the next part of the strategy before it's too late.'

'Woah woah woah, who put you in charge?' asked Nkite.

'We have!' replied Anji, Jake, Delilah, Yana and Solenia in unison.

'Fair enough,' replied Nkite sheepishly.

'What do you mean the next part of the strategy?' asked Jake.

'Er, shouldn't we be worried about the Crimson Empire coming back for more? They won't give up that easily,' said Anji.

'I've extended the shields from the Venus II to this entrance so we will be safe for a moment at least,' confirmed Skateboard. 'Now please, listen carefully. This planet's very future is at stake.'

'What do you mean, "at stake?" said Takten churlishly. 'It's gone. The Crimson Empire have won. I saw it myself.'

Skateboard was a little lost for words. 'He means,' said Jake softly, 'we saw the Sapphire Regime's HQ. It's been destroyed.'

'Ah,' said Skateboard. He watched as a kindly old man approached Takten with what he could only guess was liquid refreshment. 'I am so sorry for any and all losses that have occurred today. But the faster we act now the quicker we can save Rodas.'

'Save it!' Takten slapped the mug out of Gron's hand and ran right up to Skateboard. 'You're just an old service robot. What gives you the right to say that you can save it? If you and your Random friend hadn't disappeared years ago none of this would have happened!'

Nkite stood silently. She felt Takten's pain all too well.

Benaya and Delilah saddled up next to Skateboard. 'Hey, he knows what he's doing!'

'Oh yeah? And what gives you two any right to come here and get involved.'

We just saved your backside! signed Benaya.

'It's alright Benaya he's just cranky because he hasn't had his nap today,' said Delilah,

Takten's rage exploded and he hurled himself at the pair but was held back by Jake and Anji and Yana.

'Guards! Take him,' ordered Solenia as two burly Valkyries took over and restrained him.

'Jeez, Delilah, he's just lost his people,' said Anji.

Delilah suddenly looked embarrassed. 'Oh, sorry, I thought that you were just being ungrateful.'

'Please, sirs, madams, we really do have to act quickly, there is a lot to do. The mainframe is being defended-'

'By whom?' asked Jake.

'The Stargazer is up there now helping out the air defences. There are more battle freighters on the way,' continued Skateboard. 'But as far as I am aware there is little resistance on the ground.'

'I never thought that I would be relieved to see Admiral Bagari and the Space Seals again but here we are. As for resistance, well, there might not be,' said Anji. Takten was staring at her.

'Hang on, if I widen the communication signal, I can put out a call to any survivors. If these two bozos will let me go...' he hinted towards Solenia, who gave the nod of approval for Takten to be released.

'Sorry again,' said Delilah.

'So just how bad is it down here?' Asked Yana.

'Bad. The resistance has taken heavy casualties and was on the brink of extinction BEFORE today's attack. This latest wave is one that has been sent to finish us off,' said Takten.

'Are these the only people left?' asked Solenia.

'Oh no!' said Anji. These people are peaceful. We were helping to get them to safety.'

'They're with me, I'm Nkite by the way, not that I'm sure if this is the right moment to swap names.'

'It isn't, sadly, just be safe in the knowledge that everybody here is on the same side,' said Skateboard, who was growing impatient and slightly worried at how time was passing them by. 'Our main focus of attack will be the Crimson Empire's HQ. It'll pull as many of Kalor Maloso's forces back into one central position.'

'That's an idea, but there are hundreds of thousands of them out there, possibly millions,' said Takten, who was starting to repress his grief for the time being.

When the rest of the Space Seal Armada arrives it'll even the odds but for now that's our destination. It's the nerve centre for this entire operation and we have to help Random.' Skateboard started wheeling up the gantry again.

'Hold on, what shall we do with the river dwellers? They can't just stay here,' asked Anji.

'They won't. We can keep them safe here in the Venus II. Turn the cloaking device on and no one will know where they are, except us. They will be totally safe.'

'Nowhere is safe on Rodas,' said Takten mournfully.

'I didn't say that they would be on Rodas. The Venus II has the security mainframe code. I'll remote control it through the mainframe, alert the Space Seals to its whereabouts and then they can keep them safe in space,' said Skateboard.

'And we'll be marooned again!' moaned Jake.

'Only until the battle is won. The question is, who is going to look after everybody on board?' asked Skateboard.

'I will,' the elderly man stepped forward.

'Gron are you sure about this?' asked Nkite.

'Positive. Plus, I've always wanted to go into space!' a look of childish glee cheered on the old man's deep-lined face.

'Thank you, mister?' asked Skateboard.

'Gron.'

Thank you, sir. If you would care to lead your people up the gangway if you'd be most kind?'

Nkite hugged Gron with all her might. 'I'll wait for you,' he said.

'You better do,' she said with a tear falling down her cheek. He pulled away from her and smiled another broad smile and wiped the tear away.

'Ah, there it is,' he said.

'What?' asked Nkite.

'Your hope.'

Nkite smiled back.

'We'll help you all get on board, now come on everybody, follow us if you can,' said Yana as she started to help the river dwellers move onto the ship.

I'd better safeguard the cockpit,' said Skateboard to Anji and Jake. 'We wouldn't want someone to flick the wrong switch.'

'Er, Skateboard, could you lock my room too please?' Jake asked nervously.

Anji caught a whiff inside the ship. 'Pwoar! What's been going on in there?'

'Ah, yes, it's not the cleanest ship in the galaxy right now but it'll do,' said Skateboard.

Anji shot a look an accusatory look at one of the dosas, which stared her out in response.

'I'll update Admiral Bagari too and try and get a better understanding of how it's going up there,' Skateboard continued.

'How far away is the base?' asked Delilah.

'It's a fair way,' said Jake. 'Took us several minutes to fly there, oh yeah. Hang on, if we can't go on the Venus II then how are we getting there? It'll waste time to walk!'

'We'll ride. My dosas can carry us all,' said Solenia.

'Oh, great,' said Jake sarcastically. He instantly thought back to his last uncomfortable ride on the back of a dosa back on the planet Spectronia.

'Makes sense,' said Delilah who went off to help Yana. Benaya followed suit but not before she showed her excitement about getting the opportunity to ride one.

'Mind the mess,' Skateboard said as he passed the river dwellers who were starting to fill up in the midsection. He sealed the door to the cockpit and made his way back down the runway, calling Bagari on his portable intercom system as he went. 'Admiral, requesting an update.'

*

'This isn't the best time, Skateboard,' cried Bagari, her once neat hair now flopping in a sweaty mess over her forehead. 'The Stargazer is being swarmed. We're doing our best to see them off but there are just too many of them.'

'Oh dear,' replied Skateboard. 'Where is the rest of the fleet?'

'They are nearly here. One minute away in fact.'

'Good. I'm sending some refugees up through the mainframe to safety. They will be cloaked in the Venus II.'

Bagari grunted as the Stargazer lurched. The heli-fighters were covering the huge battle freighter like a big spider's web. Every one of them was firing on it.

'Shields at 4%' exclaimed tactically.

'Just a little longer,' replied Bagari. 'Skateboard are you still there?'

'Yes, Admiral. Request that you are also able to give us assistance when they arrive? We need covering fire as we embark on the Crimson Empire's HQ. I'm sending the coordinates now.'

'Sure,' said Bagari with a level of sarcasm that Jake would have been proud of. 'We'll bring the whole armada with us!'

'If you could, that'd be most satisfactory,' said Skateboard unaware of the Admiral's tone. 'We shall leave now. Estimate we will be there in ten clicks. Over and out.'

Skateboard left the ship and passed the final few people climbing on board.

'Some people wanted to stay and fight,' said Anji.

'They are brave people,' said Skateboard. 'Right then-'

The friends were all helped up onto the backs of the dosas, including a very excited Benaya and a still-hurting Takten.

Nkite waved Gron goodbye as the gantry hissed back into its closed position, who in turn waved back and whispered to her "You've got this." She smiled and then looked at Takten.

'Hey, I get it. I really do. Ready to take it out on the enemy?'

Takten powered up his gun. 'Always.'

'Do we have to hold on tight around their waists like last time?' asked Jake, referring to his previous experience hugging a Valkyrie to stop falling off.

'No, there are leather straps at the side of the saddle. Place your arms through these,' Solenia demonstrated, 'and you will be safe.'

Jake's face fell. Anji tried to stifle a laugh.

'Right, I have my bearings. I shall lead with Queen Solenia. Do your best to keep up all of you. As soon as the Venus II is out of the way then we can go. Ready?' Skateboard said as he warmed up his engines. The Venus II's engines whirred quieter and quieter as the cloaked ship disappeared from view, leaving Anji and Jake to collectively hope it wasn't too long before they saw it again.

'Okay,' said Skateboard. 'Let's ride.'

XIII

'I wouldn't come any closer if I were you, Random.'

Random dropped the two guards to the floor like they were trash and clenched his fists. His rage burnt fiercely, consuming him. He saw the frail old-looking figure of evil personified across the room and he wanted to tear him to shreds. The room in which they were was gloomy and dark, with a throbbing red light pulsing on and off which to Random was like a red flag to a bull. He yelled a guttural cry and tore off towards Maloso. Suddenly, Random was stopped in his tracks and was flung straight back into the air. As he crashed to the ground and skidded back towards the door, Maloso laughed like a tormentor bullying another child in class.

'I did try to warn you,' he said when he had finally managed to stop himself.

Random picked himself up gingerly. The whole front of his body hurt like hell. He felt a warm trickle of blood oozing from his nose. Wiping it away with his sleeve he regained his composure and straightened himself up.

'Putting a forcefield around yourself is a little cowardly, don't you think?'

'Not at all. Behind me are complex instruments that I would never want to fall into enemy hands.'

'Then come out. It's time we ended this.'

Maloso sighed. 'Oh, if only that were so my young friend. No, the end is already here.'

Random was getting angrier. 'Stop talking in riddles, Maloso. Why are you stalling? Giving your bully boys some time to get over their concussion, are you?'

'No Random I am well aware of the devastation that you bring with you. It wasn't just your demonstration of strength in getting to me. I know all about you.'

Random pulled a face of disgust. 'You know nothing!'

'I wouldn't be so sure. When you fled my clutches, all those years ago did you not think that I would do everything in my power to discover how you came to be? Why you were created? For a while, I obsessed over it and then when I discovered what I needed to know I knew then how this war would end. With you and me, standing here on the brink of the abyss with the war already won around us.'

Random shook his head. 'No, you see that's where you are wrong. The war is far from over.'

'Ha!' Maloso spluttered as he laughed, leading Random to try and peer closer through the gloom.

'You should be careful there you might choke.'

'And deprive you the pleasure of killing me yourself?'

Random shook his head. 'I am not a killer.'

'In all the time that you have been away from here, do you seriously expect me to believe that your powers haven't resulted in casualties? In deaths?'

Random didn't say anything. In the back of his mind, he thought of a few occasions when his actions had led to lives being lost. Then he tried his best to blot them out. Maloso was trying to get into his head and Random wouldn't let him.

'So go on then, you're clearly loving the fact that you know so much about me, I bet you're just bursting to tell me, aren't you?'

'The classic misdirection of a guilty conscience,' said Maloso dryly.

'At least I have one,' Random fired back.

'I do have one, Random. Don't you see? I have survived countless campaigns. I have been a scared child, a foot soldier, a prisoner, a Commander, a General and finally the ruler of the Crimson Empire. In all that time, fighting for supremacy, you grow attached to the cause. And there is nothing I wouldn't have done to see the Crimson Empire succeed. That's where you came in.'

Maloso struggled out of his chair. Random regarded him in what little detail he could see. A black, full-length cloak enveloped whatever was left of his body which seemed to have very little on it at all. In the years since their brief encounter Random had pictured a tall, gladiatorial figure. From the stories Skateboard had told him, the only thing that had been consistent with the rumours of the demon in the dark, the ruler who hid away was the eyes. The blood-red eyes looked like they had been born in hell.

Maloso made his way over to his tubular chamber, the one that had so recently brought about the sudden influx of soldiers in the processing plant. The very same soldiers were wiping out what remained of the rest of the population on Rodas as they spoke and were trying to break out across the galaxy of Ursa-17.

'You will find this familiar; I presume?' he asked Random. As he did, Maloso flicked a switch and a white light shone down from the ceiling onto it, bringing it fully to Random's focus.

Random recognised it instantly. 'Where did you get that?'

'It was traced back to one Professor Blent's laboratory. It took us a long time to find it. So many people were...questioned...in our quest to locate the technology that had given your life and the vessel from which you came to be and here it is, the miraculous test tube that from which you were born.'

A terrible thought began to dawn on Random. As he was thinking he became aware of a terrible racket taking place underneath him under the floor. He tried not to be distracted.

'So, that's what you've done? You've created an army of Me's?'

'No. Not an army of Randoms. An army of Malosos.'

At that moment, Maloso decided to reveal his true, hideous form to Random for the first time. Random gasped in terror at the horrifying figure of his enemy as Maloso moved into the light.

Underneath the black cloak stood a man that belonged in a morgue. A truly repulsive, ghastly zombie-like figure of a man who should have been dead a long, long time ago. His face had no flesh on it whatsoever except for an ear which dangled rotting from the side of his face. The gums in his mouth were decayed and non-existent and his torso bore the final remnants of what used to be skin and underneath his bones which jutted sharply out from his frame, Random could see his organs. Random felt a little bit sick in his mouth as he noticed his heart, blacker than the darkness of space itself, still implausibly beating.

'My god, what have you done to yourself?'

'I have given myself fully to the cause. Little by little, century-by-century, my life has been dedicated to making sure that the Crimson Empire was built in my image. In the early days, we used rudimentary cloning techniques. When I was General of the Crimson Empire, and upon the sad...murder of my predecessor, I inherited my army and piece-by-piece I allowed bits of me to go towards the making of my men.'

'You mean that you did this willingly? Centuries? You should be dead!'

'Should be, but my methods kept me alive. It was never enough though. The process was painfully slow. The Sapphire Regime – and that constrictive security barrier – kept us at bay until we discovered your creation chamber. They should have destroyed it but they had been conducting experiments – just as we had – on making organic soldiers of supreme capabilities just like you.'

'Yeah, I met one once. He wasn't too happy about what he had been subjected to. It's in-Rodasian, Maloso.'

'There are no good guys in war, Random. Only victors. Both sides took what advantage they could. It took me to make my ultimate sacrifice to tip the balance. As soon as the machine was tailored to my needs, I could input commands in the DNA that I was giving up from my own

body. I could implant ideas, and commands, in
the heads of my children. They would need no
training, no period of growth. They would be
created fully formed, in their hundreds at first,
then thousands and now...millions. A drone army
has organically grown from my own body. Every
cell is a soldier. I have not only created life,
Random. I have created a new civilisation,
programmed from conception to do one thing.
Conquer. Wipe the blue stain clean from Rodas
and then go out into the far reaches of space and
do it again and again. It doesn't matter how
many get wiped out in the process. They can
always create more now that we have the
blueprint. My DNA, you see? They all carry it.
Purely my cellular makeup. So, my clones can
keep going on and on. Now that you know why
there is a forcefield.'

'My friends are on their way here. They blow
this place sky-high to get through it, and your
processing plants. Your plan will fail.'

'If you blow the base sky high you will risk
destroying the chamber. Could you really take
that risk, Random?'

Random was well and truly stumped.

'I can see your anger. I can feel your blood
boiling. I find that good.'

'You're a monster, Maloso, death is the only
thing that awaits you now.'

'Indeed. It is. I have given my final gift to Rodas, to the Crimson Empire. I have prolonged my agony just to see you beaten at the last, Random. I am holding back the touch of death as speak, just as I have done for so many, many years. Just to see the look on your face.'

Random felt the banging below him intensify. It was like whatever was down there was reacting to whatever was being said.

'And now...' said Maloso, lowering himself in his chair. 'The time has come.'

'This is all so pointless!' screamed Random. 'All this death, everything to do with this war is utter madness! You've overseen a genocide of your own people. It doesn't matter if you were red-skinned and they were blue, you're all on the same planet! How could you be so cruel?'

Maloso closed his eyes. 'In the old times, I used to ask the very same thing of them. You're on the wrong side Random. No one is a winner here except me. I take glory in all that I have done. I have won. You can try and break in here but you never will. I will die basking in the total glory of my victory.'

Random felt the floor move, the banging was becoming so ferocious.

'And yes, to answer your earlier question, I was luring you here. And you fell for it, well you're about to.'

In that instant, Maloso flicked a switch on a command unit on his chair and the floor below Random's feet gave way. Random was not quick enough to act and plummeted into the darkness.

A giant, red arm broke its way through the void in the floor and Maloso flicked another switch electrifying it, a deep loud moan of agony coming from the arm's owner shook the room. As it recoiled, Maloso flicked another switch.

Random fell for a good few seconds before something soft broke his fall. It was dark but he could tell he had fallen onto somebody. Random could make out the face of the person as he picked himself up on the dusty floor and he gasped in horror. The creature was almost as hideous as Maloso. Then another put his arm on Random's shoulder and Random leapt again. Random was appalled to realise that he was in a pit with a few – no – a dozen of these monsters.

'I'd like you to meet your brothers and sisters,' said Maloso, evil dripping from his words. 'Well, we all make mistakes, especially in the field of science. I won't be around to feed them anymore so I hope you'll be up to the task of doing that for me.'

Random was clambering to get out but there they were too powerful. The giant, still smarting from his electrocution, peered down and snarled unspeakable slobber in Random's face.

'Look after my abominations, would you? It's not like I did, poor things. They could do with some company.'

Random was being dragged down.

'Maloso, you can't do this!' screamed Random but it was too late.

With one final action, Maloso flicked the switch that sealed the trap door shut and Random's pleading and screams still ringing in his ears, finally gave into the dark and slipped quietly away.

XIV

Jake was struggling to fathom what was more uncomfortable. The ride or the hundreds of troops firing at them. With expert skill and grace, the Valkyries were weaving in and out of the enemy fire, which had followed them ever since they had left the mountain. Even Skateboard, who was tearing it up across the dusty, harsh terrain, was giving it both barrels from his stun gun but his long-range scanners were starting to concern him greatly.

'It appears that the Crimson Empire is trying to circle us,' he yelled to Solenia, who was herself struggling to hold off the enemy fire.

'You're flying ship would have been of great help to us now,' she cried as she continued to ride her dosa and fire at the enemy. She has witnessed a few of her people be taken out by the enemy troops, something she had felt deeply in her heart. 'If we don't get help soon, I fear that we won't reach our destination.'

Suddenly high up above, a fleet of heli-fighters began to descend upon them.

'This is it; we're done for!' shouted Anji.

'No, wait!' said Nkite pointing skywards. 'They're not Crimson Empire ships!'

'They're ours!' yelled Takten. He smiled triumphantly as these heli-fighters, which were slightly different in design except for a blue emblem on their doors, tore over their heads and opened fire on the Crimson Empire soldiers below.

'Yee-haw!' cried Jake, leading Anji to do the same.

'Commander Takten,' said a voice that fizzed over Takten's communicator. 'This is General Steyn of the 43rd Sapphire Legion. As you can see, we received your transmission, and thought you needed some help!'

'But how?' he responded. 'I saw the base at Hawk 159. You were beaten?'

'We're never beaten Takten, you know that,' said Steyn cheerily. 'We have lost a lot of our people but when we received your transmission and heard that you were heading to attack Kalor Maloso's base we stopped fighting and thought we'd join you. The Crimson Empire thought that we had retreated and that they had won, seems we'd fooled you too?'

'I'm glad you did,' he replied.

'Commander, I just heard what your General said,' yelled Skateboard over the clip-clopping of hooves and heavy laser fire. 'We must not attack the base yet. Please can you inform your General?'

Takten looked surprised. 'Then why else are we going there?'

'To give Random time!' said Anji, as she ducked past a bolt of laser fire, to which the Valkyrie she was riding with shot back with pinpoint precision with his spear. 'We're driving them all to a focal point.'

'So that we can attack when he gives us the go-ahead, I guess,' said Delilah who was loving every minute of this. Benaya was too. Suddenly the horse that she was riding on bolted, throwing the Valkyrie to the ground. The gang looked back and looked on helplessly as the Valkyrie was surrounded by enemy troops who fires upon him at point-blank range with no mercy.

'Oh my god,' said Yana. 'Benaya, try and get it under control!'

The girl struggled to the front of the saddle as the dosa started to rear out of control. Luckily, using what little balance she had, she managed to hold on tight and pulled at the reigns and in doing so, brought it under control.

'Nice one sis!' said Delilah. 'Hee-yar!'

All the time this was happening Takten was speaking to his superior. 'I agree General but there is someone in that base who is our hope in finishing the war.'

Steyn paused for a second. 'The purple one?'

'Yes, sir.'

The General huffed. 'Well, if the war will end today let's make sure it goes out with a fight. Okay, we shall wait until further instruction to destroy the base. But if at any point we are in trouble then we must eliminate Maloso at all costs.'

'Agreed.'

'We're going to need help,' responded Steyn.

'We've got it,' said Skateboard.

'High above the fighting rebels and Sapphire Regime a flurry of battle freighters started to hone into view.

'Oh my god,' said Anji. 'Guys, it's the armada.'

'Skateboard, are you receiving me?' the voice of Admiral Bagari blared over Skateboard's audible receptors.

'Loud and clear Admiral.'

'I've transferred to the Titan. The Stargazer has taken some heavy damage. It appears that the attack on the mainframe has failed. For some reason all the ships just...left.'

'They've fallen back. They must have heard what was happening down here. The Sapphire Regime stopped defending against the attack and has joined our cause. Maybe that has led them to believe they must protect the base. Just as we wanted,' said Skateboard over the chaos.

'That as may be, there's an awful lot of them, Skateboard. What's your plan?'

'Draw the enemy to the base. Then, we try and take out as many of them as we can, buy Random time. Meanwhile Anji, Jake and the rest of us will try to infiltrate the base to lend assistance.'

'Do you know if he's okay in there?' asked Bagari.

'I don't. My long-range sensors are blinded by the thousands of Crimson Empire soldiers I'm picking up. I shall get a better reading the closer we can get.'

'We'll attack from the sky and try and lay cover for you guys on the ground. It's going to be a big fight, you guys had better take care.'

'We're almost there!' yelled Takten. As they continued to ride, they were getting closer and close to the ridge. The enemy was falling back all the time whilst still attacking and the soldiers started to disappear over the top.

'How many people do we have?' asked Anji.

'Just under one hundred Valkyries, the same number of dosas, seven of us on the ground including the Queen, four hundred and seventy-three heli-fighters and ten Space Seal battle freighters.'

'We're sending for foot soldiers,' Steyn overheard on the communicator. 'There should be roughly two thousand arriving shortly.'

'Since this is an open channel, I must interject that we also have 50,000 hornets ready to attack also,' said Bagari, referring to the light spacecraft that the battle freighters held. 'Multiply those ten times and you've got yourself a fighting chance.'

'And how many do they have?' asked Yana.

As the rebels reached the lip of the ridge, they had their answer.

They stopped in their tracks instantly as they saw the magnitude of what they were up against.

Down below in the valley surrounding what was the Crimson Empire HQ, Kalor Maloso's base of operations was an overwhelming number of soldiers, ground vehicles which looked like tanks and heli-fighters hovering with menacing intent high above. Not to mention twenty battle freighters of their own.

Anji started to sweat.

Jake gulped hard.

Delilah and Yana were speechless.

Takten and Benaya gave each other a look of concern.

Bagari sat back in the command chair she had acquired in the Titan aghast.

'Helm. How many are we talking about here?'

The helmswoman scanned the area. Her fingers started to tremble. 'Five million, Admiral.'

Skateboard, Steyn and Takten overheard this and the number was broadcast to the rest of the group. Even the dosas were starting to move uneasily.

'Right then,' said Nkite. 'There's no turning back now, is there?'

Yana shook her head, 'No.'

Jake and Anji's dosas were close enough to allow the pair to hold hands. 'All of a sudden I'm starting to get a little bit of stage fright.'

'Why won't they attack?' asked Solenia.

'They are trying to intimidate us,' said Skateboard.

As he spoke, the Crimson Empire foot soldiers appeared to start stamping their feet in unison. The ground started to shake ever so slightly.

'General, any chance that the rest of our army might get here a little sooner?' asked Takten. In all his years of active service, he had never seen anything like this. How had they done it? How had Kalor Maloso managed to make an army of this sheer magnitude?

The heli-fighter jets and the tanks began to rev their engines. The sound of the Crimson Empire's death cry filled the air.

'We've got to do this. Even if it means that we die trying. Death or glory,' said Nkite.

'Random is in there.' said Anji. 'We have to do it for him.'

'No,' said Takten. 'We do it for Rodas.'

Those words stirred the spirit in Nkite. She held her gun up high and shouted the final two words, the only two words that mattered to her, as loud as she could.'

'FOR RODAS!!'

Her cry seemed to stoke the fire instantly in the Valkyrie, who clicked his heels into the dosas' ribs and they tore off over the ridge.

Jake and Anji steeled themselves. They all did.

Before long they were all shouting those two words, over and over and over again.

'FOR RODAS!'

The remnants of the depleted Sapphire Regime, over Steyn's open channel on his communicator, heard the battle cry and started to call out the same battle cry which implored their heli-fighters over the ridge. Even the Titan and the other Space Seals battle freighters, and the pilots of the hornets, whose engines noisily hummed into the air as they left their ships and flew out onto the awaiting battlefield, joined in.

Admiral Bagari whispered it to herself before ordering the fleet to attack.

All of a sudden, the resistance, spearheaded by Skateboard, his two human friends, his enlisted help of the Spectronian guard and the Genocian revolutionary front, joined with the oppressed Sapphire Regime and the Space Seals, was tearing over the ridge, heading towards what was about to be the battle of their lives.

Some of the Crimson Empire – including the General who had overseen the aborted attack on the security mainframe – were taken aback at the sheer determination of their enemies.

Now that Kalor Maloso had taken leave of his communication with them, it was up to him to protect the base. They'd do it with ease, he thought. Right? There are five million of them. They'd win this fight easily, surely?

Steeling his thought, he cried through the open channel to the fleet.

'CHARGE!'

The Crimson Empire's handbrake was released and they charged head-first towards the rebel alliance that was hurtling towards them.

'Jake, Anji, stay close to me please,' said Skateboard. 'You too,' he said to Delilah, Benaya and Yana. 'We have to get inside the base.'

He wasn't sure if they had heard him and that worried him. As a torrential rain of laser fire headed their way, he knew his biggest fear had come true.

There was no way he could keep his friend safe.

This was it. It was to be the end of the war on Rodas, but as the warring factions crunched together in a hail of gunfire and physical violence, the battle for Rodas was well underway...

XV

Deep underneath the bowels of the Crimson Empire, an entirely different battle was taking place. Fighting entirely in the dark against a manner of creatures he dare not wish to see, Random was throwing as many punches and kicks as he possibly could. As he felt a vice-like grip surround his midriff, it felt like he was becoming constricted. Soon he started to gasp for air and he began to choke. Although he was in a pit of total darkness, he felt a new wave of it start to fall over his eyes and he began to lose consciousness.

'Boshy, you're holding him too tight!' said one soft voice in the gloom.

'Oh,' came the reply, 'sorry.'

With that, the grip loosened and Random felt his gasping frame be carried lower until he was placed gently on the floor.

As the soles of his boots hit what felt like a sandy, dirty floor he coughed violently and fell to the ground trying to take in as much air as he could.

'But Troyus, he was hurting us,' said the same deep booming voice that had been apologising seconds earlier.

'Well, what do you expect, being chucked down a pit with us goons?' said another gravelly voice. 'Hey kid, you alright? I apologise on behalf of us all.' Random felt a hand, well, it was more like a tentacle, move down towards him.

'Speak for yourself Postanous but I think he's broken one of my noses,' said another voice in the gloom.

'And my arms!' All four of them hurt like hell,' came another.

'Wait,' croaked Random. 'Who are you guys?' he accepted the tentacle and was helped up to his feet.

'What was it he used to call us?' asked Postanous.

'I believe it was the abominations,' came a posher voice in the dark.

'Nah, I think it was worse than that,' said Boshy. 'Something really demeaning.'

'What are you all doing down here?' asked Random, who had started to recover from the tight squeeze from what appeared to now be the friendly giant.

'Well, where else would you want to hide us?' asked Troyus. 'Would you really want us all up there roaming around with our good looks?'

'Looks don't matter I mean look at him, he's purple!' said the posh voice again.

'How can you see me?' asked Random.

'When you've been down here as long as we have, your eyes begin to adjust.'

'So does your posture,' said Boshy, 'Especially when you are as tall as me.'

'Allow me to introduce myself, I am Xiros and these are my fellow abominations. I take it that you're the latest experiment that has gone wrong?'

'Far from it,' I'm the one who went right,' said Random.

'Oh yeah, we all believed that until we were captured down here,' said Postanous.

'Who put you down here?' asked Random. 'And why?'

'Kalor Maloso. We've been trying to get out since he started hiding us,' said Xiros.

Troyus picked up the story. 'We were among the first experiments on living tissues to replicate and augment super beings for the Crimson Empire. But we were shunned, failed experiments. Maloso tried to kill us all at birth, we all have pretty much identical stories. We were created from matter from the man himself, but when we were deemed unfit to fight, he tried to have us killed, only he couldn't. He tried everything. Fire, drowning, heavy artillery, starvation.'

'The poison was the worst. My taste buds have never been the same since,' said Boshy.

'So instead, he banished us down here. Sure, he'd feed us but for years we've been trying to grab his attention, to bust our way out of here when he threw food down here to keep us alive, possibly to experiment again, or maybe until the time was right to release us, I don't know.'

'But if you're superhuman then how come you couldn't use your strength to escape?' asked Random.

'He set up a force field down here. None of us could break out. Plus, the floor is electrified. As my poor friend Boshy finds out regularly,' said Xiros.

'It tickles but hurts at the same time,' agreed Boshy.

Random started to form an idea in his head. Here, he had a readymade army, powerful enough to take out the remaining soldiers inside the base and hopefully get him to the machine.

'So, you must really hate Kalor Maloso then? And your own kind. Here you are. Shunned, kept away in the dark, a dirty little secret into the failings of the Crimson Empire.'

'Don't you start,' said Postanous. 'We've heard it all from him up there all too often.'

'But you must despise your creator. The feeling of revenge must be boiling away under your skin.'

'He's got a lovely turn of phrase, Xiros, just like you!' said Troyus.

'My dear young boy, I know what you are trying to do. You're trying to stoke our flames. You want to get us angry to help you get out of here and fight against our own kind. Well, I regret to inform you that years of involuntary confinement have corrected our murderous natures.'

'If anything, it's made us much calmer,' said Postanous. 'When I bust out of here, I want to set up a fruit market.'

'But you were trying to get out, I heard you,' said Random.

'We just try and let people know that we are here in the hope that they would rescue us,' said Troyus.

'But it never works,' said Boshy sadly.

'I can help you,' said Random.

'How? You're stuck down here with us!' cried Postanous.

'What are you proposing?' asked Xiros.

'Look, if you help me, I can put an end to this war today. We can put an end to it,' he implored.

'Does it involve any violence?' asked Boshy.

'Definitely,' replied Random.

'Hmmm. It goes against my character,' said Troyus.

'Is there anything else we can do instead? Maybe we can speak to Maloso and bargain with him?' asked Xiros.

'That monster has kept you down here in this prison for years and you want to talk with him?!' said Random aghast.

'Yeah, I mean maybe he's got a nice side,' said Troyus.

Random was astounded at what he was hearing. Here was a group of super soldiers, each one of them, despite his blindness in the dark, sounded like they were bred for war and instead they want to open up fruit markets and have a chat!

'I highly doubt that and besides, he's dead,' said Random.

There was an audible sound of gasping.

'Then how are we going to get out now?'

'Well, I think I have an idea, but it'll hurt, probably a lot.'

'Oh well you can count me out then,' said Xiros.

'Not you, me!' replied Random. 'Boshy, if you would be so kind, could you please push me up to the trapdoor? I'll prize it open.'

'You'll fry! As will I!' yelped Boshy.

'You can let go as soon as I find the groove that snaps the door open. Now it's likely that I might lose consciousness after it's opened. If you could catch me and wake me up when you are all on the surface that'd be great,' said Random.

'We've tried that before. Do you think that we wouldn't have done such a thing with a giant present?' asked Xiros.

'Yes, but I've been struck by lightning before. Years ago, my body was corrupted by a powerful element, since then my nervous system doesn't feel pain as badly as it did before. I need to see if I can withstand it. Then when we are all out, there is likely to be trouble. Big trouble. Maloso might be dead but his army is far from it. I could really use your help.'

Xiros sighed. 'Okay, if you can get us out of here then I promise I will help but I'll only use my strength to fight if I am provoked. Do we have a deal, young man?'

Random smiled. 'Deal! What do the rest of you say?'

There was a grumble amongst them. 'So, you want us to fight our own people?' asked Postanous.

'Yes,' said Random.

'Kill where necessary?' said Troyus.

'Sadly, yes,' replied Random.

'And side with you and the Sapphire Regime, our sworn enemy?' asked Boshy.

'To save your entire planet and bring about peace, yes,' said Random.

There was a pause.

'Go on then' said Boshy.

'Yeah, I'm in,' said Postanous.

'This is a stupid war anyway,' said Troyus. 'It's time it ended.'

Random smiled. 'Thank you. Oh, and I'm sorry for hurting you all.'

'Ah, don't mention it!' said Troyus. 'My arms have set already.'

'Right, Boshy, if you would be so kind?' Random prepared himself for the next phase of his escape plan. As Boshy picked him up and lifted him towards the trapdoor he could hear the crackle of electricity that stood between them and freedom. He felt the heat against his face.

'I can see the crack in the door. The electricity is giving off light. Must be powerful. Right, as soon as it snaps open, Boshy, if you could let the others use you as a ladder then get them to pull you out? Is that okay with you?'

'As long as they wipe their feet then yes,' he replied.

'Okay,' said Random, preparing himself for a world of torment. 'Here it goes.'

He plunged his hands into the crack. Instantly his body was engulfed in a bright light of energy as the electricity tried to consume him. Random snarled and spat as he grimaced against the might of the trapdoor mechanism and the pain that was flooding his body. With a huge effort, he pulled the doors open and the electricity stopped.

As the doors snapped open and the electricity died away, Random lost consciousness and began to fall. Boshy caught his unconscious body in his palm.

'Hehe, he tickles!' said the giant as he calmly placed the fizzing Randon on the floor of Maloso's room outside of the trapdoor. 'Come on up, guys!'

The abominations were shocked. They had never seen anyone withstand such power before. 'Quickly!' cried out Xiros and one by one, they started climbing up Boshy's body.

'Don't pull at my hair!' he demanded and one by one they made it out.

'The ceiling looks quite high in here, chum,' said Xiros. 'You should be fine, how's the purple one?'

Troyus was checking his pulse. 'Seems a little high, but I ain't no doctor and he's still breathing so-'

Postanous was gazing out of the window at the battle taking place outside. 'Zarks...'

Xiros and two other abominations had finished picking Boshy out of the hole and then they all turned to see what Postanous was looking at. The former was having to duck a little but he didn't mind. They were free, but they had no time to celebrate.

'Would you look at that?' said Troyus. 'There must be millions out there.'

'Millions upon millions,' came a croaky voice. It was Random. The abominations weren't paying him any attention, not the fact that he was awake or that his body seemed to have steam rising from it or that some of his purple skin looked burnt. They didn't even blink at the corpse of their captor across the way.

Random limped his way over to them.

'Kalor Maloso. Ruler of the Crimson Empire. You've heard what he was doing. You know more than I did until now. Do you really think that there is any option but to fight against it?'

'Oh my god...Sergeant they are out!'

A new voice joined the room. Random and the abominations turned and saw a lone soldier standing in the crumpled doorway. Speaking into his communicator, trembling in his boots. Far away distant sounds of more of them clip-clopping their way towards the room could be heard and they getting louder and louder.

'You good kid?' asked Postanous.

Random clenched his fists. 'Never better.'

'Good...then let's do this!'

XVI

Amongst the absolute carnage that was a battle to end all battles, one that was happening on land and in the sky, a battle that had become so bad that outside help had given the underdogs a fighting chance to survive, a little AI robot was trying to have a conversation.

Upon their charge into the valley, Skateboard noticed that the base they needed to reach was a fair distance back behind endless rows of enemy soldiers. Whilst he had been keeping a watchful eye on his two human friends, who were currently letting the Valkyries they were with do all the fighting, he was thankful to see that none of them were coming to harm. But as even he kept firing his stun gun at any Crimson Empire troops that came near him, and weaved in and out of the destructive firepower that was raining down upon them, he suddenly realised that what he really needed was for everyone to just be quiet for a second.

As he was unable to be heard by his friends over the gunfire, his open channel with Admiral Bagari and General Steyn of the Sapphire Regime was at least a blessing if for nothing else but so that he could tell them what he required.

'As I was saying,' he continued, firing off more rounds at those that were trying to kill him and his friends. 'The base entrance is two hundred metres away. It is reachable, but we may need covering fire to do so.'

'And you are sure that the purple one is in there?' asked Steyn.

I am certain of it, General. And as long as he is in there, we must not fire upon it.'

'General, Skateboard,' interjected Bagari. 'I am picking up intel that there is a massive factory of some sort roughly five miles behind the mountain containing the base. Do you think we should be firing on that instead? I mean considering there are more soldiers pouring out of the doors it might be an idea?'

Steyn was dumbfounded. 'We thought that was an ammunition factory.'

'Definitely not that from our sources. I think we've found how the Crimson Empire have been restocking their forces,' said Bagari.

'How?' asked Steyn.

'I'm a bit busy to find an explanation right now, General,' said Skateboard. 'But I am certain that the answer lies in that base. Would either of you be able to lay down some covering fire, and clear a path for us to get in?'

'We're on it, Skateboard, and yes, we shall send a squadron of hornets to bomb the factory.

Considering they are still churning out soldiers – somehow – it'd probably be a good idea if we could send them a cease-and-desist notice,' said Bagari. 'I'll get straight on it. Helm?'

'On it, Admiral,' said the helm officer.

'In the meantime, we can pick you up on our sensors. We'll make a path for you now,' Bagari continued.

'I've sent you the coordinates of the entrance now,' said Skateboard. He rounded back towards his friends who thankfully were all still alive and all close by.

'Your majesty, please continue the attack,' he said to Solenia. 'The rest of you, follow me.'

Nkite and Takten broke off from their defensive fire and looked at one another. 'You go,' Nkite cried. 'This is our fight here.'

Anji looked worried. She was sure that as soon as they were inside, they would be safer than out here in the hail of laser fire. Nkite smiled at her reassuringly.

'I'll be okay, now go!'

Anji smiled back.

'Miss Anji. Sir, please come with me,' said Skateboard. Jake and Anji ducked and weaved as the hail of enemy fire was growing nearer. They approached Skateboard and stood on his body and before long, the AI robot had clamped their feet to him.

He extended his body and allowed Delilah, Benaya and Yana on and shot off full pelt as the covering fire began clearing a path.

Metre by metre, they were gaining closer and closer on the base, closer to their friend and closer, they all collectively hoped, to the end of all the madness.

XVII

In the room that had once been their prison, the abominations were fighting against their own, against those who had shunned them. But as Boshy bludgeoned a soldier with an uppercut which sent him flying up into the ceiling, Random looked upon them for what they actually were. They were liberated.

'I say,' said Xiros as he chucked a soldier into the corridor like he was a shotput in a school sports day, 'this is really rather fun!'

Still, there was a throng of Crimson Empire soldiers who were doing all they could to keep Random and the abominations back. Some had broken out electrical prongs, designed to contain and harm those on the receiving end but Random and his new friends were having none of it.

'Everyone, with me!' he yelled and together they all charged at their enemies, sending them sprawling all ways.

'Well, that felt good!' said Postanous. They all noticed that for now, things had gone quiet.

'What do we do now?' asked Boshy.

Random got up and made for the control desk. Then he remembered the forcefield.

'We have to find a way to locate my friends,' he replied. 'Boshy, Troyus, Xiros, go to the main entrance. They should find their way in there.'

'And what do we do, boss?' asked Postanous.

'We defend this room and wait for you all to return,' said Random.

'But how do we know what to look out for?' asked Troyus.

'Well, they won't be red or blue-skinned, so that should make them easier to spot. When you do see them let them in and seal this base down. Stop any Crimson Empire soldiers that you spot on the way. This had to be our stronghold, is everyone alright with that?' asked Random.

'These friends of yours, they could be wearing disguises, so that'd make it harder. And who says they won't try and shoot us dead when they spot us? We're not the nicest looking bunch, are we?' said Troyus.

'My friends, unlike those on this planet, won't judge by appearances,' said Random.

'But they might mistake us for enemies, still,' said Xiros. 'It doesn't matter if they are-'

'A young girl,' said Boshy.

'Yeah, a young girl or a' continued Troyus.

'A blonde-haired boy,' said Boshy.

'Yeah, or a blonde-haired-'

'And a flat metal robot,' said Boshy.

Random took notice of Boshy's words and went over to the giant. He craned his neck upwards to speak to him.

'How do you know what they look like?' asked Random.

'I can see them on the security monitor,' said Boshy, pointing over to the far corner of the room. His height had given him an advantage and he could see Maloso's still active surveillance desk.

Random smiled. 'That's them!'

'And it looks like they are being chased,' said Boshy with a concerned lilt to his voice.

'Quick, go now!' said Random.

'We're on it!' said Troyus and as quick as a flash he, Xiros and Boshy squeezed their way down the corridor and off to the main entrance.

'Well, since it's all a bit quiet,' said Postanous, 'Maybe you should tell me what the next part of the plan is?'

Random frowned. 'We break in through the forcefield. Then, we end this war.'

The hail of gunfire from the hornets and the heli-fighters raged up ahead. Every now and then Anji, Jake, Skateboard and the others had to jump or avoid at the last minute a piece of debris that was falling from the sky.

As they looked up ahead, they could see that the hornets were pushing their opponents back and doing much better than the alliance was faring on the ground.

For now, though, they were unscathed and as Delilah, Benaya and Yana continued to lay down fire to repel any on-coming attackers, Skateboard did his best to reach the base as quickly as he could.

'When we get there, we may have to keep fighting so I stress that we keep our wits about us, find Random and-'

'Bagari's covering fire has worked,' yelled Delilah. 'Come on Skateboard we're almost there!'

'Let's hope we can find Random quickly!' said Anji. She had tried to keep a watchful eye on Nkite but as they grew further apart she had lost her new friend in the melee.

'Anj, she'll be fine!' said Jake. All the time they had been holding onto each other for dear life. Something they had been doing ever since they had met Random. Something that would never change for either of them.

'We've made it!' said Yana.

'You should be alright now, Skateboard,' said Bagari over the AI robot's open channel. 'Will assist on the bombing of the processing plant now. Take care.'

'Thanks, Admiral,' said Skateboard. He released the clamps on his friend's feet and as they disembarked, he folded back into his normal length. There was a flight of stairs. The gang ascended it, shooting at soldiers trying to stop them as they went. Then, as they were nearly at the top, a massive explosion ripped the main entrance apart.

They threw themselves to the steps for cover and dust and dirt showered down upon them and as Jake and Anji looked they were astonished to see a massive giant of a... creature, standing where the doors used to be.

'Oh my god!' cried Anji.

'Um...Skateboard?' asked Jake.

The red, blotchy, mutated face looked down upon them. His impossibly long arms extended outwards. Benaya hid behind her sister, and Yana screamed. Jake and Anji stood terrified at the huge, hideous creature in front of them. Skateboard readied his stun gun but knew it wouldn't be powerful enough to stop such a creature of his size.

Suddenly the stern features of the giant relaxed in a cheery smile. 'Oh, hello!' he exclaimed. 'You must be Random's friends. He is expecting you. Come in quick, you'll be safer in here.' The giant reached his arm out to beckon them in.

The gang looked at each other confused. 'Are you for real?' exclaimed Jake.

Boshy felt his face and torso and nodded vigorously. 'Yep!'

Anji and Jake looked at each other. 'It's a trap, isn't it?' said Anji sideways to Skateboard.

'Come on, Boshy what's the hold-up?' came another voice. The gang shrieked when two more ugly, mutated creatures filled the door. One of them seemed to have eight limbs like a spider. The other resembled a scaley crocodile more than a humanoid.

'Hello there, we're the abominations,' said the reptile-like one in a cheery posh voice. 'Please do wipe your feet as you come in.'

The gang didn't know what to do. Each of them looked at Skateboard for guidance.

'Let's do what they say,' he said.

'Sorry, the place is a mess. Do wipe your feet as you come in,' said the posh one again. 'We'll make introductions on the way,' he looked out at the madness of the battle that was taking place. 'My, my what a terrible racket.'

Not knowing what to make of the situation, the gang did as the abominations asked but slower than they should have been doing. Behind them, the Crimson Empire soldiers had cottoned on to what was happening and were tearing up the steps behind them.

'Oh dear,' said Boshy. 'I'll deal with this.' He slammed the door as soon as they were inside and readied himself for a fight. There was none. The soldiers took one look at him and ran off, terrified.

Boshy looked confused and sniffed under his arm. Then he shrugged and turned to follow the others inside.

'What are you doing?' asked Postanous. He had been watching Random trace around the room with a stick for a good few minutes and had started to wonder if his new friend was a little mad.

'I'm trying to find a break in the force field,' said Random, who every now and then was jolting back a little. 'But so far... nope,' he said, tossing his stick to one side. 'It's hopeless.'

'What do we do now?' asked Postanous. At that moment the door to the room burst open and Random smiled broadly as a few familiar faces came through it.

'Random!' cried our Anji. She ran towards him and threw herself at him. Jake did the same and the three of them ended up on the floor laughing, barely believing that they were all okay.

'Guys! Thank zarks you made it,' said a relieved Random.

'Hey! Don't use our lords' name in vain!' warned Postanous but his comment was ignored.

Random got up and picked his two best friends up in the same motion. 'Skateboard, you did it!'

'Thank you, sir, but the mission is far from accomplished,' said Skateboard, who proceeded to scan the room.

'Yana! Delilah, Benaya! Wow! I can't believe it's really you. It's been so long!' Random hugged each of them in turn. 'Thank you so much for coming!'

'We wouldn't have missed a party like this,' said Delilah.

'Speaking of which, it's really getting hairy out there,' said Yana. 'Shouldn't we be getting on with what we need to be doing?'

'You're right,' said Random. 'Hugs and kisses later. Oh, before I do though, you've met the abominations, haven't you? They are cousins of mine; I suppose you could say.'

'Hello!' waved Xiros. Boshy re-entered the room and used a cattle prod he'd acquired from a soldier earlier to put it across the door, in turn electrifying it, meaning that no one could break in.

'So, what do we do now?' asked Jake.

'Over there is a creation chamber tube,' said Random. 'We have to get to it that entire side of the room has a forcefield running across it.'

'What about Kalor Maloso?' asked Anji.

'He's the corpse sitting next to it,' said Random. 'He's cloned the entire army. Skateboard, I think I know what we have to do.'

Skateboard finished his scans. 'I do too, sir.'

Random nodded. 'Good, then how do we get through the force field.'

'Leave that to me, sir. I'll attempt to crack the
security network. If I can trip it, I can bring the
forcefield down.'

'Great,' said Random. 'That's when the fun
really begins.'

XVIII

As his cockpit filled up with flames and smoke, the Crimson Empire's General's hands were shaking on the wheel. Not because he was scared of the inevitable hard ground below, but because the steering wheel was going out of control. He looked all around him. Everyone else in the heli-fighter was either dead or unconscious. It was only him left.

How had this happened? Not the crashing, that had been inevitable after the Sapphire Regime had entered into battle, but first the security mainframe now this. How had the Sapphire Regime found recruitments? How were they keeping them at bay? Maloso's new clones were supposed to be indestructible. They were meant to break the mainframe and he was going to lead his new troops into space and onto further conquest whilst the foot soldiers slaughtered the remaining blue skins.

But his squadron was at a loss. When the huge battle freighters arrived, he knew that part of their plan was up. When the internal alarms had sounded for them to protect the base, they had done what, with their number, should have been unthinkable. They fell back.

Maloso had his soldiers all in a row and they hadn't heard from him since. The General tried not to think about it and as he braced for impact, trying to crash into some of the rebel alliance to take some revenge, he thought of very little. Indeed, the impact nearly killed him.

Nkite finished off her round of fire and took cover, pulling Takten down with her as the heli-fighter nearly crashed right on top of them. They held their low cover as the nearby explosion blew debris all over them. Finally, they looked up.

'You're doing well,' said Takten.

'Thanks, but I'm not sure if we are making much progress,' she replied.

'We've got to keep going. Where are those colourful horses when you need them?' he said ruing their current position. There was little cover from them and after Skateboard and the others had left them, they had lost Solenia and the Valkyries very quickly.

'We're sitting ducks,' said Nkite. 'Can you call for backup?'

Takten reached for his communicator. 'General Steyn...come in General Steyn...'

The radio was dead.

Nkite shot him a worried look.

Takten was panting hard. 'What was the name of the other one?' he asked.

'Bagari…Admiral Bagari to you,' came the reply. 'I'm afraid it looks like your General has been lost. There are a heavy number of casualties in your region, on land and in the sky.'

The Titan and its fleet of hornets were descending on the processing plant. Bagari watched on the viewscreen as the newly created soldiers continued to teem out of the factory but were immediately firing up at them.

'Tell the squadron to release their bombs on my mark. Continue to fire on anyone attacking us,' she said.

She watched on her navigation monitor as they moved into range. Lasers were exploding all around them. The tactical officer's trigger finger was getting itchy. Finally, Bagari gave the order.

'Fire.'

Instantly, the Titan released its bombs and the hornets fired their photon torpedoes. A flurry of artillery descended on the processing plant. The Titan and its hornet squadron fled instantly, careful not to be caught up in the blast.

Some of the Crimson Empire's heli-fighters tried to shoot the bombs down but it was no use, there were too many to stop them in time and it only needed a few to make a direct hit for the plan to work. Suddenly, there was a brilliant explosion.

A huge cloud of smoke and fire roared upwards into the air and within seconds the crater containing the processing plant and all that had been standing there was obliterated.

'We've done it Admiral,' said the tactical officer. 'Direct hit!' There was a whoop and a cheer around the command posts. Admiral Bagari remained cool. 'Great job, guys. Now let's get back to the front line. That goes for everyone on the Space Seals channel. One last push. This battle isn't won yet.'

Back in the front line, Nkite and Takten felt the ground rumble as a mushroom cloud of fire and smoke ripped into the sky far away.

'Great job Admiral!' said Takten.

'Thanks, now try and find some cover. We'll come in and pick you up. If you find Solenia tell her the same. We'll win this war from the air now,' said Bagari.

Nkite felt like hugging Takten but he didn't look the type. Takten looked at her wishing he could hug her but then thinking better of it. At that moment, just as he had remembered what feeling happy felt like, a sudden sharp pain blew up in his chest. Nkite screamed. He looked down and discovered a hole in his rib cage. He felt the worse pain he had ever felt. He looked at Nkite's face and gave her a smile as he sank to his knees.

Behind him was a very injured survivor of the heli-fighter crash. As Takten fell flat on his face,

Nkite picked up his gun and fired it at the assassin. She fired and fired again, tears streaming down her face, anger and raw agony overtaking her body as the body of the General lay motionless, his eyes open but still. She dropped the gun and ran back to Takten, who was just as lifeless as the General. She held him close and wept uncontrollably.

She thought they wouldn't lose any more friends today. Clearly, she had been wrong.

Before long she remembered where they were. She closed his eyes and placed Takten gently on the ground. Picking up her gun she moved away, running fast into the front line, taking on and beating any Crimson Empire soldier she came into contact with. Before long she found a Valkyrie, wounded on the ground. Her tears were still running down her cheeks when she picked up the injured Spectronian.

'Can you walk?' she asked them.

The man looked up at her and grimaced. 'Not well but I'll manage.'

'Good,' she said. 'We have to find your Queen. We're getting out of here.'

With that. She pulled the Valkyrie up. As she did, he swore as his bleeding leg and side were aggravated, words that Nkite didn't know but would one day use as they sounded just as colourful as this man's skin.

With great effort, she dragged him through the crowd of fighting red and blue soldiers and Valkyries, both fighting as they went.

'Come on guys,' Nkite said to herself. 'What's holding you up?'

XIX

'Hurry up Skateboard.'

Random was pensively walking up and down the little part of Kalor Maloso's war room that he could. His friend, the amazing AI robot who seemed able to do just about anything he could ask was struggling to hack into the security system and shut the forcefield down.

'I'm almost there, sir,' said Skateboard. 'Just 12,937 more combinations left to crack.'

'Yes, but how long will that take?' asked Yana.

'Roughly ninety-four seconds.'

'Wow, that doesn't seem so bad,' said Delilah.

Benaya elbowed Jake and pointed over at Random. She signed to him to ask what the matter was.

'Oh, something to do with that chamber. Apparently, it can end the war,' said Jake in response.

'It will,' said Random overhearing. 'At least it better do.'

Anji was sitting with Boshy and Postanous. 'So, you were created to fight the Sapphire Regime but you're fighting your own people?'

'Yeah, well, we haven't done much fighting to be fair. We were under this floor for years until your friend came along,' said Postanous.

'I'm kind of glad we didn't. I don't feel much like killing,' said Boshy. 'I don't think that I have it in me.'

'And that's why Maloso hid you,' said Anji. 'I'm so sorry.'

'Don't sweat it,' said Postanous. 'It gave us all time to think and to reform ourselves. Who knows, after this we might do charity work for a living?'

'If there is a Rodas after this,' said Xiros as he continued to watch the battle from outside the viewing window.

'Sir, Bagari has informed me that the processing plant has been destroyed. She's taking the Titan to pick Nkite and the Valkyries up,' said Skateboard.

'I wondered what all that banging was,' said Jake.

'Good, but please, just concentrate on this,' begged Random.

Skateboard spent another ten seconds in silence before finally, the forcefield disappeared.

'Skateboard, you legend!' said Random. He and the others raced over to the chamber.

Jake stood a little too close to the corpse of Kalor Maloso for his liking. 'Ewww. What did he do to himself?'

'This,' said Random, gesturing outside the window. 'So, Skateboard, you've scanned it. You know what it does?'

'I do, sir,' said Skateboard hesitantly. 'Maloso was right, sir. This machine is indeed the one that created you. It also created your new friends here. Except between your conception and everyone else's it has been augmented. It was retooled for mass production purposes. The DNA extracted from Kalor Maloso was transported through the tubes rising up into the ceiling and fed to the processing plant, creating millions upon millions of his troops. There's more. This machine was also keyed in with instructions. He found a way to teach his clones to think. He didn't programme them to feel.'

'How kind of him,' said Anji witheringly.

'So, what do we do? Blow it up?' asked Delilah.

'Far from it,' said Skateboard.

'We use it,' said Anji.

'I use it,' said Random.

'How?' asked Yana and Xiros simultaneously.

'This chamber, no matter how much it has been tampered with, has been coded to my DNA. Since it created me, I can use it again. By getting in and starting the process again it can create an army of Me's to fight the Crimson Empire and to stop the fighting.'

'But you'd be left looking like him!' said Jake pointing at Maloso's corpse.

'That's correct Jake,' said Random. 'And now that the processing plant has been destroyed that option is out of the window. Plus, we wouldn't have the time. However, this machine still can send out a psychic link to anyone who stems from it.'

'So, you can shut the army down?' asked Anji.

'It'll do more than that. It'll fry their brains. A signal from my mind to theirs, it'd probably blow them up. This machine is that powerful!' said Random.

'But sir,' said Skateboard, a tinge of sadness in his voice.

'I know, Skateboard, I know,' he replied.

Anji and Jake looked confused. 'Know what?' asked Anji.

Random looked up at her, his eyes starting to well up. 'I've known. Ever since I was born, I've known that what happens today will be the end of me.'

Jake's jaw dropped. 'You're sacrificing yourself?'

'That's why I ran for so long. I knew that coming back would result in my death.'

Anji shook her head, her eyes starting to well up with tears also. 'No. No, no, no there must be something else we can try, surely?'

Random spoke calmly. 'Anji, there is no other option. The only two that were open to us would have still led to this conclusion. That's one of the reasons why I asked for Skateboard to ask for your help,' he said nodding at Delilah, Benaya and Yana. 'Old friends who I knew could help, yes, but I wanted to see everyone again. All those people I've helped save. I wanted a reminder that it was more than worth it and it was, wasn't it?'

Jake and Anji were sobbing uncontrollably.

'Is there...no chance...you could survive?' asked Jake sniffing.

'It's practically one in a billion,' confirmed Skateboard, taking no pleasure in delivering the news.

'Even if I did, I wouldn't have much of a brain left,' said Random, tears pouring silently down his cheeks.

Jake wiped his nose with his sleeve. 'It's not like you have much of one already.'

Random laughed. Trust Jake to try and joke at a time like this. He loved him for it.

'Look, this is all very distressing for your friends. If it's tailored to DNA that has passed through it already then one of us can use it, surely?' said Xiros, about to volunteer himself.

'I'll do it,' said Troyus, who had been watching in silence. 'I've got nothing in my diary for tomorrow.'

'You can't, My DNA is made up of both the red and blue factions of Rodas. My chromosomes are split 50/50 between both races of Rodasians.

Hence the purple skin. I was designed to be the one who could end this war because of that fact. I hold within me all the good and evil of the Crimson Empire and the Sapphire Regime. I've held it off for too long. With every passing second more and more innocent people die and I can't live with that guilt anymore.'

'But Skateboard, you can tailor this machine back, surely? Please someone tell me this isn't how it needs to be!' said Anji hysterically. Jake held her in close.

'I can't miss, I'm sorry,' he said. If robots could cry, he would have been inconsolable right now.

Random moved to be next to his friends. 'You three have always been the best of me. You've given me so much happiness in my life. It was a life that was never supposed to know joy. Never allowed the privilege of love but I did. I love all of you so much. Whatever happens next, wherever I go, I'll hold it in my heart forever.'

He wrapped his arms around them. Skateboard, on his hind wheels, so that he could be a part of the hug, wrapped his arms that snaked out of his body when he needed them around his friends. They all held each other tightly, knowing that this was it. There was nothing else they could do.

Just as the Oracle of Fate had told him, Random was walking hand-in-hand, finally after all these years, with his destiny.

Those watching on held each other's hands. The abominations barely knew Random but owed him their freedom and their a chance to live.

Delilah and Benaya. The sisters who had met Random in prison down in the mines of Genocia had taken part in the uprising led by the purple one so many years back and owed them their freedom.

Yana, the rebel who had also aided in the revolution on that same planet, put her arms across the shoulders of the sisters and Troyus. They were united in their thanks for Random and not just him but his three brave friends who all stood before them saying their tearful goodbyes.

Random pulled away, his face puffy and wet with emotion. 'Skateboard, look after these two and yourself. The Venus II is yours now. Do with it what you like.'

'Yes, sir,' sniffed the robot.

'Jake, never change who you are,' smiled Random.

'You bet,' sniffed Jake again, his voice faint and croaky.

'Anj...' Random held her face in his hands. 'You be whoever you want to be,' he kissed her on the forehead, making her cry even more.

He let her go and walked back a few paces.

'Look after each other and yourselves. I love you so much. No matter what corner of the universe you are in never let the light be dimmed by the dark.'

He blew them a kiss. He turned to the others. He nodded at them all and wiped his eyes.

'Right, Skateboard, you know how to program this thing?'

'I do, sir.'

Random walked over to the chamber, his hearts thumping like mad. He pressed a button on the doorway and the chamber door snapped open. 'Okay, no more to be said. It's time to end this.'

All of his friends could barely watch as Random strapped himself into the contraption. He made himself as comfortable as could be and watched as the chamber door snapped shut again.

Skateboard hated himself for having to be the one who made this all happen. He searched his databanks, desperately trying to find a reprieve but there was none. He then calculated the odds of survival again and they were just as bleak as before. As he readied the machine he looked one final time at his brave dear friends.

Random looked at him and smiled. He then looked out and saw the faces looking back at him, their faces distraught, hopeless.

Anji. Jake. Yana. Delilah. Benaya. Boshy, Troyus, Postanous, Xiros.

Then he noticed two new faces. No, not two new faces, these looked familiar.

But how? The door was fastened shut. Then he squinted.

New faces? No. These faces, although never clear before, had been with him since he had been born.

The tall, blue man and the shorter red woman. His parents. The scientist and the freedom fighter.

They had spoken in his mind over and over again, knowing what he had to do but deep down, he knew that they didn't want him to suffer or go through what his destiny had told him to.

But it was for the good of the people of Rodas.

As he gave the command for Skateboard to switch on the machine, and the sharp, protruding implements started to penetrate his purple flesh, he kept that in his mind.

Then he remembered. He remembered the good times. Meeting Skateboard, crash landing on Earth. Meeting the two schoolchildren. Posing as a pupil in a secondary school. Travelling with his two friends. The laughs. The triumphs. Nothing but the good times.

As he blotted out the pain, he allowed himself a big, broad smile. The chamber was rattling and hissing, smoke and steam pouring out of it.

It shook violently almost like a rocket about to take off. A huge build-up of energy was collecting deep within as the machine that gave Random life and Rodas hope was about to conduct its final mission.

Random, still smiling in the bliss of a life worth lived, felt the surge of energy in his body reach new limits as he prepared to do the most important thing in his life.

Save Rodas.

As the watchers moved back, the room started to flood with a glow of purple. Anji and Jake held their hands up to their faces, the brilliant light, combined with the smoke completely obscuring any final image of their best friend.

Suddenly, with a flick of a switch on the control unit of the chamber, Skateboard wheeled back.

'Get down, everyone!' he hollered over the sound of the machine as it exploded into life. The brilliant light within the room burst through the ceiling, outside of the base and formed a fantastic horizontal beam of energy that shot up right into the sky of Rodas, stopping both warring factions in their tracks.

Nkite and the Valkyrie, who had found Solenia and were about to mount her dosa stopped and watched.

The Sapphire Regime, what was left of it in the air and on the ground watched in awe.

The hoards of the Crimson Empire stopped too.

Even the Space Seals in their battle freighters and hornet fighters ceased fighting.

The security mainframe, which had also been joining in the battle by firing on those who dare come near it again, stopped and watched as the beam of energy stopped mere metres from their location.

Slowly, the beam started to spread rapidly in the sky and before long, it covered the entire planet, turning every single corner of Rodas purple. In that instance, the Crimson Empire clones dropped their arms and held their heads in agony. Those piloting battle freighters, heli-fighters and tanks lost control of their vehicles and sent them crashing. Before long, the clones began to burst into nothing but clouds of purple dust. The sight was extraordinary.

For Admiral Bagari, watching in stunned fascination from high above, it looked as though a sea of purple was washing over the battlefield. It was happening planet-wide. Within seconds, the screaming hordes of clones who had spent so many years causing so much misery, butchering millions upon millions of people were suddenly no more.

In a matter of moments, the purple clouds ascended up towards the beam's wave of energy over the planet and when all of it had been sucked up, the wave started to recede back towards the energy beam. Seconds later, the beam of light shot back down into its location below in the base and in the room where for so long Kalor Maloso had carried out his heinous acts of genocide against his own people, there was suddenly peace.

The chamber stopped shaking. The beam of light was gone.

All that remained was silence and smoke.

Those who were left behind, be it in the air, on the ground, in the mainframe, anywhere on Rodas were left stunned.

It had taken centuries for the war to end.

Now, in a hushed room at the centre of the Crimson Empire operation, it had taken seconds to bring about what the repressed people of Rodas had wanted for so long.

Peace.

XX

Silence spread over Rodas. It was as though time had stood still. Nkite dare not move in case it was all a weird side effect of being shot by an enemy soldier. Some people on the battlefield barely drew breath; forgetting to do so in the shock of it all until they began sobbing. Some cried tears of joy, others cried tears of relief. Nobody, not one Rodasian was not moved by what had happened.

Nkite let out a yell of pure elation and her fellow men, women and others who had joined the alliance followed her lead. Aboard the Titan, indeed, across all the battle freighters that the Space Seals had brought to Rodas, there were similar scenes of raw emotion and relief. Admiral Bagari sat in her command chair and allowed her guard to drop for a brief moment. She smiled. She laughed. She almost wept.

They had done it. No, Random had done it. The Crimson Empire was no more.

The war on Rodas was at an end.

Amongst the jubilation, Solenia dismounted her dosa and took a brief head count of her army. She was saddened when she realised that some of her Valkyries clearly hadn't made it. She was disturbed in her grief by an elated Nkite, who was picking her up and throwing her around, all the time repeating that they had done it.

Solenia was happy for her, but the cost of battle would be something she would have to face when they went home. Happily, however, they were going home. She hadn't thought it possible at the moment leading up to the Crimson Empire being wiped out.

Back on the Titan, messages were being relayed between the Space Seals fleet. The situation was being broadcast across the planet. War was over.

Before long Bagari, despite being beckoned by her peers to a team briefing, flipped a switch on her command chair. She had to know if they were okay.

'Skateboard,' was all she could say.

'Admiral,' was all that Skateboard could say back.

She detected a note of sadness in his voice.

'Random?' she asked.

Skateboard couldn't respond. His two friends were kneeling in the dust, sobbing and holding one another. The chamber was a mess. Inside there was too much smoke to see if Random had defied the odds but Skateboard already knew the answer.

Anji and Jake broke off for a moment when the former of the pair tore herself away from her friend and made for the chamber.

She wanted to touch it, to feel some form of connection with Random but her hand recoiled a couple of feet from the glass.

'An insurmountable energy had passed through that tube,' said Skateboard. 'We shouldn't go anywhere near it until it has cooled.'

'But Random...he could be?' asked Anji.

'Anj,' whispered Jake, his eyes streaming with tears. 'We'd know.'

Anji looked back at him and wanted to hit him. Know what? If he was alive? All she could do, however, was pull Jake back in and hug him.

The others stood motionless, not knowing what to say, knowing that there was nothing that they could say. Words were not even a crumb of comfort to the two young humans who were united in their grief for someone who had made the ultimate sacrifice, someone who most definitely was never going to make it...

...Random opened his eyes. He was surprised to find that he was still breathing. He was even more shocked to learn that he was still all in one piece. That was nothing to the astonishment he felt when he realised that he was standing in some sort of white void.

'Hello?' he called out. Nothing, not even an echo replied back.

He regarded his current position. Was he dead? Had it worked? Where on Rodas was he? Was he even still on Rodas? Finally, a voice did call to him through the void, one that he had heard very recently and was surprised to hear once more.

'See, that wasn't so bad, was it?' called the voice of a woman. The woman who had sent him back to Rodas after he had answered her call for help.

'Stung a bit,' he replied. 'Where am I? What are we doing here?'

The woman walked through the void and arrived fully formed in front of him. It was the Oracle of Fate. Random knew it was her the moment he had heard her but he was still very confused.

'I found you at a point in your time stream when you stood on the very edge of life and death.'

'So, I'm not in the afterlife?'

'What is an afterlife? It's not the same for everybody, no, you are in a point of limbo. You have yet to pass beyond the point of life and cross into the realm of the dead.'

'Okay, well, what am I doing here then? I take it the plan worked? Please tell me it worked.'

The Oracle, with dozens of pairs of eyes blinking intermittently and her tasselled dark hair matted over her shoulders, smiled at Random.

'You fulfilled the prophecy. Rodas is free once more from tyranny. The battle was won and your plan indeed worked.'

Random choked and began to well with emotion. 'Good,' he smiled. 'I'm happy that my death wasn't for nothing.'

'Death, such a finite word,' said the Oracle. 'Now that you have fulfilled your destiny my vision of Rodas' future is no longer impaired. I can see it flourishing, its people living together in harmony. Red and blue, hand-in-hand, for the rest of time. I have seen it, Random. What Rodas will one day become because of your actions. The billions upon billions of souls who shall echo throughout time who before your sacrifice would never have been given a chance of life. They shall flourish now forevermore, as will the planet. Eventually, it'll take time, but Rodas, the once shunned and ashamed planet of Ursa-17 shall take its place amongst the stars once again. It has an important part to play in the history of the universe, as you do too.'

Random scoffed. 'If what you say is true then I think you'll find that the only thing I am is history.'

The Oracle walked closer to Random and held his cheek in her palm.

'So why can't I rest now? Why can't I be at peace? Surely my work has been done? You're just here to see me off over the bridge, yes?'

'At the dawn of time, my fellow gods and I swore an oath. An oath not to interfere in the peoples of the universe's affairs but as the millennia have passed and I am now along the last of my kind, those who have survived the ravages of time with me will look upon my gift to you as a minor discrepancy.'

Random looked confused. 'You're talking in riddles, Oracle, what are you saying?'

'As you know Captain I am forbidden to interfere. But the tragedy of Rodas was so severe, indeed your part in its tale was so strong that I needed you to fulfil your destiny. If Rodas had fallen, then the universe, billions of years from now, would have been a darker place. It is for that, on our final meeting together, that I bestow to you the greatest gift I can give you as a way of saying thank you.'

Random shrugged. 'Nope, still lost me. Am I getting a medal? I mean I'm grateful but what I'll do with a medal in the afterlife I've no idea-'

The Oracle placed her palm on his chest. 'Goodbye, Captain Random and thank you.'

Suddenly, what felt like an electric bolt through his hearts sent Random reeling out of the void.

Back in Kalor Maloso's war room, a light tapping could be heard. Skateboard picked up on it first but it soon became stronger. Anji and Jake stopped crying and looked towards the chamber.

'It can't be?' said Jake.

The tap was becoming a thud.

'It is!' exclaimed Anji.

They, along with everyone else in the room circled the still-burning hot glass chamber.

'He's alive!' cried out Anji.

Skateboard instantly ran a physical scan on the chamber but it was suffering some interference.

'He can't get out!' shouted Jake.

'We'll help with that,' said Xiros. He, Postanous, Troyus and Boshy, ignoring the searing heat of the glass chamber, used all their might to tear the entrance door clean off its hinges. The glass shattered as they did and they tossed it to one side.

As the smoke cleared, the charred, injured body of Random looked back at them, smiling.

'Oh, thank god!' cried out Jake. He and Anji threw themselves at him. Random groaned loudly but reciprocated.

Skateboard was able to complete his bio-scan and he, along with the others stood disbelieving what they were seeing.

'You did it Random, you did it!' cried Anji, her tears now those of utter joy.

Random, unable to do much but hold his friends close to him looked at Skateboard. His body was still sizzling, a vapour rising from his frame like he was a meal freshly emerging from a microwave.

'Skateboard,' he said in a weak dry, husky tone that was not his usual one, 'what were the odds again?'

'About a billion-to-one, sir.'

Random smiled. 'I think I met her.'

Jake and Anji heard this and looked bemused at the comment.

'You must rest sir,' said Skateboard.

'Is he going to be okay?' asked Anji.

'It'll take time but his injuries will heal,' confirmed Skateboard.

With that, Random smiled again, allowed himself a little chuckle and sank back into the chair. 'Must rest,' he muttered.

'Admiral, we need a medical freighter here immediately,' said Skateboard to his communication channel.

Random sighed, relieved and tired, and looked up at the faces of his best friends, some old and some new and shone a smile that he had never smiled before.

'Thank you,' he sighed as he closed his eyes and drifted into a long overdue and much-needed heavy sleep.

XXI

For the next fortnight, Random spent most of his time asleep in bed. When the Titan landed on the now calm planet of Rodas it had scooped up those who had fought in the battle and took them in to tend to injuries and to generally look after those who had fought so valiantly.

The other freighters also landed on the planet and distributed aid where it was needed. There was much that Anji and Jake helped with whilst their friend recovered. Along with Nkite, they assisted in getting food and clean water to the many who had been made homeless by the constant shelling and destruction.

Skateboard, upon the return of the Venus II, had handed the river dwellers over into the care of Admiral Bagari and commenced an emergency deep clean of the ship. After seeing the terrible conditions that it had endured in transporting the dosas over from Spectronia, he was relieved to discover that it didn't take too long at all and he could set up an automatic cleaning system which worked in tandem with the self-repair nanobots.

Plus, as soon as it had been confirmed to him that Solenia and her Valkyries would be going home on one of the Space Seals battle freighters it was more than a comfort that his friends had never seen the mess that they had left behind, especially in Jake's room. It would take a while to get their home looking spick and span again but they were in no rush.

After a couple of weeks, the rehabilitation of Rodas was in full swing and Random was well enough for the debriefing with Admiral Bagari, who stood at the foot of his medical bed as Anji, Jake and Skateboard listened on. She'd already explained some of the details and Random was keen to hear every word.

'Your friends from Genocia have spent the past fortnight out on patrol across the planet with the people you found trapped in the war room,' she explained. 'They have been helping us to look for those who are homeless and in aid and spreading the word that we are here to help.'

'That's great,' said Random, his voice a little croaky still but apart from a few grazes on his face almost back to his very best. 'I'm happy that whatever I did meant that the abominations didn't perish, too, we've really got to call them something else, haven't we?'

'I can explain that away, sir. Maloso's earlier cloning experiments were given free will. When you destroyed the psychic link, it only obliterated those who were directly under his control,' said Skateboard.

'The Crimson Empire didn't fall?' asked
Random.

'It did,' said Jake, 'but with the clones no longer
around those who were left were outnumbered.'

'And as Yana has told us those that they are
finding out in the wastelands aren't bad,' said
Anji. 'They were after peace as much as the
Sapphire Regime were.'

'It's something you've always got to remind
yourself in a war,' said Bagari. 'There is good and
evil on both sides. But a treaty will be signed in
due course by the highest-ranking officials from
both the Crimson Empire and the Sapphire
Regime to formally conclude the conflict. After
that we hope, in time, that sides will no longer
need naming. Hopefully, as soon as the ink dries
there will be one society of Rodasians and the
division will be at an end.'

'Quite; it'll take a while for that trust to be built
but they will get there in the end,' said Random
happily. 'Is there anything else?'

'The dismantling of the security mainframe has
begun. They will remain on the planet, as will
some of our men, to oversee the transition from
tyranny back to democracy. But Rodas will need
help, and lots of it, to stand on its own two feet
again. I spoke to my peers earlier this week and
they confirmed that we are willing to commit to a
long-term programme to restore this planet.'

'So much needs to be done,' said Random. 'The whole place will need building up from scratch.'

'And the people of this planet will learn to trust each other again,' said Bagari. 'We'll do what we can. I myself have been placed in charge for the foreseeable future.'

'Ah wow, congrats Admiral!' said Anji.

'It's a tough job but someone's got to do it,' she said. 'Also, there is just one more thing. The Space Seals have decided to give you four, among the associates that you recruited, congressional medals of honour.'

'No way!' beamed Jake. 'Really? What does that mean then?'

'It means that we shall have the freedom of the universe,' said Skateboard giddily.

'I thought that we had that already,' said Anji cheekily.

'Unofficially,' replied Bagari dryly. 'Congratulations. I know it probably hasn't sunk in for you four yet but what you have done here has saved an entire planet, possibly even the universe. Great work.'

'All in a day's work for us, as you know, Admiral, but thank you, and the entire fleet for what you have done too,' said Random with a wink.

Admiral Bagari snapped to attention and saluted them all. 'I shall see you at the ceremony.'

As she left the medical bay, Random looked down at his surgical gown.

'I suppose I'd better find something better to wear for it,' he joked.

'Yet another medal of honour to add to the collection,' said Anji gleefully.

'I need to find my others. I think they might be down the back of one of my drawers,' said Jake.

'She is right you know,' said Random, 'What we did here really was incredible.'

'What you did, sir,' said Skateboard. 'We just assisted.'

'No,' said Random. 'You gave me a reason to come back. You made me face my fears and you did it by my side, no matter how much I tried to convince you to go somewhere safe. In the end, I couldn't have done it without you guys.'

'Group hug?' asked Anji.

'Why not?' said Random. All four of them embraced as Nkite walked into the room.

'Am I interrupting something?' she asked.

'Not at all, Nkite,' said Random, 'care to join?'

'I'm not really the hugging type,' she said. 'How are you feeling?'

'Much better thank you,' said Random. 'How about you?'

'The shoulder feels as good as new. I've just heard from Gron. He said that he and the rest of the river dwellers all want to go back to where they came from.'

'Back to the river, you mean?' asked Anji.

'Yes. It's a community there. Hence why I've decided that I shall be joining them. It's the only family I have now. I know you'll all understand when I tell you that it isn't something that you can't take for granted.'

'Definitely not,' said Jake beaming at his friends. 'Have you heard about the ceremony?'

'Heard? I'm getting a medal too,' she grinned. 'Admiral Bagari said that she wants to talk to me about the rebuilding of the planet too. I think she wants to keep me involved.'

'She'd be a fool not to,' said Random.

'And what about you, Random?' she asked. 'Do you know what you will do? I heard they might make you King of Rodas.'

Random's face turned serious for a moment. In truth, no he didn't. He had been thinking, in his hours lying awake, that since the voices of what he now understood to be his parents had gone and his mission was complete, he was a free entity again. There was no millstone around his neck, pulling his conscience this way and that. But did he owe it to the Rodasian people to stay with them and help rebuild the planet or to continue on his adventures with his friends?

Jake and Anji's faces fell. It hadn't occurred to them that Random may want to stay on his home planet. Random said nothing and simply smiled.

The night of the ceremony was a low-key affair. It was held in the shadow of Kalor Maloso's base and attended by hundreds of thousands of civilians. The Space Seal fleet, the surviving soldiers for both sides, well, the ones that hadn't been thrown in prison for war crimes or had shown an inkling of creating trouble, along with the rebel alliance that Skateboard had assembled all stood on the battleground where the war was finally ended.

The base, and the chamber from which Random had ended the conflict, were in the process of being demolished. Under a new act, such cloning techniques were to be outlawed on Rodas as much as it was in other parts of the galaxy as the security teams wanted to bring the planet in line with the law and order among the rest of Ursa-17. As delegates from neighbouring planets stood on the lip of the cliff that dropped into the battlefield, handing out medals to all who had fought, the ceremony was a long one. Random, Anji, Jake and Skateboard, along with Delilah, Yana, Benaya, Troyus, Boshy, Postanous and Xiros had all spruced up to look their best and were called in turn to receive their medals. Solenia and her Valkyries had elected to remain in their Spectronian armour and the Queen was awash with pride for her people when she and they were given a special recognition award for their part in the battle for peace.

Random had stood in his tuxedo, feeling slightly foolish, still pondering over what to do next. Anji, who look stunning in a flowing aqua blue ball gown alongside Jake, who had taken the effort to slick his hair back and wear a smart three-piece suit, and the two couldn't stop feeling happy for what they had helped achieve. Even Skateboard had been given a polish and was sparkling. As they received their awards the entire congregation cheered and applauded.

As the medal draped around his shoulders, Random shook hands with the Ursa-17 delegate and turned to wave at the crowd, who celebrated so loudly that Jake thought it sounded like they had all just won the Premier League! But he gave no speech and unlike his friends, Random just wanted to slip quietly away.

A little later, as the food and drink that had been provided by the Space Seals was being enjoyed and a party-like atmosphere had swept around the entire planet, Random was taking some time alone, something that was hard to do on a night like this, as everyone wanted to speak to him and hug him and thank him profusely for what he had done. Through the party goers, Nkite spotted him and made her way over.

'Hey,' she said.

Random noticed her dress. 'You look nice.'

'Thank you! Your friend Anji lent it to me.'

There was an awkward silence.

'Random I... I just wanted to say that I am sorry for the way I spoke to you back in the cave.'

Random scoffed. 'Honestly, Nkite, people have said far worse. I hurt you. It's okay I understand totally.'

Nkite bit her lip. 'So, we are good?'

'Good? We're more than that,' smiled Random. 'We saved a planet together. In my book that pretty much makes us family!'

Nkite smiled and then stared at the floor. 'We won't hold it against you, you know.'

Random looked puzzled.

'If you did decide to go?'

Random's eyes stared at the floor. 'I haven't decided yet. The thing is Nkite I'm very good at all of this revolution malarkey but I'm not one for bedding down somewhere. This might be the place of my birth but that out there,' he pointed at the stars, 'that's home to me.'

'The people will understand if you don't want to be King, I'm sure, but we all owe our lives to you Random. Just, promise me that whatever you decide that you won't forget us.'

'Forget you?' How could I ever do that? Take a look around you. The Space Seals, Spectronians, Genocians. I've never forgotten any of them. Sure, I should drop in on them more often, well, I had my reasons for not going back to one of them especially, but forget? Nkite I never will.'

Nkite smiled and took his arm. 'You know, when I saw you escape all as a child and saw the purple ripple in the sky, I thought it was the most beautiful sight I had ever seen. But this,' she guided him to look at the party. 'Red and blue Rodasians together, in peace. No, this is the most beautiful thing I've ever seen. We'll work to maintain it. Improve it even. But I don't think this as a spectacle can be bettered.'

Random smiled at her and placed his arm around her shoulders. 'You and me both, Nkite. You and me both. Then they looked down a level onto what had been a battlefield and was now a dance floor and saw two familiar figures embraced in a slow dance.

Jake's hands were a little clammy and he was thankful that they were on Anji's waist but he could tell that she was nervous too as her heart was thumping against his chest. Slowly they shared in their first dance, both a little scared of putting a foot wrong but both equally in the knowledge that the other person wouldn't care if they did.

As the Rodasian music swelled around the party, and a colourful array of fireworks exploded high ahead against a backdrop of the neon moon and the night sky, Anji let her lead roll onto Jake's shoulder. She shut her eyes, totally content in the moment. Jake never wanted it to end.

'Well,' he said, 'this sure beats prom hands down.'

Anji laughed. 'How would we know?'

Jake spotted Random and Nkite watching them from afar and gave a knowing smile to them.

'I think,' he replied. 'we're going to find out together.'

XXII

It was the morning after. Everyone was feeling a little worse for wear. Jake and Anji had spent the whole night talking, laughing and dancing and now they were knackered. As they walked towards the Venus II, they noticed that many of their friends had lined the open gangway, wanting to see them off. There were the abominations, whose footloose dancing the previous night had caused all sorts of dance-offs to ensue. Nkite and Gron, two of the river dwellers they had helped save stood smiling at them. There were the Spectronians, who had now pardoned the crew of the Venus II and were only too happy to see them back on their planet soon. Then there was Admiral Bagari, who had sent them on so many missions since the Space Seals had helped them defeat Stratos the planet destroyer. The Genocians, who like the Spectronians had found another mode of transport home, shared in their first adventure on an alien planet.

'Blimey,' said Jake as he walked hand-in-hand with Anji with his suit jacket slung over his shoulder and his hair back to its shaggy normality. 'Feels like I'm walking through some kind of intergalactic Facebook!'

At the top of the gangway stood Skateboard, who hadn't attended the party after the ceremony and had hastily made off to make sure that the repairs would be finished in time and that the dosa poo was now completely cleaned up. If only the bio fixing that meant everyone else's excretions were transported from their bodies when they needed to go had extended to Solenia's cavalry but alas, it was all a terrible memory for Skateboard now.

'She's looking better than ever, Skateboard,' said Anji. She wasn't wrong. The Venus II's gleaming metal glistened in the Rodasian sun.

'Hey, where's Random?' asked Jake. They both looked around.

'It's probably better if you come on board,' said a sorrowful Skateboard. Anji and Jake looked concerned but bid a heartfelt goodbye to each and every one of their friends who had come along to see them off.

'Don't be strangers, please come back anytime,' said Nkite.

'Yes, drop in on us too when you're passing. I think you owe me a few rounds, Jake,' said Delilah.

'Take care out there,' said Bagari, shaking their hands.

'We will,' replied Anji. 'Seriously, though, where is Random, Skateboard?'

Skateboard said nothing but goodbye to everyone who had assembled and led his two young friends onboard. As soon as they were safely in the mid-section, he started up the engines remotely and shut them in.

'You're not telling me he isn't saying goodbye, Skateboard, he wouldn't do that!' said Jake.

'Who said anything about goodbye?' came a voice from the cockpit.

Anji and Jake's jaws dropped as Random came bounding into the mid-section, a silly grin beaming from his face.

'Ha! Gotcha!' he cried.

'Random that was mean!' said Anji playfully slapping him.

'But I thought they were going to make you King!' said Jake.

'Me? King? Crowns don't suit me, Jake,' said Random.

'You're not staying?' asked Anji, wanting confirmation that this was indeed for real.

'Nope.'

'But your people are here, and they are free, and yours Skateboard?' asked Jake.

'It almost sounds as though he wants us to stay,' said Skateboard.

'Exactly, Jake, they are free. Mission accomplished,' said Random who was making his way back into the cockpit. 'Besides,' he said plonking himself in his familiar old pilot's chair.

'Now that the security mainframe is gone, we can come and go when we like and we will. If I've learnt anything from our visit here it is that we have more friends than we care to remember sometimes.'

Jake leaned over to look out of the dashboard. There they all were, dosas and Valkyries were roaring upward in salute as their engines neared take-off velocity.

'Also,' said Random, tapping his congressional medal of honour that was hanging from the steering column. 'This gives us the freedom of the universe. It'd be a shame not to use that freedom, wouldn't it?'

'Indeed, sir,' said Skateboard. 'Where shall I set our coordinates for?'

'Guys?' asked Random.

Anji and Jake took a look at each other. 'Anywhere,' they said in unison.

'Cool, Skateboard, set a course for anywhere.'

'I'm not sure I'm aware of that one, sir, but I'll do my best.'

Anji pulled Jake in closer and leaned forward to hug Random who in turn put an arm around her as he lifted the steering column. 'Right, gang. Let's see what else is out there.'

Anji suddenly caught a whiff of something unpleasant. 'Skateboard, what's that?'

The AI robot stayed silent in shame as the Venus II took off. Its occupants waved to their friends down below as the ship was brought around and then with one final jolt, Random, who counted himself the luckiest man in the universe, stepped on the accelerator and the Venus II and its crew of heroes sailed away from Rodas, off out into the unknown.

Their adventures were mapped out in the stars, just waiting to find them.

THE END

ACKNOWLEDGEMENTS

To **Sophie** – my wife
William – my son
Anthony – the illustrator of biblical proportions
Viki – cover designer and blurb writer
extraiordinaire
Steve and Mark – podcasters supreme
David Kitchen and Jonny Dab – feedback
curators
Mum and Dad for the obvious
Mrs Bell – the teacher who encouraged me to
write
Una McCormack – who told me after writing one
Captain Random novel that I had to complete the
series, here it is!
Nicci Currie for proofing and advice
**Thomas Savill-Owen, Anna Brown and Stephen
D'Costa** – the writing gang
Eve Hopley - support

And to you for following my work and the
adventures of Captain Random.

Also Available:

Don't Panic! The Unauthorised Dad's Army Handbook

ISBN: 978-1739375201

For nearly six decades the adventures of the Walmington-on-Sea Home Guard has delighted generations of viewers. Classic quotes such as, "Don't tell him Pike!" have been copied time and again as more and more people have tuned in through repeats that continue to this day.

In this unofficial book, through an in-depth episode guide, favourite lines, memorable moments, behind-the-scenes stories from the people who made the programme and much more, Hayden Gribble discovers what really makes Dad's Army one of British television's greatest creations.

Available from all good bookshops.

Journeys in the Randomverse

ISBN: 978-1999865986

The adventures of Captain Random continue in this special collection of FIFTEEN new stories.

Join Random, Anji, Jake and Skateboard as they encounter a planet that gets inside the mind, giant bug-like creatures on a mysterious world, alternate realities, holiday planets as relaxing as being stuck in a cupboard during a fire alarm and the Oracle of Fate.

This is the FIFTH Captain Random book.

Available from all good bookshops.

Captain Random and the Stratos Conundrum

ISBN: 978-1999865979

From the darkest depths of space comes an enemy of the universe that plans to wreck havoc across the stars.

In his blood thirsty quest for revenge he will crush entire star systems and his name will make all who hear it shudder in terror.

Whilst the biggest threat the cosmos has ever known forms his master plan the only person who can possibly stop him is lying in a coma on a hospital moon that orbits a planet that is in his line of fire.

Random, Anji, Jake and Skateboard face a race against time to save the lives of all who stand in his way whilst trying to unwrap the mystery of who he is and why, in particular, he wants Random to watch the universe suffer.

His name is Stratos...and he is the destroyer of worlds...

This is the FOURTH Captain Random adventure.

Available from all good book shops

Captain Random and the Rainbow Chasers

ISBN: 978-1999865962

The Zedron Flux is the most powerful energy source in the known cosmos. In the right hands, it has the power to end all suffering. In the wrong hands, it could bring an end to all things. After a narrow escape from an army of ancient gods, Random, Anji, Jake and Skateboard crash land on the beautiful planet of Spectronia, a paradise of colour and home to a peaceful race ruled by the elegant Solenia and her Valkyries. Upon recovering they ally themselves with a band of explorers led by Lon, who is hell bent on finding the Flux after it was taken from his grasp by a rival archaeologist. But nothing for the crew of the Venus II is ever simple. As the quest continues, danger is not far away and, as the Flux gets closer and closer, Random is left with a terrible choice that will have major consequences, not just for him and his friends, but for the entire universe...

This is the THIRD Captain Random adventure.

Available from all good bookshops

The Lurking

ISBN: 978-1999865955

Rob is a hopeless loser in the game of life. With work, his relationship with his long suffering girlfriend Claire, with everything in general. Tonight he will change for the better, make a fresh start by taking it to the next step and propose to her.

But fate has other intentions.

After an accident that leaves him stranded, Rob takes shelter in an abandoned aircraft hangar and soon discovers that he is not alone. There is something lurking in the darkness, taunting him, haunting his every movement.

Soon trapped in a living nightmare, Rob must learn the terrible truth of his tormentor and escape its clutches before it is too late...

Available from all good bookshops.

Captain Random and the Eater of Souls

ISBN: 978-1999865931

Following their explosive battle with the Sandman, and struggling to come to terms with life out in space, the crew of the Venus II decide to throw themselves into a spot of retail therapy on the friendly planet of Genocia.

But almost as soon as they arrive, they realise that this new world is not all that it seems. Outside the splendour and vast wealth of the Grand Chamber lies a neglected wasteland where terror lurks within the poisonous gloom whilst deep within the bowels of the planet lies a terrible secret.

At the very heart of it all is the ruthless leader Consula, whose designs for supremacy mean ultimate devastation to all of those who oppose her. But the greed and corruption of the government is nothing compared to what lurks in the shadows for Random and his friends. Separated and fighting for their lives, Random, Anji, Jake and Skateboard must work quickly to save the lives of the prisoners stuck in the mines deep below the surface, where death is very close by...

What is the Soul Destroyer? What part does it play in Consula's diabolical plan? Will Anji ever see her friends again? One thing is for sure. The Eater of Souls is hungry...

Available from all good bookshops.

Captain Random vs the Sandman

ISBN: 978-1999865924

Rodas. The scorned planet of Ursa-17. Ravaged by centuries of war between two factions, the villainous Sapphire Regime and the ruthless Crimson Empire. The reason behind the conflict of red and blue? The people of Rodas were unable to make the colour purple.
Until one day, when two rebels, one from either side, combine to create the ultimate warrior. A being who could put an end to the battle of ages and bring peace to the volatile planet of Rodas once and for all.

There is one tiny drawback. The warrior is a boy.

***** Fantastic book, enjoyed every part of it!
Highly recommend it for Dr Who/Red Dwarf/Rick and Morty fans.

***** Hayden Gribble's writing is witty and clever with an essence of Douglas Adams in there too. Would thoroughly recommend for anyone with an adventurous spirit.

***** I really enjoyed it. I can well imagine Kids getting swept along with the interstellar, action packed adventure and chuckling along with all the funny scenarios and characters and wanting to know just what happens.

Available from all good bookshops.

Child Out of Time: Growing Up With Doctor Who in the Wilderness Years

ISBN: 978-1999865900

For 26 years, DOCTOR WHO was a British institution, capturing the imaginations of generations of children. But then, in 1989, it was cancelled. The Doctor and his on-screen adventures were no more. There was no longer a hero, a champion for the outcasts who struggled to fit in. It was as though he had walked into his TARDIS and set his controls for dematerialisation, never to return: a whole generation lost to the powers of Science Fiction's greatest creation. It was in this Doctor-less world that I grew up. This is the story of how one little boy would try to find the Doctor in any way, shape or form and the obstacles he faced in doing so. This is the story of growing up without Doctor Who in the Wilderness Years...and how I lived through it.

***** An engaging and enjoyable insight into a fan discovering Doctor Who during the wilderness years

***** A very passionate account of one fans discovery of the greatest science fiction of all time.

**** Perfect for fans of the Doctor in any of his or her forms.

Available from all good bookshops.

The Man In The Corner

ISBN: 978-1500549862

A mysterious assassin wants out of his life as a cold and ruthless killer but must face one last assignment before he flicks the escape switch. As he closes in on the biggest criminal mind in the country, he is reminded of what he left behind and how getting closer to the light at the end of the tunnel might also reunite him with a person from his long and distant past. Who is the Big Chief? Why must he be brought down and will it be the end, not just for himself and his superior, but also to the only link to the life he has lost.

***** An exciting book! Whilst focusing on the dark story of an unnamed man, you find yourself sucked into a city of criminals. The chapters contain their own stories which really draw you in and make you want to read more. Great read! The only negative is that it was over too fast.

***** Brilliant read. Did not want to put the book down.

*** This book is a great little read about the path to redemption; not too long, in fact in some places I found myself wishing it might go on a little longer. It's got a sort of style all its own.

Available from all good book shops.

Hayden Gribble was born in Cambridge in June 1989. He has always loved writing and released his debut novel, The Man In The Corner, as an eBook in 2013 before it went paperback the following year.

Since then, Hayden has managed to top the Amazon best seller list on three occasions, although the Booker Prize still seems some way off.

The Battle of Rodas is Hayden's eleventh book and the sixth and final story in the Captain Random saga.

Away from writing, Hayden loves reading, walking, sports, music, film and TV.

He has also been a regular member of the Diddly Dum Podcast, a show about Doctor Who, since February 2015.

He lives with his wife and son in Suffolk.

You can find out more about Hayden and Captain Random at www.haydengribbleauthor.com